A CIRCLE OF SHADOWS

Also by Lou Paduano

Signs of Portents
Tales from Portents
The Medusa Coin
Pathways in the Dark

A CIRCLE OF SHADOWS

Greystone Book Five

Lou Paduano

Eleven Ten Publishing LLC

GRAND ISLAND, NEW YORK

Eleven Ten Publishing LLC
282 Fareway Lane
Grand Island, NY 14072

Publisher's note: This is a work of fiction. Names, characters, places, and incidents either are the product of the author's imagination or are used fictitiously. Any resemblance to actual events, locales, or persons, living or dead, is entirely coincidental.

Printed in the United States of America
Edited, formatted, and interior design by Kristen Corrects, Inc.
Cover art design by Kit Foster Design

First edition published 2018

Library of Congress Cataloguing in Publication Data
Paduano, Lou
A Circle of Shadows / Lou Paduano

LCCN: 2018906689
ISBN-13: 978-1-944965-54-9 (hardcover)
ISBN-13: 978-1-944965-12-9 (paperback)
ISBN-13: 978-1-994965-11-2 (eBook)

For Samantha Riley, who completed our circle.

PROLOGUE ONE

Ten Years Ago

The snow danced in the sky. Multi-colored lights hung along the row of shops dotting the block. The holiday season was in bloom and the weather was finally catching up. The sharp drop in temperatures held no effect on the crowds rushing along the lane, feeding into downtown in a mad dash for last-minute shopping.

Soriya would have loved it. She always preferred to be surrounded by the people of the city—to witness their joy, to sympathize with their sadness and grief. She was much more connected to Portents even at such a young age. It surprised the man known as Mentor to no end how different they were, despite their shared purpose.

The coffee cup shook in his hands. A long night filtered into a longer day, a case of demon spawn hatching in the coves offering more of a challenge than he originally considered. He should be resting. His right leg ached—his knee locking up mid-stride. It was getting worse.

He wasn't ready to return to the Bypass chamber, though. He needed to think through things, needed to figure out the signs. He should have done so alone, or with his charge who waited patiently tucked underground off the C-Line in the heart of downtown.

Instead he came here, to an elaborate coffee house, dimly lit but showered by the twinkling decorations adorning the street outside. Not alone, though he knew better. He kept his gaze locked on the coffee cup, the warmth of the black liquid surging through his fingers and up his arms. His level of comfort ended after their greeting. When she asked he told her the story, regretting the act immediately. However, he needed to talk to someone about it.

And Karen was a friend.

"They were humming?"

Karen was his junior by almost a decade but had seen much in her lifetime—witnessed the extraordinary and the terrible in the same instance. In that, they were the same.

She cradled the Greystone, a finger grazing the surface. He reached out and waited for her to drop it against his palm. Reluctantly she did, a roll of her eyes answering his unspoken request. Mentor tucked the stone away as more patrons filtered into the shop.

"You should have felt it," Mentor said. "The electricity in the air."

"And when you pulled them apart?"

It was an accident. He had been busy working, noting occurrences on the vast map of the city pinned to the wall of his room in the quaint underground domicile off the sprawling chamber. New pins of one color for discovered threats, another used for possible problems down the line. A good system and one that was typically straightforward. However, something else was out there recently. Something that gave him pause. He noted it in black, leaving the small circle pinned to the board.

A Circle of Shadows.

So lost in thought over the new addition, he failed to realize what Soriya was doing in the room. She had come to finish her studies, the same as every day: heavy reading with required analysis to gauge her understanding of the material. She called it punishment. He did the same at her age, though he hoped he hadn't sounded quite as annoyed as the twelve-year-old pre-adolescent.

Her stone rested on the table, his own at the other end. Curious, she shifted the Greystone closer to its brother. With the simple movement the room changed. It drew him away from the map, back to the small table in the center. She pushed them closer together, light sparking along their surfaces. For a brief moment they appeared to occupy the same space.

Then he ended the experiment. Harshly. Perhaps too harshly, but then that was how he tended to react when Soriya operated on her own. The pressure of being her teacher, and more, at times wore him down.

"What happened?" Karen asked again.

"Silence."

Karen rubbed her chin. "What did you tell her?"

"Soriya?"

"No." She grinned. "Your other daughter, Christopher."

Christopher. A name left behind years earlier. A name he tried to forget as often as it came crashing down upon him. A name with a past, with connections. A name that pulled him back to the world, one he wanted no part of, not with the tasks ahead.

No one noticed his discomfort at hearing the appellation. No one noticed the pair in the corner of the coffee shop at all. They lived their lives without a care to the shadows among them, without any knowledge of the secrets kept in the darkness of Portents. The way Mentor intended to keep it; always for their benefit.

Karen understood the sudden uneasiness and the thin glare shot her way. "Right. Sorry. Your adherence to the teacher-pupil dynamic is commendable, but you realize the child feels differently."

"I do."

The snow fell harder, large flakes sticking to every surface. Soriya enjoyed the winter months, bundling up and walking through the deepening drifts. She wasn't the only one. His daughter loved it as well. Julie. She must have been almost twenty now, a young woman. College bound, possibly at Portents University—his previous employer before abandoning the line of work.

Before abandoning his family for a higher calling.

"If anything were to happen—"

Mentor shook his head. "It won't."

"A promise you can't keep," Karen said. She reached for his hand, squeezing it lightly before letting it slip. Her smile warmed him better than the coffee. "You know that."

"I didn't tell her anything."

The questions came rapidly. Queries about the stones, about their power, about their purpose. About *her* purpose. He did his best to answer them, turning the situation into a teachable moment.

In time, the stone will be the one to tell you. If you will listen.

He made it about her, keeping her looking inward to strengthen her spirit, all in the hopes she would never look elsewhere for the truth behind the stones. The truth about her past.

"I didn't have anything to tell her," Mentor continued. He finished his coffee, running his finger along the lip of the cup. "Even after all these years."

"The same questions. I could help, you know."

He started to shake his head and she stopped him with a smile.

"Let me help, Christopher," she said. "The Bypass. The stones. The library offers a wealth of untapped knowledge."

"The library is shuttered. Why did you stay?"

Stark amber eyes shifted for the window and the darkening sky. "I had my reasons. And no fear of the truth."

"Don't—"

Karen leaned closer. "The stones are calling each other and you deny it. The Bypass opens its door to you and you lock it away."

"It isn't safe," Mentor shot back. "What you would ask of it would pull you away from the world, as it almost did me."

"A mistake. One you haven't repeated. Yet haven't learned from either."

"Standing too close to infinite knowledge is dangerous. Having that access could—"

"Do good for so many."

"That's not..." Mentor stopped. He shook his head, pulling away. "I didn't come to argue."

"I know." Karen rubbed her eyes. "You came for advice. Tell her the truth. You have to tell Soriya about the other stones."

"She's not ready," Mentor muttered. "The danger involved..."

"You'll need them."

He sighed. "At the end. If it comes."

"*When* it comes."

The evil on the horizon, always out there, always waiting. One more night. One more week. One more year. It haunted Mentor, the waiting game. One that put the entire city at risk.

That threatened the world.

"Do you know where to find them?" Mentor asked. "Who the other bearers are?"

Karen grinned. "Are you asking for my help, Christopher?"

His eyes thinned. "A name. A location. Nothing more."

"I can do that," Karen said. She slid from the bench, pulling her coat down from the hook beside the booth.

Mentor watched her curiously. "What do you do now? Without the others? In Portents?"

She tucked her hands in her pockets, eyes to the growing storm outside the window. "The same as you, old friend. I hope for the light. And I plan for the darkness."

PROLOGUE TWO

Five Years Ago

Beth Loren raced down the Knoll, her bag slapping along her back with each footfall. The summer sun blazed overhead, the heat of the day scorching the ground beneath her sandals. The brick edifice of her apartment building towered in front of her. She finished her mad dash across the block for the small hallway inside.

She slammed the door shut and clicked the lock. Taking a deep breath, Beth rested against the frame. Her eyes closed, willing the day away, but a knock ended that dream. The tenant from Apartment 3-B banged on the metal entryway, frustration and anger barring his path.

"Sorry about that," she mumbled under his curses after opening the door and clearing the way. His anger faded with her glowing smile.

The door closed once more but she didn't bother with the lock. Traffic in and out of the apartment building was constant and the next entry would undoubtedly leave it unlocked. Instead, she took to the stairs for her second-floor domicile. An elderly woman wearing a fluffy blue bathrobe waited at the landing, any warnings of her constant curiosity lost on arrival.

"Beth, dear, is everything—?"

"It's fine, Mrs. Arbogast," Beth said, fumbling with her keys. The scent wafting from the woman's apartment threatened to topple her back down the steps. More burnt cuisine, a specialty for the mainstay at the complex, thanks to a reduced capacity to smell anything after a lifetime of smoking. The other tenants complained but little was done. The old woman had a gift for circumventing trouble, something Beth envied at the moment.

"Are you sure?" Mrs. Arbogast pressed. "I could—"

"No," Beth replied over the woman. "I'm fine. Rough day is all."

Beth continued to her door, jamming the key in place and twisting hard. The frame stuck, warped from the mounting heat of the summer, then fell away. She threw the curious neighbor a quick wave before entering the apartment. The door scraped against the wood, the lock put in place and deadbolt secured. The young woman dropped her bag and slid to the floor.

"Very rough."

What was she thinking? How could she not have known? Two years of work, researching what was actually going on in the city, and she remained as clueless as the rest. Unable to see the growing shadows in Portents.

Even though they stood right at her side.

Beth rushed for the phone on the end table. She dialed quickly, the number embedded in her brain like so many facts of the history of Portents. A city she loved more every day and hoped her husband would feel the same someday. Hoped he would still love her as well after all she had hidden from him.

"Come on, Greg, pick up," she said, the ringing in her ear continuing. "Don't be saving the city for once."

Save me.

His voicemail chimed in, his words strong and deep. It forced a smile, just the sound of him against the emptiness of the apartment. She waited for the automated instructions to take over then ended the call.

The message would come too late to do any good. Greg was lost in another case. *The Kindly Killer.* Another headline grabber, but a deadly one from what her husband offered in their scant conversations. His duty to protect and serve trumped all when it came to work, his obsessive nature giving him the advantage over other detectives on the force.

But it pulled him away from her. It kept them apart. And she did the same. Beth walked to the mantel and lifted the image resting in front of the pristine mirror hanging above.

Their wedding photo. A promise made and one she had subverted with lies and omissions, unable to find the right moment, the correct way to show Greg the truth.

About everything.

About her.

"How could I be so stupid?" Beth cursed. Delicate fingers grazed the clean-cut image of her husband. "I should have told you. And I will. I promise."

The sun crested, inching toward the west. Beth checked the time. Greg wouldn't be home for hours, despite the extra hours clocked from his usual overnight shift. Late, no doubt, with promises of a home-cooked meal offered before he left the night before.

Like a bag of salad is really dinner?

She grinned, clutching tight to the wedding photo against her chest. The real reason behind the grocery stop was clear. He needed cigarettes. Another last pack, one she wasn't supposed to know about. A secret of his own; one Beth accepted when they made their vows. Would he be so accepting of hers?

It didn't matter. He needed to hear the truth. And she needed to be the one to tell him.

She placed the photo on the mantel, straightening it with care. Then she reached for the phone once more. Nervously dialing, she reached out to the only other person who could protect her.

"Hello?" the young woman's voice answered.

"Soriya. I need your help."

PART ONE
THE GATHERING

CHAPTER ONE

Night fell over the city. Darkness surrounded every act, every conversation, every hushed whisper of fear and terror. Portents had seen plenty of it of late. The city was distracted, lost in the latest crisis. Someone was slaughtering innocents throughout the downtown district, images of burned-out eye sockets filling the front pages of the major news outlets.

The police had leaks—too many and all in the right places. Rumors turned to protests turned to outright horror at what was happening, yet none faced the nightmare head on. They cowered in homes, apartments, and their favorite bar to wait it out.

The distraction was necessary.

Their fear kept them indoors, surrounded by loved ones with the hope that the stories were just that and nothing more. That when the sun rose, Portents would remain and their lives could continue as they always had. It kept the streets clear—from the alleys to the thoroughfares, from subways to the bus lines. No one ventured out of the coves to the north or the warehouse district to the south. The city was vacant, a wasteland of potential.

One the cloaked figure desired more than anyone.

She stalked up the Corridor, the failed attempt to blend the citizens with their place of employment. Homes lay in ruins to the left, the businesses on the right long since abandoned. One building remained pristine and untouched. One that had been there for longer than any could recall.

A historical center that saw no attention was the building of her desire, the one that brought the cloaked figure in the white mask to the Corridor in the first place. The stone columns hid the double bronze doors at the apex of the wide steps. Two expressive statues adorned the base of the stairs, resting on short pedestals of marble.

An old crone, her eyes blindfolded, and a tiger reaching out with sharp claws.

The woman hesitated, eyeing the statues closely. Too much planning had gone into the night's activities to stop here. It had been hard work to bring the people of Portents to their knees, tucked in their beds early, to keep them from spotting her in the darkness.

Nothing would stand in her way now.

She started up the steps, her flats clacking against the stone without a care. The cloaked woman scurried up three then four steps before turning.

She left the center of the steps, the secret path of safety installed to ensure privacy above all else. The statues lit up at the act, leaving their pedestals for the intruder. The tiger roared, drawing near his prey. The crone removed the blindfold, eyes of black glowing and nails stretching out at the cloaked figure.

"Not tonight," she whispered to the scratching tiger and his crone. "Not here."

She did not relent, did not shift. She waited until the two statues were close enough. Pulling back her sleeves, she revealed the sigils marking her skin—half on the right, half on the left. The masked intruder put them together just as the tiger and the crone reached for her.

Light shattered the silence of the street. With it, the statues crumbled. The crone screamed, the tiger whimpered, before both fell to dust at the base of the steps. Larger chunks scattered along the sidewalk and the street beyond.

Dropping her arms, the cloaked figure continued up the steps unhindered. Runes carved on small pieces of stone marked the wall on both sides of the double bronze doors. Different characters, different languages. A pass code hidden behind the wall.

Ignoring them, the figure moved for the single golden image at each side of the doors. The small flame rose from the torch insignia, one that matched the etching on the shoulder clasps of her cloak. First, she twisted the right sigil until it clicked. She followed with the same for the left, waiting for the loud snapping sound of the dial beneath the surface.

Holding for a moment, she counted to seven then moved back to the right side and returned it to the original position. The sigil clicked once more and the doors opened. The secret hidden behind them stretched before her.

The Courtyard.

Twelve city blocks tucked in a single structure, a gateway to a hundred worlds filled with legends and myths that spanned centuries. The buildings related to different eras, castles of the Middle Ages to tenements from the early twentieth century. At its height the Courtyard housed hundreds if not thousands of beings living between worlds, traveling as they pleased.

The massive microcosm was now deserted, the threat loose in Portents too great for those residing in the hidden city. The shadows grew in their midst, a perfect storm causing them to flee. She couldn't have planned it better if she tried.

Or had she?

A smile spread beneath her mask, beady eyes scanning the street. The site was acceptable, the pillars adorning the sides of multiple structures easily reconditioned for the purpose ahead. The doors to the other realms would be locked and secured from interlopers, the need for solitude essential to the plan. A quiet immediately broken.

"You cannot be here," a winged beast cawed. "This place is not meant for you."

"Ah, the raven," the cloaked woman said. "I have plans for this place."

Kok'Kol perched above her position in the street. She was well aware of the beast's tendencies, being a First One of the Miwok, and of his need to assist the city when required. He was a god in animal form, lording over everyone, feeding them tidbits of information while keeping the narrative a secret behind his snapping beak.

Secrets earned by man, knowledge to ensure humanity's next step toward perfection. Secrets she required for the future.

"I've seen your plans," Kok'Kol remarked. "She will stop you."

"The child?" the woman laughed. "The so-called Greystone bearer? She knows nothing of this. So blinded by the moment. By doubt."

"You underestimate her. And me."

Kok'Kol screeched, swooping from his perch at the woman. She ducked, her movements too slow for the raven. Talons sliced through her mask, and the bottom half fell and shattered against the street.

The woman howled, blood lining her right cheek from the raven's scratch. "Insipid spirit!"

"What you seek cannot be taken," Kok'Kol said, circling the street overhead. "It is not yours."

Kok'Kol launched at her once more, talons at the ready. A smile grew on the woman's face as she stepped sideways, muttering words of darkness under her breath. The raven missed the target but she did not. Her hand shot into the sky and caught the beast by the neck.

"Yet," she snapped. "It is not mine *yet*, First One."

"How?"

She squeezed tighter, watching as fear filled the raven's green orbs. "Knowledge is power."

She tossed the raven aside, sending Kok'Kol to the ground. The First One of the Miwok scrambled, attempting flight without success. He clawed at the pavement, struggling for the alley—his home and spiritual center in the Courtyard. The cloaked figure followed close, watching the bird's writhing agony from her assault. Kok'Kol flailed to escape her, talons scratching at the street.

Her foot ended his efforts, stomping down on the spirit guide. Green eyes flared then dimmed to black. Feathers flew as she crunched the beast into submission.

Kicking aside the raven, the cloaked figure turned toward the open street and the four pillars adorning the block. Pride swelled in her chest, her hands firm on her hips. And a plan in her thoughts.

"All your secrets will be mine."

CHAPTER TWO

Six Months Later

City Hall was in chaos—the normal operating procedure for the hundreds locked within the twelve-story structure. Mayor Reginald Dunn prided himself on the situation, using it as a message to the people of Portents that work was always "Getting Dunn." One of the many uses of his last name he annoyingly worked into conversation.

Bernice Caplan hated it. Hell, her dislike of the man grew by the hour. His personal aide for over four years, the middle-aged woman wanted nothing more than to send the email saved in her draft folder announcing her resignation. It would have made her waistline happier at the very least. Dunn, however, needed her. So did the city. Or so she was constantly told when complaints arose.

With Dunn's reelection campaign in full swing, the word *chaos* understated the situation on the seventh floor of City Hall. Papers flew from runners delivering the latest in poll numbers and articles written by both the left and the right in opposition to Dunn's various policy positions. Public opinion universally damned the man, yet no one saw a better option.

And Bernice saw no way out. She closed out her email window and the waiting resignation letter. *Tomorrow. Maybe tomorrow.*

"Bernice?" Adam called from his desk on the other side of the makeshift wall separating their workspaces. She managed to go four whole minutes without a question being asked. Without another task dropped on her lap. Best four minutes of her day. "Do you have the agenda for tomorrow?"

She sighed. "Sent it to you ten minutes ago, Adam."

"Damn server."

Vince skirted the corner, pointing accusingly at the cursing aide. "Did you try turning it off and on again?"

"Don't," Adam snapped, pushing away from his desk. He walked over to the shared printer, another of his favorite four-letter words slipping out over the jammed mess awaiting him. He ripped the loose-leaf free and the device whirred back to life. "Don't use your IT voice with me, Vince. Not today."

"Campaign woes?"

Adam waved him back, intent on waiting for the printed schedule for the next day. Vince turned toward Bernice, who passed over another dropped paper from the latest runner.

"Approval ratings tend to drop when the crime rate rises."

Vince shrugged. "Shouldn't live in Portents then."

The thought was there, tucked in the back of her mind, growing louder every day. Three murders in the city with no end in sight. The police, a constant sticking point with the constituents, appeared unable to protect their own asses let alone the people of Portents.

"Speech ready for the Friars Club tonight?" Bernice asked, pushing aside her despondent thoughts.

Adam and Vince shared a glance, unable to look at her. Adam grumbled, locked on the schedule in front of him. "Dunn's had it since this morning."

"Why?"

"Bernice…" Vince started then fell silent.

She grumbled, standing from her desk. Her back ached and her constant need for a protein bar frustrated her further. She used to get by on a piece of fruit in the morning and three cups of coffee. Now she needed fuel for the growing tire around her midsection at all hours of the day. All because Dunn took their simple job and complicated it at every turn.

God, I hope he loses.

"This isn't the time for him to try out a new stand-up routine," she said, steadying her voice.

"He likes to add a joke or two," Adam replied.

"They aren't funny."

Vince grinned. "That's what makes them funny."

"To you," Bernice said. "Not the rest of the city. Hell, he made the late-night shows with that one about the president and the flying monkeys or whatever the hell he was trying to say."

"It was poor delivery."

"Screw the damn delivery, Adam!" Bernice yelled. Eyes glared from all directions and she let loose another sigh before shifting down the hall. The two men followed close. "It was poor. Period."

The security team rushed by. "We're rolling in ten."

"Great." Two speeches and a dinner party. Another late night. And Dunn was missing all day, locked in his office, screwing with precisely prepared remarks for each function. All for another laugh from the audience—or in his case, a forced one.

"You want me to remove the jokes?"

"Yes," Bernice said. She let out a long breath and smiled. "But I'll talk to him first."

"Deputy joining us tonight?" Vince inquired, peering down the hall for her.

"She's promoting gun control legislation in the coves."

"Good."

Bernice laughed. "Winters hassling you too?"

Six months. That was how long Deputy Mayor Winters had been with the team. Six incredibly strained months where she interjected on every major platform and minor event to offer her perspective.

Her predecessor's death was a shock. Heart failure during one of the worst weeks of their term. Everyone was so focused on the murders plaguing Portents, from the Saint Sebastian's incident to the bowling alley massacre, that no one noticed an elderly man with a heart condition.

The team went from a man who was more a sounding board than an active player in policy to someone with ambition. Too much ambition.

"You'd think she was running for mayor with the pressure she's putting on everyone," Vince said, reading her thoughts.

"No one likes to lose," Adam chimed in.

"That's what my waistline tells me," Bernice said.

Adam laughed. "See? It's in the delivery."

Their laughter followed her down the hall. Bernice stopped outside the mayor's office, hand hovering over the frame. She steadied herself, forgetting the anger and the letter of resignation saved on her computer. Work needed to get done. After knocking on the frame, she turned the knob and stepped inside.

"Sir? Car is waiting for—"

She fell back into the hall. Adam and Vince rushed to her side. "Bernice?"

"What is—?"

Silence took over, their eyes wide at the office of Reginald Dunn. The bookshelves and knick-knacks accumulated over the last four years were untouched, but the center of the room told another story.

The window was shattered, glass strewn along the ground behind the desk. A black circle of char and ash was etched into the cherry wood tabletop. Long scorch marks trailed down the leather chair, black as night.

The same as Reginald Dunn. His eyes were open, terror and surprise forever embedded on the lenses to his soul. He sat in the chair, his pale skin charred and burnt, his clothes singed. Dead. The sudden act left him horribly and grossly disfigured.

"My God."

Bernice fought back the swell of vomit from her latest snack attack and crossed the hall away from the office. She took out her cell phone and held down the saved contact programmed to the number 7. It rang twice, then clicked over.

"It's me," she said to the man on the other end of the line. "We have another one."

CHAPTER THREE

The Walker Complex was a fifteen-story structure that covered a city block on its own, an illuminated clock adorning the edifice. It served as the hub for the city's financial district, firms branching out from the historic landmark on all sides. A quiet nook that controlled the daily financial fate of Portents.

When the bell tolled, ending trading for the day, the world exhaled. The masses fled from the downtown area. They took to the line of cabs, ready to make their fares for the evening. Others started for the subway, the bus routes, and the parking garages down the lane.

One, however, stayed, heading up the stairs instead. Exiting at the roof, the sweaty executive with his tie much too tight around his swelling neck joined the company of three waiting women.

"Another friend has joined us, sister." A dark-haired woman grinned as the door opened.

The second, with locks of scarlet, but sharing the same ravenous eyes, silenced her song and joined her sister at the door. "How shall we thank him, Pei?"

The man's movements were staggered, his eyes vacant. Pei drew him to her with a waving hand. He stopped short of her lips, her fingers running down his back to the wallet in his pants pocket. Keys jangled and slipped to the ground, quickly lifted by her scarlet-haired sister, who helped herself to the man's briefcase as well.

"I can think of a few ways," Pei said. Her sister laughed, snapping open the case to thumb through the files within. Pei's fingers grazed the man's sweating cheek. "You have lovely accoutrements, gentle soul. Don't you agree, Thel?"

The third sister sat uninterested, staring out at the city, her hands buried in the pocket of her hooded sweatshirt. Thel shrugged in response.

"What's with her, Aglaope?"

The scarlet sister shook her head. "Don't let her bother you, Pei." She clapped her hands, victoriously removing a small key from the briefcase. Sauntering over to the dazed man on the rooftop, Aglaope held the key before him. "Or you, my sweet."

"Who…?" The man struggled to speak.

"Why you, of course," Pei cooed, her voice a song. "You'd do anything for us, wouldn't you?"

"Y—Yes."

Agloape cleared her throat, the key still in hand. "Safe deposit box?"

The man's eyes flared, terror filled. "I…"

Pei rubbed his cheek. Her song grew with each word. "For us."

"127th and Main," the man answered. "Box 985. My grandmother's jewels."

"I love jewels," Aglaope said, pocketing the key. Her fingers ran the length of the locket around her neck, the purple stone shimmering in the dim light of the rising moon. "Almost as much as what comes next."

Pei nodded, directing the man forward. He inched toward the ledge then climbed, his eyes screaming to wake up from the nightmare.

"Please…"

"Begging," Pei said. "Mmm, tasty."

"Thel?" Aglaope called.

The young blonde refused to look. "Let's go already."

"You heard our depressed sibling." Pei smiled. "Let go already."

Thel's dark eyes flared, suddenly awake. The man crawled closer to the edge. "Wait… No, please…"

"I hate to be kept waiting, don't you, Pei?" Aglaope yelled over the rush of wind running the length of the Walker Complex.

"Goodbye," Pei said.

"That's far enough."

A thin pink ribbon snapped through the air, catching the man by the waist. The young woman with the dark skin and the fire in her eyes pulled and the man fell back to the rooftop.

Soriya Greystone had been tracking the sisters for weeks. After their sudden arrival during the Night of the Lights there was a spike in activity followed by a lull until recently. Now the nightly routine of the three sisters, commonly referred to in historical texts as sirens, consisted of murder and mayhem—a Portents specialty.

"Greystone," Pei seethed.

"I hate spoilsports too," Aglaope said. She ran at Soriya, who slammed her to the ground with a solid right cross to the face.

"And I hate sluts on parade," Soriya snapped. "How many has it been? Ten? Twenty?"

"Oh, at least."

Aglaope wiped the blood from her lip. "It's difficult to keep track when you honestly don't care."

"No more," Soriya replied. The ribbon of Kali left the man resting along the roof and flew for the pair of sisters, catching their ankles and pulling hard. Both fell to the ground, the ribbon retracting like a living creature, resting along her left arm as she pressed the attack on the sirens.

Pei and Aglaope scattered, narrowly avoiding the driving kick from the Greystone bearer. The dark-haired sister bellowed to her sibling, "Thel? Thel!"

Soriya shook her head, pulling Pei up and knocking her down. "She doesn't seem interested."

Aglaope jumped on Soriya's back, then immediately flipped over her shoulder to land on a surprised Pei. The sisters struggled for breath, fighting for a moment to recover. One Soriya refused to allow.

The stone slipped from the hand-woven pouch at her side and settled along her palm. Energy coursed up her arms, heat and cold brewing beneath the surface of the ancient weapon.

"Dammit," Thel muttered from across the rooftop. Her voice carried a song, her hand waving to the unconscious man in the corner. His eyes shot open and he stood, moving for the ledge once more.

"What?" he asked, eyes flaring with renewed terror. "What are you doing——?"

"Sorry," Thel said. She raced to the access door to the complex below. "Sisters?"

"Don't you——" Soriya lowered the stone.

Pei helped Aglaope to her feet. "Tick, tock, Greystone."

"Watch that first step," Aglaope sang to the man at the ledge. She ran to gather the briefcase and the stolen goods before following Pei to the door.

"Banter later, idiots," Thel said. "Let's go."

Soriya started for the sisters then paused at the staggering of the man on the ledge, fifteen stories up from the ground. Thel hesitated by the door, her head bowed in sorrow, before slipping into the darkness of the stairwell.

The man's right foot extended to the open air. "I…I have to do this."

"You don't," Soriya shouted over the rushing wind, racing toward the ledge. "You really—"

He jumped, his scream booming through the chasm between buildings.

Soriya slammed into the ledge. "Crap."

She followed, wind whipping her hair back as she dove like a bullet after the man. The ribbon snapped loose from her left arm, catching the large clock adorning the front of the Walker Complex. Another strand soared to the man, wrapping around his wrist. The sudden jolt interrupted his shriek.

Soriya's own cry took hold, her body wrenched between slowing the man's descent and the clock threatening to tear her in half.

The man continued his fall, screams of terror shifting to confusion before cutting out completely. He touched down softly on the sidewalk as if brought down by a parachute, his feet settling along the pavement.

The ribbon let go of his wrist, returning to the hanging Soriya Greystone, who watched the man stumble down the block for home, as if the last few minutes of his life had been nothing more than a dream.

The clock shifted and the ribbon slipped from the minute hand. Soriya dropped, the street threatening to greet her at terminal velocity. Reaching out, she caught hold of a small ledge jutting from the edifice of the Walker Complex. She slammed into it, fingers digging into the stonework until they held. Lifting her lithe frame to the ledge, Soriya sat against the building and wiped her brow.

"I need a vacation."

CHAPTER FOUR

"Did you see the look on her face?"

Cheers and hollers echoed in the alley from the emergency exit to the Walker Complex. The three sisters bolted from the building, rushing into the alleyway for the adjacent block at the back of the structure. A few steps from the exit they stopped, their cheers growing.

"So much anger," the scarlet-haired siren giggled.

Pei joined her. "So delicious."

Both peered at the building, congratulating each other in the form of an embrace and cajoling over the stolen goods. Thel rolled her eyes. She wanted to keep going, wanted to keep running but Aglaope's hand fell on her sleeve, holding her up.

"Seriously?" Thel said, pulling from her sister's embrace. Her hands fell into the pocket at the base of her sweatshirt, blond locks washing over her bowed head.

"Thel?" Pei asked, the cheers fading behind their sister's solemnity.

"What is your problem, sister?" Aglaope called, fed up with Thel's moods. She played with the locket around her neck.

"You two," Thel shouted. "You two are my problem, Aggie."

"Not this again," Pei said, throwing her hands in the air.

"I hate that name," Aglaope seethed. "And I thought we were past this."

"Centuries lost and you idiots haven't changed at all." Thel recalled the old days with a clarity that gave her nightmares. Their exile from the world, lost to mankind for their selfish acts and the dead left in their wake, all for a pittance or prideful revenge. In Thel's eyes, their end was justified.

Then they came back, returning in a flash of green light that rose from the streets to the obsidian tower at the heart of Portents. Thel hoped their second chance had finally arrived.

"What do you expect us to do?" Pei asked.

"We are who we are."

"Says who?" Thel said. It was the same argument, the same glossed-over stare from her sisters. "Why play by the old rules? Why not try something else? Something new?"

"Like what? Get a job?"

Aglaope huffed. "Live with the rabble? Like commoners?"

Thel shook her head. "Still so blinded by arrogance."

"And you are by your guilt," Aglaope snapped. "When there should be none."

"Well, there is," Thel said.

"Hey," Pei said. "*We're* your family. Not them. They brutalized and betrayed us for our gift. Demonized us as witches. Deprived us of life."

"So we take theirs?" Thel asked. "Is that how you justify it?"

"It is our way."

Aglaope nodded. "It will always be our way, Thel."

She slapped Pei's hands away. They took her in centuries earlier, gave her a purpose and celebrated her gift, one they each shared. They were sisters, family—in another life.

"Not anymore," she said. "Not for me."

She turned for the street, the roar of the traffic pulling at her. Everything in Portents pulled at her, leaving her awestruck in the presence of the metropolis. They slipped into the future yet their eyes remained locked on the past, something her sisters embraced and she detested.

"Where are you going?" Pei yelled over the flow of traffic.

"Thel? You can't change who you are."

Thel shook her head. "I can try."

Aglaope paused at the mouth of the alley, catching her departing sister turning the corner at the end of the block. There were disagreements before, arguments of tactics and the lives taken when none were necessary.

Thel came late to their collective. She didn't understand the population's fear and terror at their unique gifts. She didn't experience the torture and humiliation to the extent of her sisters. Not until the end.

But they had a second chance, another life offered to them and they would not relinquish it by squandering their talent or hiding among the peasants.

Pei pushed ahead, starting to give chase to their errant sister. Aglaope's hand fell across her arm. "Let her go."

"I can't believe Thel would—"

"She'll come around," Aglaope said, leading the pair back into the alley and the waiting briefcase. "She always has. Once she sees the truth of the world."

"What's next, then?"

Aglaope smiled, reaching into her pocket. The safety deposit key glistened against her painted nails. "Jewels. And then?"

Pei clapped. "More fun."

"For us, maybe."

Four men stepped out of the shadows, surrounding them. Pei reached for Aglaope who clutched tight to the key and pulled her sister close.

"But not for you," another shadow said. "Not anymore."

"What is this?" Pei shouted.

"You can't," Aglaope warned. Her voice shifted, her sister joining her growing song. Aglaope's hand shot out at the approaching men. "I said, don't!"

They continued, grins on their faces. One tapped the base of his ear. "Sorry, ladies. Earplugs. You understand, don't you?"

The sirens ran, hoping to reach the door only to be met by a pair of shadows inches from freedom. Swift blows took out their legs and they fell before the group closing in on them.

Pei lost her sister's hand. Her eyes pleaded, her voice a screech—all ineffective against their attackers. A black bag settled over the dark-haired siren's face, ties wrapped tight against her wrists and ankles.

Her sister clawed at the first assailant to approach, sending the man reeling with a cry. A kick from his colleague knocked her down and a third grabbed a fistful of her red hair, pulling her to her knees. Her locket snapped loose, falling in front of her. She tried to reach for it, but another kick sent her to the ground. Blood ran from her lips, the zip ties tightening around her hands.

"Don't..." she whispered. To no avail. The earplugs made her proud gift useless—as useless as her struggle. Two of the men surrounded her. A third lifted Pei over his shoulder and started down the alley.

The fourth paused at the brick wall of the Walker Complex. He shook a can of spray paint then let loose, an image taking form along the crimson structure.

"Shadows..." Aglaope said before the bag fell over her eyes and the world darkened.

CHAPTER FIVE

Greg Loren leaned against the concrete wall and sighed. His eyes burned—the cumulative effect of days without rest. He rubbed them, shifting the blur away for mere seconds before forcing them open once more.

The moon skimmed the horizon. Loren used his time poorly—another day lost in his apartment, stuck in the past. The image of Soriya Greystone sat on his coffee table, begging for an answer. A reason for why she would have been in his apartment the day his wife fell to her death. It demanded a response, one he was unable to ask for let alone conceive. Instead he focused on sleep, only to find rest unattainable.

His dreams refused to allow him that luxury.

When they started, they came infrequently, mostly muddled whispers in the dark of an otherwise peaceful night of sleep. After Evans and the so-called Night of the Lights, things changed. Beth's message, his wife's ceaseless warning, rang louder and louder. Dreams turned to nightmares, from monthly to nightly in the span of weeks. The intensity shifted as well, her warnings growing with each visit.

Someone was going to die.

Loren slipped a stick of gum between his lips. His dreams had to wait. He was too busy worrying about the living at the moment.

When Mathers shoved the dozen missing persons reports on Loren's desk during the Erikson affair, the delinquent captain had no clue what they would lead to. Nor did he care. The goal was simple: remove Loren from the case, from anything having to do with the headline-grabbing slaughter of the citizens of Portents. Tuck him in a corner and forget about him.

Instead, Loren found a link between them and dozens more that went unreported. He found it hidden in apartments, tucked behind shifted dressers and tables. Always present if you had the wherewithal to look.

A Circle of Shadows.

After Erikson died, when the dust settled, the cases were pulled away. Loren refused to let the matter go. He couldn't, not knowing that someone was out there, some group, taking people. Including Hady Ronne, the former head coroner. Including his friend, Dominic.

Dominic might have only been a bartender, but to Loren he was a confidant. Someone who shared the burden that came with the day-to-day existence in Portents. Someone to share a laugh or even a secret.

No one cared, not about those missing. Reports never arrived from loved ones or friends. They came from bosses or landlords, angry over time or money lost.

Leads dried up quickly. The people taken were ghosts in the city. They held few connections and too many secrets. With the last question asked, Loren took to the streets, finding the forgotten places in Portents as the next viable option.

His exhaustive research brought him to the abandoned cross-town station outside the Grove. Once home to the F Line, bringing passengers from the outskirts of the city downtown, now the station lay empty, the tracks blanketed by thickening brush.

Old posters dotted the walls of the aboveground platform. Films lost to time and old stage plays performed at defunct theaters. Locked in the past.

Like Loren.

He wondered how many more empty and forgotten places existed in the city. How many more would he visit before he found what he was looking for? Before he put the dead to rest and faced the future? Before he followed his wife's desire for him to live?

The platform led below ground. Electrical panels were concealed behind the stairs, out of sight from anyone passing through the defunct space in the Grove. Loren started down, flashlight in his grip. His other hand rested along the holster at his side. When his phone rang he nearly ripped the pistol loose and fired. His heart pounded and his eyes flared, scanning for signs of life.

He let the phone ring twice before shuffling it over to his voicemail. Lifting the device from his pocket, he read his partner's name on the screen. Myers. Her third call on the day. He noted and immediately ignored her concern.

Work needed him. Almost as much as he needed it. Hell, he *was* working, the only one attempting to find so many who had gone missing from the city. Loren cleared the message before sliding the phone back into his pocket.

Inching through the cobweb-infested underground terminal, Loren struggled to keep his eyes open. He pushed too hard, working too many long hours. Holding things back from Myers even after everything, hoping to have more answers in hand before bringing her into the fold.

That had to change. He needed someone to trust about the missing. About his dreams. About everything. Myers had been by his side for months, their partnership solidified the night Richard Crowne took his own life. Loren fought through hell to save her, hoping to do the same for his old friend. Not everyone could be saved, though, the lesson offered by his new companion. She trusted him and he could do no less.

The smell hit him first. Fierce, like a wave, battering him back against the handrail at the bottom of the stairs. He knew it well: decay and death. His sidearm was primed before his next step.

Turning the corner, Loren found them.

Bodies filled the hall of the station, stacked on top of each other like kindling. A mass grave from floor to ceiling. Loren almost dropped the flashlight. Once he composed himself, he put his gun away to examine the dead. Some bodies exhibited visible gunshot wounds. Others, stab marks on rotting flesh. A myriad ways they met their end, all with the same result. And all hiding a secret.

Dominic's body was obvious: gills along his neck. When Loren stumbled on his friend's corpse, he cried out. He tried to pull him loose from the pile, his hands and feet slipping along the mound of the dead. The secrets were written on them all. A third eye; hair coiled like rope. Freaks and monsters.

He continued to dig through the bodies, relieved Hady Ronne was not among them. The sensation faded as Loren settled at the end of the hall, exhausted tears dotting his cheeks. He found them, the missing and the lost. A step toward resolution for the lives taken. But it wasn't the end.

Not yet.

So many gone and the culprits remained at large. A group Loren worked to bring to light for all to see.

A Circle of Shadows.

CHAPTER SIX

Noah Jordan hated sneaking around. Nineteen years old and his entire life was filled with secrets. He should have been in school. His first semester went well enough, though he had yet to settle on a major. Mathematics was always his strong suit—solving problems, tackling puzzles. He loved his professors as well.

Then life cast its shadow over everything. School, friends, even the ladies in his life disappeared. No longer a priority, he searched elsewhere for meaning—for answers to the one problem that mattered.

He was still looking for that answer.

The lock clicked, the keycard clutched tight between aching fingers. His body always hurt after a full day of work—after he used the tool at his disposal. He should have practiced more, tested out new ways to implement the device, though it was funny to think of it that way. The tool held no controls and carried no instructions. There was only his will.

A will that needed to be stronger. Nothing would stand in his way of getting the answer he sought.

The lights were off in the hotel room, a downtown suite that was larger than his home. A bathroom sat to the left of a short hallway that opened up to a vast living area. The bedroom was vacant, the two full-size beds still made from the morning.

Only the beaming of the television illuminated the room. Gabe sat on the couch, enthralled by the action on the screen. Guns blazed, blood flowing freely at every goon standing in the way of a modestly-built action star with too many catchphrases to be believed. The comedian sidekick turned damsel in distress offered his own commentary to the obscenely violent display until Noah lifted the remote and turned off the film.

"Hey," Gabe yelled. He reached for the remote and Noah tossed it to the opposite couch. Noah opened the curtain, moonlight filling the room.

"You shouldn't be watching that garbage."

"That garbage has *Best Picture* written all over it," Gabe said. Sixteen and he believed he was right no matter the subject.

Noah smiled, enjoying the back and forth despite the occasional aggravation. "Speaking of garbage..."

He reached into his bag and pulled out the meal purchased on the way home. Gabe's eyes lit up. "No way. You brought it?"

Gabe snatched the sub from his hand and moved for the table near the windows. He unwrapped the plastic, then pulled the foil away. Hot sauce dripped on all sides, the buffalo finger sub steaming.

The heat stung Noah's eyes. "Hey, I'm your brother, Gabe. I'll never let you down."

Gabe took a large bite, satisfaction running along his lips and down his chin. "Sweet deliciousness."

"I'll take your word for it."

"You need to eat something too, bro. You look skinny."

"I ate earlier."

"Where?" Gabe asked. "Where have you been?"

"Working."

The sub settled against his salivating lips but Gabe resisted, putting the sandwich down. "Why here, Noah? Why now? Two weeks here. That's longer than Philly, longer than Santa Fe, even Miami. I could understand staying longer in Miami, but Portents?"

"Not enough bikinis for you?" Noah grinned.

"Not even close," Gabe replied, his mouth full.

Months of moving, tracking down leads, everything brought them here—to Portents, of all places. Little sun, way too many damn clouds, and growing shadows at every turn.

"We should be home, Noah," Gabe said.

"What home?" Noah regretted his words immediately. Whenever Gabe asked, it hit him like a hot poker through the chest. Images of the fire filled his vision, the house unrecognizable beneath the blaze. It burned as hot as his rage over the loss of his parents, both who had been trapped inside.

Unable to escape their fate.

"Sorry," Noah said, flickers of flame dancing in every waking thought. "Just tired, I guess."

"I miss them too."

"I know." Noah cracked a smile, his brother by his side. There were brief moments of adolescence in the kid but more often than not were glimpses of the man he would one day become. Strong. Resilient. Then Gabe wiped his greasy fingers along Noah's sleeve with a devilish laugh. "Hey!"

"What?"

"Ass!" Noah punched Gabe against the arm, before pushing him away. "Grow up."

"Make me."

"This shirt is always going to reek like hot sauce now."

Gabe nodded. "I'm waiting for a thank you."

"Keep waiting."

The pair laughed, collapsing on the couches of the suite—a gift from his current employer. Their voices echoed, the sound that used to fill their old homestead. Before the flames and the tears. Before they lost their old lives in a flash of burning tragedy.

Gabe caught his brother's quiet pain. "I miss you too, Noah. We're still a family. We can still be a family. If you let us."

"We will." Noah reached out to his younger brother, who shook his head. "Hey, I'm serious. Listen. I'm close, so close to finding out what happened and then—"

Gabe jumped to his feet. "They died! The fire—"

"Was never explained."

"Noah…"

"Don't," the older brother snapped.

"I can't stay here. All day, every day! How the hell can you afford it? And what about school? For both of us? And our friends?"

Knocks rattled the wall, their conversation carried on too long and too loud. Noah waved Gabe down. "Soon. It will all be fixed soon."

Gabe shook his head. He heard it all before.

The fire was deemed an accident. Only Noah thought differently, without any evidence to contradict the ruling. But it was out there. It had to be. If only Gabe believed him for an instant, saw his resolve in making things right. For their family, both past and future.

Instead, Gabe collapsed on the couch, remote in hand and turned the television back on.

"Gabe…"

"I'm fine," his brother grumbled. "Go shower or something. You smell like hot sauce."

"Ass," Noah said. "I actually can't stay. Just stopped in to bring your dinner. Work—"

"Right," his brother said, turning up the volume.

He started for the door. "I'll make this right, Gabe. I need a little more time. I promise."

Gabe refused to acknowledge the admission, locked on the screen in the darkness of the suite. Noah nodded, then headed out for the streets, his task not yet done.

But close. Very close.

CHAPTER SEVEN

"Guess I can forget about eating today."

Detective Samantha Myers stopped at the entrance to the mayor's office, a thick case file clutched under her arm. The smell was pungent, reminding her of the burnt bagel she accidentally left in the toaster for a three-day stretch. Dunn's body continued to rest against his chair, the desk locking him in place.

"I appreciate you coming in, Myers," Captain Gerianne Wexler said. She held the bridge of her nose, fighting a chronic headache that spiked when a new case arrived. Calling it persistent was an understatement.

Myers didn't mind. She had nothing else to attend to anyway. Making her way through *Breaking Bad* for the sixth time wasn't enough of an excuse to share with the agitated captain when it came to another murder. Especially the death of Reginald "Getting it" Dunn.

More like Reginald "Getting it Well" Dunn.

Wexler stared at her. "Something funny?"

Too soon?

Myers wiped the smile from her face. "No. Of course not."

"Loren?"

Myers snapped a pair of gloves into place and crept deeper into the room. She stepped to the back of the office, leaving behind pristine carpet for the circle of black.

"Myers? Is Loren—?"

"He's on his way," Myers said without looking. "Traffic or something."

"'Or something' is right," Wexler said. "He didn't answer again, did he? Quit covering for him, Myers."

"He'll be here any minute, Captain."

"Right." Wexler removed the small bottle from her pocket, dumping three tablets into her palm before downing them eagerly. Myers ignored the grinding of the captain's teeth, focused on the corpse in the room. "I figured this related to your other victims."

Myers nodded. Four dead now. All charred. All taken without a fight. "Does Mathers know?"

Wexler huffed, rolling her eyes. "He's busy preparing an official statement. His favorite task."

"Figures."

Wexler offered a nod then left for the hall, giving Myers the room. Alone, the young detective sighed and removed the glove on her left hand. She pulled out her cell. No calls. No messages. She started to dial, but stopped midway.

There was no point. Her last three calls went to voicemail, the last obviously ignored. Sure, they were off the clock. Sure, they were supposed to have their own lives. But they didn't. Neither of them did. No circle of friends, no close family. They had work and each other.

Or so she believed. After months of building trust, Loren appeared intent on pulling away. His secret work—the cases she chided him over—took precedent, leaving everything and everyone else behind.

She knew about them. Of course she did. She was an obsessive neurotic with control issues. She *had* to learn what he was hiding. But she wanted him to be the one to tell her about it, to open up and let her in.

Not that she offered the same in return. Thoughts of the gun sitting in her nightstand drawer plagued her. Loren's gun, taken from the scene of Richard Crowne's death. The madman killed himself with it and she retrieved it. *For control.* That was her belief and the reason offered to the voice on the other end of her weekly calls, the voice that truly controlled the situation.

And her fate.

They wanted Loren contained, and she held all the cards to make it happen. Yet she hesitated at each turn. She was tired of waiting, tired of being ignored. She risked more than her own secrets by waiting even one more day, knowing the whereabouts of her father—held in witness protection—could be released at any time by the voice on the phone. Myers refused to let all her years of protecting the only man who ever meant a damn to her go to waste. Something had to change.

"Need anything… Myers?"

The confused voice brought a grin to her face. John Pratchett filled the frame of the door, his six-foot-four figure casting a shadow over the scene.

"I thought this was your night off," Myers said, drifting toward him. "Miss me?"

"They called me in."

"I can tell."

"What are you—?"

She reached up, standing on the tips of her toes, to fix his collar. She dabbed her finger with her tongue and wiped a smear from the top as she patted it back into place.

"Lipstick," Myers said. "Things going well with…what was her name? Freddie?"

Pratchett cleared his throat and stepped back, causing her to laugh.

"Frankie," he replied, his voice cracking. "Frankie Gibson and you know her name very well."

"Not as well as she knows you, apparently." They had met the bubblegum-addicted IT tech during their investigation into Edgar Rusch and his familial ties. It was love at first poorly timed joke.

"Need anything?"

"A giant billboard with a photo of the killer that says 'I DID IT.'"

Pratchett smiled. "How about Anderson? He's getting impatient."

"Tell him to wait. I want to check—"

She stopped. Loren stalked down the hall, his shabby Superman shirt and stained jeans combo giving her cramps at the sight of them. His presence was one thing, but to show up to the mayor's office—deceased or not—like a hobo was the last thing Myers needed. Not with Wexler looking for every excuse to rip him a new one because of his recent behavior.

Myers punched Pratchett's arm lightly, slipping out of the office. "You know what? Go ahead and give our esteemed coroner the room."

Pratchett started to speak then fell silent, nodding at the arrival of Loren. His goofy grin faded, youthful eyes turning sad. Myers thought to ask before noticing Wexler approaching from the opposite end of the hall.

"Myers?" Loren asked. "Why the hell am I learning about this third hand?"

"This way," she snapped, continuing past him down the hall. She smiled politely at other officers working the area, searching each room they passed. Finding an empty space, she led him inside.

Loren stopped at the door. "The scene is down—"

"In here, Loren. Now."

She closed the door behind him. He reeked, small stains coloring the red *S* on his chest in black. In his eyes, the shirt's wrinkles and holes added character. To everyone else, it was a sign of a larger problem. One quickly seen by his ruffled hair, long since in need of a cut and the thickening beard on his cheeks.

"Well?" he asked. His arms crossed his chest as he impatiently waited for an answer.

"You look like crap, Loren."

"Long day," Loren said. "Quit stalling."

"Quit making me stall," Myers answered. "With Wexler. With Mathers. Hell, everyone wants to know where the great and powerful Greg Loren is hiding out."

"I wasn't hi—"

"I called," she continued. "You ignored it. If not that, the damn phone is turned off. Been that way for weeks."

"I've been busy."

"Yeah, well, while you've been skipping briefings and ducking calls someone else has been pretty damn busy too."

Myers dropped the case file into his waiting hand. He rounded the desk, laying out the images within. He flipped through them without a word, running over the preliminaries and the backgrounds. She let him take a moment, pacing the length of the room.

"Four of these?"

She nodded. "Place is burned. Victim too. No physical evidence left behind."

"Arson?"

"No accelerant," she said. "Too focused as well. Just the victim and their immediate surroundings."

"Any connections between the victims?"

Softball questions. Each asked at every scene over the last two weeks. The answers were in the reports. They were in the investigation, one he should have been involved with since the beginning.

"Last one was a damn dishwasher. No clue how he would connect with Dunn," Myers said, struggling to keep calm. "You're really going to focus on the victims here?"

"What are you talking about?"

"Come with me." He needed to see the office that served as Dunn's resting place. Loren was distracted, lost in his own case. If she couldn't snap him back, force him to ask the right questions and to make the correct conclusions, he was useless to her.

And to Portents.

Loren followed close behind. "I'm getting tired of being dragged around."

"And I'm getting tired of carrying your ass lately." Stray glances flitted their way but she no longer cared. She stopped short of the crime scene. "The late nights. The secret work. It ends now. Look at the damn scene, Loren. Same as the other three. What do you see?"

He entered the room, sticking to the perimeter. Gloves in place, he inched toward the victim, pulling at fibers along the chair. "The marks. The glass—"

"Came from outside," Myers said. "Shattered in. What does that?"

"What are you getting at, Myers? What do you—?"

She groaned. She pointed at Dunn's charred corpse. "What do you know that can do something like that to a person, Loren? It's a simple enough question."

He stood, eyes flaring. "You can't be serious."

"I've tried to figure out another angle but they're all the same."

Loren shook his head, heading for the door. "Try harder."

She stopped him, her hand hooking tight to his arm. "I did. Out of respect for you. But you know exactly what did this and what she is capable of doing with it."

"She wouldn't," Loren muttered. "The photo—"

"Is enough proof that she is capable," Myers finished. "You can't deny that."

Loren peered at the dead man in the room. "I know."

"Dammit, Loren. It's her." Myers showcased the room. The charred victim, struck from outside. The glass from the window showered the carpet behind the desk, fused from the heat of the explosion. A hole blasted in the back of the chair from the blow. Dunn's body was scarred from the strike of a single shot—not from a gun, and not using a bullet. A single shot of lightning—channeled and controlled.

By only one weapon known to them.

"Soriya Greystone is our killer."

CHAPTER EIGHT

The high-rise complex adorning the corner of Fulcrum and Vermont met its end in a blaze that consumed three floors of the unit. The fire sent people screaming for the streets and then fleeing for safer pastures and new homes. Dozens lost their belongings. Hundreds lost their residence.

All thanks to Soriya.

Her Greystone was out of control, a side effect of merging her own stone with Mentor's. The lightning bolt sent to end the threat of a single vampire started a blaze that took the entire night to contain.

Thankfully there was no loss of life. Soriya's guilt over the event remained, however.

The wail of the sirens brought her to the high-rise. Their path of death circled the abandoned structure, those fallen at their whims all within a certain radius. Why go far from home if you didn't have to?

Tarps covered doorways. Tools littered the blackened space. Repair crews did what they could after the blaze, working tirelessly to restore the property. All efforts fell short, the management bleeding money with each passing day. Selling the complex failed, loans were turned down, and the structure languished in limbo ever since.

The perfect place to hide.

Soriya crept through the space, starting from the darkened corner apartment she last visited. From the sprawling burnt-out husk of a luxury living space, Soriya surveyed dozens of apartments: who lived there, how they lived, their joys and failures.

She only hoped to rectify the situation by not allowing another threat to inhabit the despondent property.

She found a light when she arrived on the ninth floor. Candles dotted the unit, a corner loft overlooking the avenues. The sound of traffic slowed to a dull roar, the wind whipping through the shattered windows at the end of the hall, sending a chill along the level.

A siren sat in the corner, surrounded by light. She held a book in her hands, trying to get comfortable with her back against the wall.

Soriya crept into the room, sticking to the shadows.

The woman stirred at the shifting of feet along the worn floor. She lowered the text. "Aggie? Pei? You there?"

"No." Soriya stepped into the light, the Greystone in her hand.

"Oh," the ageless woman muttered with a nod. She closed the book and set it down next to her. Then she pointed to the kitchen and the water boiling on the stove. "Do you mind?"

Soriya eyed her curiously. "Go ahead."

"Thanks," the woman said. She removed the pot from the burner and poured a cup, steam rising up and permeating the teabag inside. "Always calms the nerves."

"And a good book," Soriya said.

The woman beamed at the copy of *Alice in Wonderland* on the floor. "Who would have thought that with all the technological advancements throughout history, libraries would be our greatest achievement?"

The siren took a long sip of her drink, letting it fill her. Soriya retrieved the book, passing it to her waiting hand. The woman shook her head.

"Return it for me?"

"Really?"

"My sisters wouldn't appreciate it," she replied. "Someone else should."

Soriya put the book down. Scanning the apartment cautiously, she paced the room. "Where are they?"

"No idea."

The Greystone bearer's brow furrowed, recalling the name shouted earlier atop the Walker Complex as well as Mentor's teachings. "Thelxinoe, right?"

"Thel," the siren answered. "Easier to say."

"True."

"Like I said," Thel continued. "I left my sisters in the alley after we ran. I meant to pack, to leave them, but—"

"Family."

Thel took a deep breath, the scent of jasmine rising from the steaming cup. "I'm not like them. Not anymore."

"People are dead. You sent that man over the ledge—"

"And you saved him," Thel said. "But I know. I do. I shouldn't have…" She finished her tea, then took a long breath. "That's not who I am. I should have said something sooner, stopped them somehow. But you will, won't you?"

"Yes."

"Good. We deserve it," Thel said. She lifted the book, grazing the cover before kneeling on the ground before Soriya. "A second chance and we earned none of it."

The young woman closed her eyes, waiting for the end. Soriya lifted the stone, feeling the light grow along the surface. Thel was a siren, a threat to the city. She and her sisters killed people. Yet Thel didn't take control of Soriya. She didn't resist or run from her fate.

Soriya lowered the weapon, the stone growing silent. The young woman at her feet opened a single eye, then cocked her head in confusion.

"What are you doing?"

Soriya tucked the stone into the pouch at her hip. "Earn this chance, Thel. Or I'll find you."

Thel stood, nodding quickly as Soriya moved for the window. She opened the makeshift curtains, a stiff breeze blowing out the closest candles. Soriya jumped into the whipping wind, the ribbon down her left side connecting with the closest building, swinging her toward the street.

The spared woman yelled into the night, her promise caught on the breeze. "I will. I…I will!"

Soriya let the ribbon drop her at the end of the block, falling into a full run before slowing to a brisk pace through the city streets. Thel may have been looking for a fresh start but her sisters remained killers.

Backtracking their movements brought Soriya to the Walker Complex. The alley Thel mentioned was her first stop, noting the sign painted in thick black on the wall. Soriya recognized it, the image marking a number of notes in the Bypass chamber.

A Circle of Shadows.

Walking over to the sigil marring the brick, Soriya heard a crunch under the sole of her sneaker. She pulled back, bending low. A locket lay smashed, the gold chain glinting in the moonlight.

"She was wearing this," Soriya whispered. Aglaope. The scarlet-haired siren. This was her locket and one that was cherished, as all her possessions appeared to be. Small scratches dug into the concrete surrounding the fallen object.

And blood.

"Who did this?"

"Like you don't know."

A kick followed the proclamation. Soriya was barely able to duck under the strike. She leapt over the next blow, the world a blur of motion as her feet connected with the black mark on the wall before she bounded over the threat in the alley.

She caught his stare, wonder and awe mixed with anger. He was younger than her, a muscular frame hidden behind oversized clothing. He jumped at her, giving her little time to react, but enough to cushion his blow with a well-placed block.

"Hey!"

The boy pressed his assault. "Who did you take this time? Who else is suffering because of you and your damn shadows?"

His fist connected with her side, driving her back. He grinned, his spirit vibrant and in tune with the dance. She refused to fall, prepared for his next assault.

"That's enough," she snapped, catching his fist in her hand.

"How?"

"You're good," Soriya said with a grin. "I'm better."

She twisted hard on his arm, sending him spinning through the air. He rolled with the blow, dodging her strike, but slamming into the alley wall.

"Try this then," the boy said. A small object fell into his grasp, light growing along the surface.

"It can't be." Soriya's eyes widened. "A Greystone?"

CHAPTER NINE

Soriya knocked the stone aside, blocking a jab from her attacker in the process. Keeping his main weapon at bay was her primary focus. She ducked under a second strike before spinning out in a kick to knock him off his feet.

The ploy failed, the young man leaping to avoid her. The stone lit along the surface and Soriya dove out of reach as the sigil took hold.

The shockwave shattered the alley, debris ripping from the walls of the surrounding buildings. Soriya fell to the ground, skidding along the pavement as she covered her face from the brick slamming down on the wide path.

A cloud of dust from the devastation wafted in the air around them. Soriya coughed, standing among the wreckage.

A Greystone. He had a Greystone. Another piece to a greater whole, just as Henry Erikson alluded to months earlier. She never thought it possible, never imagined his discovery coming to pass, even with the evidence offered by the deranged professor. She carried on as if nothing had changed, alone in the world, the power unique to her.

His symbols were not the runes displayed on her stone. His tactics changed, ebbing and flowing with the rhythm of the conflict. He was not stuck in a pattern, following a playbook handed down by Mentor. The young man and the stone were one.

Soriya peered through the debris. She tried to clear her lungs from the dust settling over her body. A light slipped through the cloud and she ducked seconds before the air sliced above her.

A concussive blast broke the ground, knocking her back. Leaping toward the right, Soriya bounced from the wall, her leg coming down hard on the young man's position. Or what *had been* his position.

He was already on the other side of her, his arm shooting out in defense against her strike. Soriya's leg slammed against the ground; the man's fist connected with her ribs.

"Enough!" she yelled, holding the wound. She stood defiant to the stone's glowing light. A kick to his chest sent him reeling but he held his ground. "I said, knock it off!"

His stone was ready for another strike. So was hers.

"You..." He stopped, the light dimming along the surface. "You have a—"

"A Greystone," she said, sweat dripping into her eyes. She refused to blink, wary to wipe it away with his weapon still in play.

"I..." He paused, raising his free hand before lowering the stone. He inched to his feet, slipping the stone in his pocket. "I didn't realize there were others. When I saw you in front of the sign I just—"

"It happens," Soriya replied. She lowered her weapon but kept it in hand. "How did you—?"

"My parents."

"They passed it down?"

"In a way," he said, his head low. "They died. There was a fire."

"A fire?" Flames danced behind her eyes. The image of the van burning, half-smashed into the trunk of the charred tree at Olcott Curve. The final moment of her previous life and the birth of the new. She found the stone in the wreckage. The only link to her parents, to who she was before that fateful day.

"You?"

Soriya managed a nod but little else, lost to memory.

The young man understood, pulling the stone out again. He smiled as he passed it between hands. "It took months to figure out. I'm sure I'm not even close to understanding the thing but… Well, it's been strange to say the least."

She didn't realize at first, the slow motion of each toss back and forth between waiting hands. Then the stone appeared to hover in mid-air, spinning of its own accord. When he dropped his hands, the Greystone danced in front of him, spinning and whirling, the signs and symbols shifting with each motion.

"How are you doing that?"

"You've never—?" The ancient weapon fell into his hand. He shook his head. "Sorry."

He had the stone for months and managed to unlock more of its secrets than she had in decades. Her focus had been so split between the teachings of Mentor and the threats to the city. But that was only an excuse. She never pushed herself, never worked hard enough to learn more. No wonder Mentor always displayed such disappointment.

"Don't be," Soriya said. The wreckage settled in the alley and they paced the length of the Walker Complex. "Those sigils? The signs on the stone? Was that math?"

He nodded. "Languages seem to be its thing. Dad always thought I studied too much. Just felt natural."

"In an unnatural world."

"Exactly."

"Balance."

"Pardon me?"

"Something Ment—someone used to tell me," Soriya said. She stopped at the black circle along the brick edifice, cracked but still identifiable after their battle. "Balance is the key. The natural and the unnatural. The stone and the Bypass."

"The Bypass?"

"A door," Soriya clarified. "A crossroads to the infinite."

"For real? And it's tied to the stone?"

Soriya held the Greystone up. "Protection. A weapon and a shield in one. I'm sorry I—"

"Don't have all the answers," he finished. "I get it."

She smiled. He understood more than he let on, following her ramblings, taking in each and learning. A teacher and a student. Both with the same gift, the same talent at their disposal, the responsibility of it all. In mere moments together, he understood her world like no other.

"Maybe together?" he started, rubbing his neck. "I mean, the two of us? We could figure this thing out, this Bypass?"

"I don't even know your name."

He chuckled and held out his hand. "Right. Talk about rude. Noah. Noah Jordan."

"Soriya," she answered, offering a firm shake.

"Like Cher?" Noah asked. She didn't answer and he waved the awkward stare away with a laugh. "Sorry. Something my dad says. Said." He sighed, kicking at the ground. "So this Bypass—"

"Is my responsibility." She pointed to the symbol on the wall. "Like this city."

She regretted the words immediately. The hurt spread from his faded grin to his solemn eyes. "Right."

He started down the alley for the street. "Wait."

Noah stopped. "I'm looking for answers, Soriya. That's all. I could use someone on my side. Someone to trust. You look like you could use someone like that as well."

"Noah…" She raced after him as he turned the corner. The crowd had lightened, the late hour encouraging people to go home. Still, she failed to find him through the darkness. "Dammit, I…"

He wasn't wrong. He was a stranger to the city and needed her help. With the stone. With the Bypass. With the symbol marking the wall of the alley. And he could provide the same.

Balance.

She started down the street, hoping to catch him, halting at the sound of a voice in the alley.

"Don't even think about it." Greg Loren waited in the shadows, fingers inspecting the painted symbol on the wall. "We need to talk. Now."

CHAPTER TEN

Loren took a sharp breath. His body shook—seeing the woman before him unsteadied his nerves. Every instinct screamed at him to take action. To ask the question that had haunted his every waking moment since being handed the photo.

Soriya Greystone. The shadow in the window the day Beth fell.

Following Soriya was never an issue. Detective work rarely entered into it—only the ability to glance up to catch a flash of lightning against the clear sky. Tonight's came with a bonus light show, flaring colors and a brisk wind that continued to swirl the length of the alley.

"Do I want to know who your friend is?" It slipped from his lips. The old trap he always fell in with her—the banter. The camaraderie came from years of trust, years of partnership against the darkness that infested the city. Her secrets, however, outweighed those notions.

Secrets that culminated in the deaths of four men.

"I wish *I* knew," she said. Facing Loren, a smile returned. It cut through him, her joy at their time together. He tried to avoid her for months, working within the system, working with Myers, in order to keep his distance.

Even her answer gave him pause. The doubt stemming from the single image locked in his mind. As well as the one adorning the alley wall. His hands fell to his hips, his eyes dipping to the debris-ridden concrete.

"This doesn't work anymore, Soriya. It hasn't in a long time."

"Loren?"

"What have you been doing?" he asked, tempering his anger. At least, hoping to—although the confusion in her eyes told a different story. "Don't hide it, don't deny it. Just tell me."

"The sirens?" Soriya held out a locket, letting the gold chain dangle between her fingers. "They got away. Is that what this is about?"

Sirens? What the hell was that now? How could she see the image on the wall and not know what it was? Not understand the connection with everything hidden in the city? Or did she already know the truth and she kept it from him? It wouldn't be the first time.

"Dammit," he muttered. "I thought just once you would play it straight with me. No lies. No secrets."

"I am," she shot back. "Loren, I know I've screwed things up in the past but I have no idea—"

He reached into his pocket to retrieve the image given to him by Myers. "The damn *mayor*, Soriya."

She snatched the photo away, her gaze locked on the dead man at the center of a charred maelstrom. Loren gauged her reaction.

"What?"

"No? Nothing?" The photos of the other victims flew from his hand, scattering along the alley. She followed them to their resting place, crouching to lift the closest. Loren pointed to the image, picking at the wound. "How about Dennis Carmichael? A *dishwasher*, for crying out loud."

"These marks—"

"Glad you noticed," Loren pressed. "Care to elaborate on your previous statement, considering only one weapon is capable of making these marks?"

"Loren, you can't—"

"I get it. We don't see every threat like you do. But tell me what the hell these people did to deserve this?"

She dropped the photo and stepped away from him. His chest heaved, his heart pounding in his ears. Sullen eyes greeted him. "You think I did this?"

"I came to find out the truth."

She shook her head. "No. No, you didn't. You made up your mind long before coming here. I knew it was bad between us, Loren, but how did it get *this* bad?"

"You killed—"

"I didn't kill these people!" Soriya rushed to his side, reaching for his hand. "Look at me, Loren. Please. Just look at me."

"Don't, Loren."

Myers stood at the mouth of the alley, gun leveled on the woman with the torn jeans and ribbon whipping down her left side.

"Myers?"

The detective inched closer. "Step away from her, Loren."

"What the hell is this?" Loren said, blocking Soriya from view.

"She's dangerous."

"I saved your life." Soriya tried to push Loren aside but he kept her back, their dynamic upended by Myers' arrival.

"And taken how many others?" Myers asked. "Right, Loren?"

"What is she talking about?"

Loren shook his head, tossing Myers a narrow glare. This wasn't what he wanted. Not like this. Not at gunpoint.

"Ask her, Loren. Ask her about Beth."

"Beth?"

The name on her lips sent rage through his weary body.

"No," he snapped. "Dammit, Myers. Why did you follow me?"

"To make sure this ended the only way it can."

"Not going to happen, Detective." Soriya pulled away from him, fists clenched.

"Soriya."

"I won't let it, Loren."

Hands spread, Loren inched toward Myers. "This isn't necessary, Myers. We can—"

"*Four people*," Myers said. "How many more will it take?"

"You don't know—"

"Yes, we do," Myers yelled. "And you do too."

The evidence was in front of him, scattered along the ground. Charred marks ran along the edifice of the buildings surrounding the alley. Everything condemned the woman at his side. Everything begged for him to do his job.

"Let me talk to her," Loren pleaded, trying to find a way out of the confrontation.

"You can," Myers replied. "At the precinct."

The precinct. He recalled the last time she was taken into custody and the disaster that ensued. She never fought the system, never stepped out of line. But for this, she would. There would be no taking her in. Not without a fight. Not without unnecessary bloodshed.

Something Loren hoped to avoid. "No. Not like this."

"There's more going on here," Soriya said in a hushed tone. "I can't help behind bars."

"Move away from her, Loren," Myers said, cocking the hammer of her sidearm.

His eyes implored for more time from Myers. His partner. He meant to trust her with everything that had been going on: about the image on the alley wall, about his dreams. All with the hope that he would finally have someone to help find the answers.

Like the woman at his side.

For so long he believed Soriya to be that person. The one who would always be there for him, who would always help him find his way out of the darkness. She had for so long, sometimes pulling him along kicking and screaming. Soriya gave him purpose, pushed him to be a better man more times than he could count.

No matter what the evidence said, no matter the image locked in his mind. There remained something else.

Hope.

"Go."

"Loren?"

He stepped toward Myers, barring her path. "Just go."

The air snapped, the ribbon of Kali snagging the cornice of the Walker Complex and its neighbor. Soriya soared overhead, feet running along the wall before leaping across the way. He stopped, watching her flee, her nimble shadow dancing back and forth in her climb for the roof.

Shots erupted. Myers unleashed an entire clip at her fleeing suspect.

"Don't," Loren shouted. "Myers! Hold your fire!"

Bullets marred the walls, ricocheting across the gap. None came close to catching the leaping figure before she disappeared out of sight.

"Dammit, Loren." Myers grimaced. She jammed her pistol into the holster and locked it in place. "We had her."

"As what? Target practice? Is that what justice is in this city now?"

"Tell it to the murderer you let escape."

"There was a better way to handle it," Loren said.

"Yeah, there was," Myers said. "Now I have no choice."

"Myers?"

From both sides of the alley they came. A pair of officers on each end approached Loren, pistols aimed. Confused, Loren failed to notice the cuffs hanging from her fingers before Myers slammed the gleaming pair against his wrists. He tried to pull away, the shock of the impact stunning him. She held tight. The officers, suddenly closer than he realized, remained silent, witnesses to his inaction.

"You're under arrest, Loren, for obstructing a murder investigation."

"You can't be serious."

"I am."

He stood in disbelief. "Myers. Come on. This is a mistake."

She shook her head, pulling him close. "No," she whispered. "This was your decision, Loren. You should have trusted me."

Her eyes were cold, the woman he thought he knew gone. He tried to find a reason, tried to fight to make sense of what happened, of how to explain everything... But it was far too late for that now.

"I'm sorry it came to this," Myers continued, prodding him toward the flashing lights of the squad cars. "I think you will be too."

CHAPTER ELEVEN

Soriya watched Loren's arrest unfold from a rooftop a block over. She crouched low to avoid more shots fired into the air by a trigger-happy Samantha Myers.

Why the woman hated her so much was beyond belief, especially having saved her during their struggle with the Charon. Sure, there was that bit about stealing evidence in the middle of the investigation, and also her inaction in preventing the death of Jeremy Bennett, an act fated to occur long before their arrival to the small ranch home in Tolliver's Grove.

But other than that?

It took all her willpower to stop from jumping back down to the street. She could easily rectify Loren's incarceration, but in the process make him a fugitive in the eyes of the law. Not exactly a win for them, but a situation they would then share.

She was a murder suspect four times over. She was shocked—not only at the outrageous allegations at her involvement in the recent deaths, but who brought them upon her. Loren truly believed she killed four men, four ordinary people. He blamed her. How could he even *think* such a thing, let alone level it against her?

That was not the only revelation of the night. Not by a long shot. *Beth.* A secret long held. How much did he know? Had he finally learned the truth? Soriya's jaw tightened, her fist slamming against the ledge. She was a fool for not telling him sooner, for not being honest about what happened that day.

The day Beth fell. The day everything changed for Loren.

"I'm sorry about your friend."

Instinct took hold and she grabbed at the shadow looming behind her. She connected with his wrist, pushing his arm across his chest to drive him back along the roof. Noah Jordan slammed against the closest air conditioning unit. Soriya clutched tighter to his caught appendage.

"You're *sorry?*"

"Hey, listen—"

"What the hell have you done?" she yelled, squeezing tighter. "The mayor—"

"Wasn't who he said he was," Noah finished.

"So you killed him?"

"What?" He stopped struggling, eyes flaring at the accusation. "What are you—?"

"I saw the marks," she said, stepping back. "The scorch marks. The victims were charred like they had been struck by lightning."

"Victims?"

"Four of them. You're really playing this game?"

"I didn't kill him…them…whoever!" Noah nursed the strained arm, pushing off the air conditioning unit. "I was keeping an eye on Dunn but that's all."

"Why?"

"Because of the group he's working for. People who aren't looking out for Portents' best interests."

"And you are?" she asked, watching him intently. He was rattled, visibly horrified at the news. But how else could the cause of death be explained? She saw the photos. A Greystone was involved…or was it meant to look that way?

"These people deal in manipulation, blackmail, and murder," Noah said. "They work in the shadows and have for years. You had no idea?"

The marking in the alley. The same one from Mentor's map in the Bypass chamber. Shadows falling over events in the city and never brought to light. At least by them.

"How did you?" Her fists remained tightly fixed at her sides, her body poised and prepared. Too many surprises had come her way tonight. "How did you know about them? You just show up and suddenly understand this place better than me?"

"My parents. These people…" Noah shouted. "They killed my parents."

Lost in a fire. Like her own.

"I'm not buying it," she said. "What aren't you telling me?"

"I can prove it," Noah answered. "I came back to help you see what is happening here. You don't have to do this alone anymore."

"I'm not alone."

"Really?" Both peered at the departing patrol cars. Myers remained on the street, staring into the darkness. Waiting for another opportunity to drag Soriya away in cuffs. An opportunity the dark-skinned protector refused to give. "That's not how things looked from here. This thing we do? This Greystone? No one else gets it. Hell, I barely understand it."

"But you do," Soriya said. Their previous altercation proved that much. His talent with the stone surpassed her own, the methods behind it outside of her own thinking when it came to wielding the great weapon. "How?"

He held out his hand. "She can help you too, Soriya. She wants to help everyone."

"Who?"

"She found me at my lowest, helped me keep going, to keep fighting for answers."

"I need a name."

"You wouldn't recognize it. But her title? Well, former title at any rate…"

"Who, Noah? Who is helping you?"

He smiled. "She calls herself a Luminary."

CHAPTER TWELVE

She followed without a word. Hearing about the Luminary's presence rattled her to her core. She hadn't seen one since her singular visit to the Library of the Luminaries, long since abandoned by the group. To have one still in the city, with access to the knowledge and the wherewithal to use it, was exciting to Soriya Greystone.

And worrisome.

If such a force was present and had been since the doors to the great library closed, then why hide in Portents? Why not reach out to her and Mentor? Why not make a difference? Was it their code of non-interference that held her back?

Noah Jordan offered no insight to her unspoken questions as he led her uptown to the Corridor. When they passed the marketplace at Allure, she realized their destination. Her curiosity spiked, but she held her tongue.

"It's through here," Noah said, leading her up the steps to the Courtyard. He ran along the railing, taking them two at a time, while Soriya paused at the base. The statues once adorning both sides of the wide stairs lay in ruins. Small pieces of debris remained along the gutter. The marble base of each was broken, offering nothing more than a lump of a once-proud figure.

"What happened?" She picked at the rubble.

The sight of Noah returning from the double bronze doors surprised her. "You coming?"

She nodded, leaving behind the sacred place's safety protocol. The stairs faded and the doors opened before her. The Courtyard spread across her field of vision, twelve city blocks contained in the structure, hidden from the world yet connecting to so many more.

When she brought Loren there was a rush of movement, a circus of myths and legends scrambling about the place. Up and down the street, into the shops and housing—a cornucopia of creatures spreading good cheer as they walked between worlds. Living.

No more. The place was empty. The street was vacant, devoid of life, except for one. She smiled at their arrival, crow's feet around her thin, amber eyes. A scar ran along her right cheek.

"Soriya," Noah ushered her into the open space. "I'd like you to meet—"

"We've actually met before," the woman interrupted, cutting in front of Noah. "Haven't we, Soriya?"

Soriya hesitated, lost in the woman's face. She heard the words again, remembering days long since passed yet never forgotten.

"The library. The Medusa coin."

The woman nodded. "The coin was marked by death."

Soriya chuckled, astonished. "A Luminary."

"Former member, anyway."

The two crossed the street, Noah following at a distance. Soriya peered across the road, searching for some sign of life, but found none. Four pillars branched from the buildings in the road, small carvings scattered along the beams. Tools and scaffolding rested at the base.

"They are not the group we are here to talk about today, though, are they?" the Luminary asked.

Soriya shook her head. "You're helping him. Helping Noah against these shadow people."

"A Circle of Shadows," she confirmed, throwing her hands up in front of her. "Their name for it. Very macabre."

Soriya smiled. "Slightly dramatic."

"Not as much as black cloaks and white masks, I'm sure, though it doesn't make them any less dangerous."

"Noah believes they killed his parents."

The Luminary nodded. "The Circle has a hand in everything. From politics to the courts to the barista at your favorite coffee shop. They manipulate events for their personal gain, all to finance their operation."

"Which is…?"

The woman's eyes dimmed. "This place is empty for a reason, Soriya."

"The Charon—"

"Which you stopped. So where are they?"

Soriya paced toward an alley off the main path. "The shadows?"

"Are everywhere."

The Greystone bearer stopped at the mouth of the alley. Kok'Kol's words echoed in her mind, their visit atop the Rath during the Charon's reign of terror the last time she spoke with the black raven.

There is more going on in the shadows than you know.

"Kok'Kol tried to warn me," she muttered. Her sneaker caught on something and she shifted away from it, curious. A black feather slipped free, skittering along the pavement. Beneath it lay a series of scratches along the ground.

A shadow loomed behind her and she stood to face the waiting Luminary. Soriya wiped her hands clean along her torn jeans. "So you're taking them down."

"Bringing them into the light."

"Someone is killing them."

"What?" She shook her head as Noah confirmed the situation. "Forcing these people to face their choices was our goal. To see someone else pervert our intentions—"

"So you have no idea who might be behind this?"

"None," she replied. "We are not violent people, Soriya. We seek the truth in all things. Surely you understand that better than anyone."

"I do." Soriya grinned, pulling her hair back behind her ear. "I'm sorry. What do I call you? Luminary? Miss?"

The woman laughed. "The apology is mine. Karen."

"Karen?"

"That's what Christopher always called me."

The name gave her pause. The name she never learned until after his passing. "Mentor? I didn't realize he was close to anyone from the library."

"Christopher had his secrets."

"Too many," Soriya said.

"He met with me quite often," Karen remarked, the pair pacing steadily along the street. "We would talk about the city, our roles in it. I tried to help when I could."

"Like with Noah?" How did he fit into it? Did Mentor know about him? About his stone? What other secrets did he hide over the years?

"Christopher asked me to locate other bearers," Karen said. "It took some doing."

"Why bring in others?"

"In case." She smiled at the lack of an answer. "He always believed in being prepared for any eventuality. The Bypass needed to be safe. Protected."

He always acted that way. Ten steps ahead of a threat, so blinded by the path he forgot who else walked with him. Afraid to let anyone in, except he did with this woman. He trusted her with the notion there were more stones and in effect, more bearers of the Greystone. More people to help. More people to trust. Only he didn't trust the one by his side all those years hidden underground in the Bypass chamber.

He didn't trust Soriya.

"I see."

"He wasn't wrong," Karen continued. "Rarely ever was, in fact. Except about the Bypass. We can help, Soriya."

"I don't—"

Karen stopped her. "I remember the arguments of old. Fear of abuse. Taking advantage of all that knowledge locked in the orb. I always thought he was being paranoid."

"He wasn't," Soriya answered. The Night of the Lights proved as much. The city almost paid the price for Nathaniel Evans' abuse of the stone.

"I realize that now," Karen said. "But he also always had something no one else had when it came to safeguarding the secrets of the infinite. He had you. Who do you have, Soriya?"

"I—" There was a clear answer to the question once. Not that long ago Soriya would have blurted out Loren's name with ease, the detective proving to be every bit as capable of holding the line. Until now. He believed her to be a killer, a murderer. After all they fought for together, to have that laid at her feet, to witness his true feelings, proved how divided they truly were.

Karen's hand fell on Soriya's shoulder. "Think about it, Soriya. That's all. We know the city, the true city, and we cherish that knowledge. We can help—with the Bypass, with the shadows surrounding everything in Portents. Now more than ever, we can help."

"I will," she said, her voice quiet against the thoughts coursing like a river. "I'll think about it."

Noah rushed over as she moved toward the exit. "Leaving? I'll walk with you."

"A minute, Noah?" Karen called from the street. Soriya continued for the Corridor beyond the open door then stopped, turning back to the pair.

"About the Circle… You said something about proof?"

"Of course," Karen said. She removed a slip of paper from her pocket and passed it over. "Follow him. You'll understand."

Noah cleared his throat. "Are you sure I can't—?"

"I'll be fine," Soriya said, reading the name before crumpling the paper between her fingers. "I should handle this myself."

CHAPTER THIRTEEN

It was time.

Karen saw the look on the young woman's face as she departed from the abandoned Courtyard. How her head hung low and her gait slowed. Soriya's doubts crippled her on all fronts, and Karen seeded those doubts to a satisfying conclusion.

Noah Jordan hesitated, the words threatening to spill out with each caught breath, with each dramatic sigh. Karen rolled her eyes. She forgot how it was to be young. For her, it had been decades since feeling like every day was filled with gut-wrenching heartache and overpowering desire. Desire turned to ambition turned to focus, the end result now within her grasp.

"I don't like lying to her," Noah muttered, the entryway clear of the Greystone bearer. She was off to discover another secret kept in the darkness of the city she trusted so fully. A difficult lesson to learn, one Karen confronted throughout her life.

Secrets destroyed.

Everything turned in Karen's direction, starting with the columns at the heart of the Courtyard. Four pillars of stone rose out of the buildings lining the central street hidden away from the rest of Portents. Each sat equidistant from the others, a container awaiting its cargo.

Karen knelt beside one of the stark white pillars, reaching for the tools resting at the base. Lifting the chisel she began her work, following the lightly sketched rune etched along the palette.

Noah cleared his throat. "I said—"

"It is necessary," Karen said. "I wish it wasn't."

"She might decide differently. You don't—"

"I do." She dropped the tool and jumped to her feet. "I know a Greystone very well at this point. She needs to witness what can happen when you stand alone. To see the truth. That's what this is all for, isn't it, Noah?"

His eyes wavered for a moment. "Of course."

She patted his shoulder. "That is all we are offering Soriya. A chance at understanding. She's not there yet, though."

"She's not?"

"No." The doubt remained but so did the lessons programmed into her by Christopher Eckhart—lessons that refused to abate no matter the secrets learned about his past. And they were numerous.

Including Soriya's entry into the world.

Karen was positive that secret was kept from the naive girl. She could shatter all illusions of the man. But there was a better way to do it. A better push—not only for her but for everyone. One that assured the desired outcome.

"Then let me talk to her. I can—"

"No."

"I think I—"

Her cold stare stopped him. "It's time, Noah."

"Time?" he asked. Realization set in and he staggered back a step. "Wait. Are you sure?"

Karen walked with him toward the entrance of the Courtyard. "Soriya Greystone is not the only one in Portents in need of a wake-up call," Karen said. "The runes are almost in place. It is time."

After so much planning, a decade of quiet manipulation in the background of the city, she would not allow herself to deviate from her intentions.

Knowledge was power, hoarded by the desperate few, intent on damning the rest. It was time for a change, one she would bring to the people of Portents and the world at large. Her role as Luminary centered on discovering secrets, on spreading truth. For the betterment of all.

Content with his silent acceptance of her request, Karen peered out over the street. The skyline of downtown lit up the distance. The dawn approached, and with it a new day. The day of the Luminary. A day of truth above all. No matter the price paid, no matter the sacrifices.

And sacrifices would be made. So many sacrifices…
"Send the signal, Noah. Tonight."

CHAPTER FOURTEEN

Loren beat the back of his head against the wall of the cell. He tried to relax in the holding area of the precinct, even attempting sleep. Unfortunately, the dream came right away, the concept of rest fast becoming foreign to him.

Beth continued to reach out, to try to relay some crucial piece of information. But he didn't understand anything, a fact that frustrated him and tired him all over. Something escaped him, *everything* did, while he lost hours in holding.

Dozens were dead, buried in a mass grave. He wanted to relay the information, but Myers wasn't exactly making the Christmas card list at the moment, and his lone ally in the department, Captain Alejo Ruiz, was still on a leave of absence to reconnect with his family after sacrificing decades for the job.

Alone, isolated, Loren's thoughts ran in circles, ridiculing the lack of answers in the dark.

When the cell opened, it startled him. He rubbed at his eyes, pushing back the bleariness. Sloane stood at the door, pity on his face.

"Bail's been posted."

"Fantastic," Loren said, his ass numb from the bench.

"Sorry about this, Detective."

Loren smiled. Not long ago any sympathy would have been a surprise. He stood as the department pariah, the lone wolf causing nothing but problems when no one needed another one to handle.

Since the Erikson case, things shifted. Old friends returned, new ones introduced themselves—though Loren had trouble remembering their names—and the precinct almost felt like home again.

"Not your fault," Loren said, patting Sloane on the shoulder then heading down the hall.

"I'm sure it will get cleared up," Sloane called.

Loren knew better. Rufus Mathers grinned at the end of the hall, a maniacal laugh waiting to break out in the face of Loren's situation. The vengeful day shift captain hated Loren, constantly reviewing his reports. Always on the hunt to find an offense and remove him from duty.

Was he the reason for his stay in holding? Myers was gone, having departed as soon as she passed him along to the first floor crew. She wouldn't have done that, wouldn't push him away like that, not after months of coming together as a team. But Mathers?

Loren's jaw tightened and he shifted for the sneering captain. Fortunately, Wexler cut him off. "A word, Detective."

Loren sighed, rubbing the kink in his neck. Wexler took over for Ruiz during his extended leave. A good cop, always backing up the officers under her command.

"Captain, I—"

"Shut it, Loren," she snapped. She was, however, not the biggest fan of Loren, whose constant scruff and inability to appear presentable for the job remained a sticking point between them. And the cause of more than one migraine for the woman. "Just save the explanations. They're not going to help."

"Looks that way," he muttered.

Wexler shook her head, hands to her hips. "You're a smart cop, Loren. The sooner you realize the spot you're in, the sooner you figure out how to dig your way out."

"I've been here before, Captain."

"No," Wexler said. "Not like this. Someone is out there picking people off. Rich, poor—no one is safe. And you protected our chief suspect."

"We don't know—"

"Soriya Greystone," Wexler jumped in, stopping Loren. His head fell. "Yeah, she's no longer your little secret. She's involved in this and no matter your history, no matter the deal you and Ruiz worked out in the past with this woman, you are on the wrong side of this."

They found out about her, about the work being done over the last five years. How? Loren winced. *His files.* Myers shared his office. She had access to all his files, even the ones tucked in his desk in the bottom drawer.

"What do you want me to do, Captain?"

She leaned close, her voice low. "Stay the hell out of it. Let your partner do her job."

"Myers is wrong."

"No. Working with an unsanctioned vigilante was wrong. Myers showed us the cases you've hidden."

"Captain—"

"The hearing is set, Loren," Wexler said, backing away. She pinched the bridge of her nose, another migraine on the rise. "There's nothing I can do."

Another hearing. Another censure. Another hit on his record—the one thing he excelled at above all others. People didn't turn to him for his winning personality. All he had was the work, the cases to keep him moving.

Including Beth's.

"Dammit."

Wexler left him in the hall. Mathers caught up with her, the pair exchanging heated words before rounding the corner. Glares from his fellow officers followed Loren as he headed for the exit. The same stares from years ago.

Questioning everything. Questioning him.

Ruiz made it possible for Loren to work, to handle the cases no one could understand given the threats involved. Ruiz kept his head off the chopping block, using his position to keep Mathers at bay. With Ruiz gone, no barrier existed. Myers didn't have his back in this. Neither did Wexler, it seemed.

At least he still had Ruiz as a friend. He hoped word would get to him about the weary detective's arrest. The two of them could figure out their next move and how to handle not only the hearing but the other mysteries plaguing the city.

Loren stopped short of the lobby and the man waiting to take him home. Ruiz was nowhere to be seen. In his place stood a towering officer and his pink-haired girlfriend snapping gum between her teeth.

Filthy habit.

"Pratchett?"

John Pratchett grinned at the door, holding it open for confused detective. "Let's take a ride. We have a lot to talk about."

CHAPTER FIFTEEN

Streetlights beamed overhead, the orange luminescence leading the SUV deeper into the downtown district. Loren stared at them, lost in thought. His silence brought with it a never-ending array of questions. Jail time had that effect on him.

Myers left him to rot, refusing to offer an explanation or an apology over his arrest. To her, he was the betrayer and he felt the exact opposite held true. He thought he knew her, believed her to be the one to pick up the flag dropped by Soriya in their marathon struggle against the threats to Portents, the cases that defied all logic. He planned to tell her everything, from his investigations into the uncovered missing person's cases to the organization behind their deaths.

The opportunity, however, slipped away. She stood against him when he needed time and support to understand the current dilemma. Four deaths, four seemingly innocent citizens, struck down by the power of the Greystone—Soriya's weapon of choice. There was a reason behind it, an explanation.

Now lost thanks to Samantha Myers' actions.

Perhaps she wasn't the one he should have trusted, after all. It was possible he didn't know Myers at all. Perhaps the same was true for the man driving the vehicle.

Pratchett was silent, keeping his eyes on the road. Loren knew from years of working together how the officer disliked the quiet that came from being on patrol. Pratchett was frequently reprimanded for being spotted talking to the people of Portents, rather than working his beat.

To have him so silent was disorienting, like the orange light washing over the darkening skyline. Another day missed. Loren wondered if there would be another.

No more sunrises.

His wife's warnings echoed his own. He was exhausted, visible in his bloodshot eyes and his thickening beard. He looked like he'd stumbled out of an alley, rather than served the city in an official capacity—though that appeared to be coming to a close, if Myers and Mathers had their way.

So many sides against him. And now secrets from Pratchett. For so long, the lumbering prankster at the department had shown no depth, no capacity for any hidden layers beneath his goofy grin. Something had changed.

"Want to tell me where we're going, Pratchett?"

Forty-five minutes had passed since they dropped off Frankie Gibson at her place in the coves. Promises were made to meet later, cemented in a deep kiss that flushed even Loren's cheeks. Pratchett wore it like a badge of honor, glowing from the exchange.

Then the silence came. Loren peered back to the fading exits of the expressway, the SUV dipping into traffic along the concourse for Evans.

"What do you mean?" Pratchett asked, taking a slow left to avoid last-minute pedestrians rushing for home.

"I realize your sense of direction has never been up to snuff, but you passed my exit two miles back."

"I know."

Loren rested his head against the seat. "Is this part of what you wanted to talk about?"

"Yes."

"This is fun, Pratchett. Maybe we can do this when you're feeling chattier and I don't feel like the Loren Revenge Squad is out to get me."

"The what?"

"Did no one read *Superman* comics when they were kids?"

Pratchett laughed. "Only when they were kids?"

"Point."

Loren returned to the window. The city shifted, the car slowly crossing over Main and heading through Grant Square and the Walker Memorial. Loren rarely headed this way, typically cutting through the Knoll to King's Lane or skirting north for the marketplace at Allure.

This was an older district, one of the first in Portents after the expansion from the docks. Beth took him on a tour once, focusing on the impact of Walker and his architectural styling that had endured for more than a century. Saint Sebastian's Church marked one border, the place of worship serving as a prime example of the man's design sense.

The SUV drifted through the tighter lanes of earlier streets. "I know, Loren. That's what I've been trying to say. I mean, I wasn't saying anything before, but it's what I wanted to say this whole time."

"You're losing me."

Pratchett sighed. "I mean, you might think I'm a moron only capable of driving a squad car—though Myers doesn't even think that well of me—but I know what you've done for this city." His eyes sparked, sharper than Loren ever noted in the past. "What you continue to do for Portents."

"You do?"

"You're not the only one." The car left the pavement for brick roads, slowing further. "I'm sure it feels that way with the Evans Tower thing and the Erikson situation, but there is help away from the department."

The SUV made another turn, bumping Loren around the passenger seat. A wall straight ahead barred the way, not that Pratchett seemed to notice. Loren gripped the door handle tight, pressing back against the seat.

"Pratchett?"

"Yeah?" The vehicle stopped, jerking the pair forward.

Loren caught his breath then let it loose. "I appreciate the drive and the sentiment of whatever it is you're trying to tell me. Do you mind getting to the point soon?"

"Right." Pratchett smiled. He hit the gas and turned through the small inlet barely visible from the outside right before the dead end. A thin brick bridge connected the buildings above before opening up to a circle. Pratchett coasted to the front of an extensive manor before braking. He shifted the car to park and the engine died with the turning of the key. "We're here."

The Franklin Center. Another testament to the brilliance of Walker, the center was built in the 1920s. For a long time it was known simply as the Heritage Home, a place of history, a meeting place for feuding parties to come together to work out their differences. It was boarded up at the turn of the century, the city never sure how to renovate or revitalize the district.

Loren stepped out of the SUV, the cool night air surrounding him. "Cozy."

"It does the job," Pratchett replied. He circled the vehicle, joining Loren on the passenger side. "I've been working with people like you, Loren. People who see what's happening in Portents and want to help."

"Pratchett—"

The officer waved him toward the door. "Come on, Loren. I'll show you around."

Loren refused to budge. "Why are you telling me now, Pratchett? I imagine there were plenty of opportunities for this chat."

"There were," Pratchett agreed. "But I see what's happening. With Myers. With Mathers. Their way doesn't work but they don't care. Too blinded by regulations, by guidelines that can't work in Portents. They've never worked here."

"You have a better way?" The Center loomed over Loren, ancient gargoyles adorning the cornices, watching his every move with sneering, wild grins.

"Maybe. I'd like to think so. We help where we can. Finding threats before they spill out onto the streets."

"Ambitious," Loren said, following Pratchett's glances to the waiting door. Wondering what was inside. Who was inside, awaiting his arrival? "I still don't—"

"Dunn was a member."

"The mayor?"

"The other three victims as well," Pratchett said. "Someone knows about us. Someone is targeting our group."

Our group? A secret organization kept hidden from law enforcement and everyone in power, where the influential and the poor came together for a common cause. Loren stared at his waiting colleague, arms crossing his chest.

"Say it, Pratchett."

"Say what?"

"The name of your little club. What it really is." Loren paused. He left the comfort of the SUV, pacing the length of the Center.

Beside the stoop, tucked in the darkness with the moss and the cracked brick was a sign painted in black.

"A Circle of Shadows."

"You know?" Pratchett asked, stunned at the revelation.

"Of course he does," a man called from the steps above. He held the same wide eyes as Pratchett, vibrant compared to the rest of his tired, old frame. Worn from decades on the force.

Julian Harvey was a legend at the Central Precinct, one Loren recognized as more than just another member, but the head of a growing circle surrounding Portents. "That's why we could use a man like you, Loren."

CHAPTER SIXTEEN

The scrap of paper rested between Soriya's fingers. She hesitated at first to believe it held any meaning, that the name could possibly hold any secrets from her, or a small hidden truth from the world. Every experience with the man was straightforward, offering little insight into anything deep behind his actions. Nothing more than half-baked jokes and nonexistent ambitions. He never questioned her presence at a crime scene, never asked about Loren's work no matter the discussion overheard.

Yet John Pratchett knew more than any of them.

The Luminary was right. Following Pratchett offered a new path to understanding her presence in the city, as well as her training of Noah Jordan. A good starting point for Soriya. However, it failed to explain Loren's presence at the Franklin Center.

Hiding behind the brick wall that bridged the small entrance to the forgotten manor, Soriya watched their conversation unfold. Loren was more aware of their presence in the city as well, revealing their name before the stunned officer had the chance.

A Circle of Shadows.

The notes decorating Mentor's map in the Bypass chamber suddenly held a new clarity. Citizens ranging from the top official in Portents to the everyday blue collar worker were part of the organization, a growing one that spread like a virus right under their noses.

Was Loren part of their group? Did they manage to secure his release from jail? Was he holding back another secret, keeping them apart rather than working to put their partnership back together?

Soriya closed her eyes. Noah and the Luminary stood at one side, working to save the city and uncover a greater threat in their midst. Loren, on the other hand, was being chummy with them. None of it made sense.

She sat in the center, unsure which side to choose, or if it was as simple as choosing a single side. *There is always a third path.* Mentor's words rushed over her, but they offered no solace.

She needed someone to talk to, someone to reach out to, to work through the situation. Loren once held that place—her friend, her confidant. And more. But the distance of late, the questions asked of her drove them apart. Now she wasn't sure where he stood, how rooted he was in the shadows that surrounded everything happening in Portents.

Gilgamesh would have been an alternative, but he was in the wind. His presence, outed by unknown parties, forced him to flee rather than stand by her side in her time of need. Ruiz was another choice, one taken off the board through his leave of absence. After working for so long to bring him to the table, to bridge the gap between their ways of thinking, she had finally succeeded only to watch him walk away from the life.

As if it was that easy.

Frustration grew, anger welling through her muscular frame. Every instinct begged her to jump down to the parking lot below and force the answers from Loren's lips and whoever else stood with the so-called Circle of Shadows. To demand a chance to make things right.

An impossibility now. They were no longer partners. No longer even friends in Loren's eyes.

She was alone in this. She stood, falling back into the rising darkness surrounding the circle. Loren entered the Franklin Center, an old man's hand on his shoulder, guiding him into the shadows.

Soriya rushed from the scene, leaping through the twilight over Portents. She needed help, and only one place remained to find some.

It was time to go home.

CHAPTER SEVENTEEN

The lobby of the Franklin Center was dimly lit despite the ostentatious chandeliers hanging from the ceiling. A bearskin rug carpeted the vast space, with two curved staircases leading to a large landing overlooking the entrance. Two men carrying semi-automatics paced the length of the upper floor.

Loren paused at the entrance, his comfort level dropping rapidly.

Julian Harvey ushered him into the grand hall off the foyer. Landscapes, photos, and other assorted artwork dominated the wall space, alternating with wall sconces that improved the lighting in the room. Images of Nathaniel Evans and Patrick Hennessey hung in golden frames. Evans' crimson eyes burrowed through Loren, who turned from them. Hallowed halls dating back to the start of Portents, each decade documented in the Franklin Center. All forgotten over time.

An oak table took the majority of the space in the center, seating available for two dozen. The layout branched in various directions at the back of the room, leading to the multiple wings viewed from outside.

A big place to fit their needs.

A Circle of Shadows.

They were real. A group bent on keeping the city safe by following their own rules, their own code. Now, Loren was surrounded by them, their presence filling the periphery with each step into the structure. Loren continued to pace the room, Harvey dogging his steps. Pratchett stayed behind near the lobby, subservient to his uncle who appeared to be the ringleader of the hidden circus.

"If I put in as many years on the force as you did, Harvey, I would have been happy with a ten o'clock tee time and some daytime soaps. Or Ellen. She's pretty hilarious."

Harvey stopped at the head of the table, holding tight to the back of the leather chair in its place. "Not a golfer."

Loren shrugged. "No love for Ellen?"

"I'm a cop who couldn't jump through hoops any longer."

"Smart move," Loren replied. "You might break a hip."

"I get your discomfort, Loren. But please consider leaving the sarcasm at the door. At least for a few minutes."

"Might be asking for too much there, Unc," Pratchett said.

"You too, smartass."

Loren and Pratchett shared a smirk, the former glad to have his colleague with him in this situation, despite allegiances to the contrary. Pratchett's smile faded, the shadow over his face growing as the evening wore on.

"This is all for a membership drive?" Loren asked. "Bodies not even buried and you're looking for new blood to fill the ranks?"

"Nothing so callous."

"Loren," Pratchett called. "It's because—"

"I've got this, Johnny."

"But…" Pratchett fell silent, offering a nod to his uncle's cold glare. "Right. I'll be outside."

The officer departed, the lucky one of the pair. If anyone was going to make a winning sales pitch, it would have been someone Loren knew. Harvey was smart enough to recognize that, just as both men were quick to see the young man's heart wasn't in it tonight. Whether it related to his involvement in the group or the idea of recruiting Loren, the detective didn't know for certain.

"He tries," Harvey muttered as the door closed. "Sometimes he needs a little nudge, a little guidance. Not unlike Portents."

Loren huffed. "And your Circle of Shadows provides that?"

"I've never been much for the drama of it." Harvey walked with Loren through the grand hall. "There are circles wherever secrets lurk. We keep the secrets so no one else has to be burdened by them."

"How noble."

"You do the same. Your work with the Greystone."

Loren stopped, thrown off guard with Harvey's knowledge. The staggered step caused the elderly man to smile devilishly.

"Yes, we're aware of Soriya. I knew her predecessor."

"Did Mentor know about your work?"

"He never approved of outside help."

Loren nodded. "Understatement of the decade." In front of him, on the wall leading to a series of branched halls hung an image of the Portents skyline. The obsidian tower sat off center, and the remaining towers adorning the city's rich history sparked with fresh light as the sun rose behind them. A unique perspective of the city, one rarely seen.

Loren remembered a similar experience, one taken from the Old Mill in Tolliver's Grove from the thin platform built out of the peak of the structure. They captured the moment with a photo of Portents.

The exact same photo.

"One of Beth's favorite spots, if I remember correctly."

Loren's eyes flared. "What did you say?"

Harvey pointed to the small timestamp along the corner of the image. The day Beth took him to the Old Mill. "Your wife was a member of our little circle."

Loren struggled to catch his breath, shaking off the words with a laugh—one easily seen through by the retired detective.

"She didn't tell you."

"Another understatement." Loren shifted from the cityscape for the oak table in the grand hall. He leaned on it, his jaw tightening. "I figured she knew about the city but—"

Harvey nodded. "We pretend it's to protect our loved ones but they're always the ones hurt the most by our secrets."

"All secrets come to light," Loren whispered. Soriya said the same thing months earlier in the Library of the Luminaries. The truth always shone through. *And damn did it hurt.*

"The city better hope the hell not," Harvey said, catching his whisper. "The darkness in Portents? You might handle one or two, but for every Evans there are ten other freaks lurking in the shadows."

"Freaks? Is that how you really feel, Harvey?"

"Don't you?" Harvey answered. "How else do you see creatures that were never meant to return to the mortal plane? What else do you call the monster that slaughtered dozens under the influence of a damn coin?"

"Hady," Loren said. "I call her Hady."

Harvey fell silent, confused.

"Hady Ronne?" Loren pressed. "Former head coroner?"

Harvey shook his head unwilling to discuss the subject further. But Loren needed the clarification. For months he assumed the Circle was responsible for Hady's disappearance. Harvey's reaction and the fact she failed to turn up in the mass grave placed that theory in doubt. If it wasn't the Circle, why was the wall marked with their signature? What else was going on in the city?

"I miss her, you know. Beth. She was a true asset."

"Like the gun-toters upstairs? Is that what Beth did? Hunt down monsters?"

"No," Harvey said without looking at him. "She handled research. The lore of the city and of the dangers we faced." His eyes were distant. He was hiding something. When he caught Loren's stare he turned away once more. "This is our city. We intend to keep it that way. Keeping this city in the dark about the truth protects them."

Loren couldn't dispute the argument. It was one he heard often from Ruiz—and one he made himself when it came to Hady Ronne's rampage as the Charon. So many were left dead, and the threat centered on those meant to *protect* the people of Portents. No one would understand that, no one could. Keeping everything in the shadows offered them an alibi, gave them a way to work the cases too dangerous to be seen on the evening news.

"Except someone knows about your work," Loren finished.

"The first was a surprise," Harvey said. "The second, unfortunate. After Dunn? There's no denying who this killer is targeting. Your skills could be invaluable to us."

"To save your own ass."

"Dozens are affiliated. From all walks of life. And yes, I'd like to save my own ass. There's nothing wrong with a desire to survive."

"Tell that to Henry Erikson," Loren snapped. "Desperation makes people dangerous. How desperate are you, Harvey?"

Loren had seen the truth in the actions of a dying man who would have done anything, made any deal, to keep from meeting his ultimate fate. His actions led to Hady's rampage, to the countless dead that ripped families asunder. Loren wondered what the cost would be for Harvey's life.

"Get off your high horse, Loren."

Loren turned to the darkness as the voice bellowed through the hall.

"Who?"

He stepped into the room, a smug look on his face. The last time Loren saw the man he wore a uniform, a gold badge pinned to his chest, none of it deserved. His actions stripped them from him as proof. Now he wore a simple shirt that did its best to hide his burgeoning gut. But Robert Standish still wore that damn grin on his face. The one that made Loren's blood boil just at the sight of it.

"I told you he wasn't needed, Harv," Standish said. "Loren's not a joiner. He's too good for the rest of us. Isn't that right, partner?"

CHAPTER EIGHTEEN

"You son of a bitch!"

Loren's fist slammed into Standish's cheek, forcing the robust figure back. He hit the wall, the image of Nathaniel Evans slipping from the hooks and crashing to the floor beside him. Loren delivered a blow to the man's gut.

"Loren!" Harvey yelled from behind the fight.

The raging detective ignored him, his fist swinging out. Standish fell from the blow, blood spattering from his lips. Loren picked him up and tossed him to the center of the room and the waiting table. He lifted him by the collar.

"How a piece of garbage like you manages to survive astounds me, Standish."

Standish grinned with blood-coated teeth. "You missed me, didn't you, Loren?" He sprayed Loren with spit, soaking his attacker's shirt with crimson.

Loren dropped him, Standish's heavy frame slamming against the tabletop. Fists flew wildly, more blood covering Loren with each assault. He didn't care, didn't hear the cries from Harvey in the background. Not over his own screams.

"Damn you!"

Laughter filled the room and Loren ended his assault. He fought for breath, trying to slow his pulse. Standish always had that effect on him. From their first meeting at the Second Precinct to their time together at Central, Loren's first instinct was to beat on the man, knowing he deserved every blow. Rage always won, even now.

Standish's enjoyment filled Loren's senses and he let go of the man's collar. Slowly, the bloodied former officer rolled off the oak surface. He held tight to a nearby chair, his feet unsteady. Wiping the blood from his lips, Standish sneered.

"Still the same old Loren. So much anger," Standish said. He inched closer, locked on his former partner. "And so much to lose."

Loren screamed, fist raised. One more blow, one more strike—anything to silence the man, to put his words to rest. Every single one was true. Everything Standish stood for was anathema to Loren but he was right in this regard.

He hadn't changed. Not after his fall. Therapy only took Loren so far. His time away from the city did the same, but when he came back he believed he could make a fresh start of it. A new beginning. The same promise. Instead, he fell in the same trap.

Standish. Always Standish.

His fist fell, his scream silenced. Loren shook his head, putting Standish behind him. "You have no idea who this man is, Harvey."

The old man at the head of the table stood, splitting the room between them. Standish straightened at his approach, settling along his right side. "I know exactly who Robert was, Detective. And who he is to the cause. He serves a purpose, as you could. The city needs us."

Loren shook his head, unable to glance at the man without feeling his fist clench tight at his side. "You're wrong."

"I'm right," Harvey replied. "Especially now."

"I know what you've been doing, Harvey. I couldn't understand it. But seeing him at your side?" Loren leaned close to the retired head detective. "My answer was never going to be yes."

He started for the door. Nothing more needed to be said, the flare of recognition on Harvey's face enough to confirm Loren's suspicions. He didn't need to show him the image tucked in his pocket. Didn't need to question him the way he had Soriya the night before.

His cold eyes made it clear how guilty Julian Harvey was.

Loren reached for the door, the shuffling of feet dogging his exit.

"Our people are dying, Loren," Harvey called at the edge of the foyer. The lights blinked in and out; the shadows surrounded him.

Loren's head fell to his chest, his hand hesitating at the handle. "Oh, I'll find your killer." He turned, catching the light and

Harvey's gaze. "Then I'll do everything in my power to shut you down."

Standish grinned from behind his new employer. One that fit much better than the Portents Police Department. One that allowed the rabid beast his fair share of blood. One that needed to be put down—permanently.

"All of you."

CHAPTER NINETEEN

Loren slammed the door behind him. The night breeze filled his lungs and he savored every breath. The air was stifling in the Franklin Center. It reeked of death, the same feeling he had every time Robert Standish showed up.

Shuffling away from the building, grateful the door remained closed, Loren wiped at the blood along his shirt. His knuckles dripped, spreading the crimson liquid along his chest. Desperate fingers swiped at the mess, failing in the attempt.

Pratchett stood beside his SUV, turning at the sound of the approaching detective. His patented grin faded at his arrival, concern rampant in his eyes.

"What happened?" Pratchett asked.

Loren ignored the question, unable to speak, unable to think clearly. All he saw was the red spreading across his shirt, the anger at the men inside the hall. And the secrets kept from all. He continued to walk for the open road.

Pratchett reached for his arm. "Loren, are you—?"

Loren jerked away, staring out at the emptiness of downtown Portents. "Did you know?"

"What?"

His eyes were heavy and red. "About him? About Standish?"

"Loren, I..." Pratchett fell silent, running his fingers deep along his brow.

Loren shook his head. "What are you doing here, Pratchett? You're a good man doing good work. Honest work."

"I do good work here too," Pratchett shot back. "Someone has to."

"We do," Loren said. "At the precinct."

Pratchett chuckled.

"Hey. We do our best. And Soriya—"

"That woman?" Pratchett scoffed. "The so-called Greystone? She causes more problems than she solves. How many of these nutcases would never have come back if she didn't let them roam the streets? What the hell does she actually accomplish?"

"More than just death," Loren admitted. Despite all his anger, for all his doubt over their work together, that was one thing he could admit. Soriya Greystone did not serve some agenda. She didn't fight for someone else's cause, following someone else's rules. She fought for what was right.

Unlike the men hiding in the shadows. Reaching into his pocket, Loren removed the image taken the previous night.

"What's this?" Pratchett took it between his fingers.

"Your good work."

The officer's eyes shot wide. The sight of dozens dead, piled high in a mass grave tucked in the abandoned rail station in the Grove had that effect on people. Even those responsible.

"I didn't—"

"No," Loren snapped. He shoved the photo hard against Pratchett's chest. "You're part of this, Pratchett. *'I didn't know'*? Pleading ignorance? That doesn't work. Not with this."

He waited, holding out hope that Pratchett didn't agree, that he stood for something. From Myers' betrayal and his overwhelming doubts about Soriya, there was still a chance to have someone stand for something better. There had to be.

Pratchett's silence, however, was damning. His long, hollow breath was more an admission than anything words could say. "Loren…"

"There's a better way," Loren continued. "Maybe it isn't Soriya's. It sure as hell isn't Harvey's."

Pratchett extended the image, unable to look at it any longer. Loren refused to take it back. He could keep it as a reminder. Loren started for the road and the quiet of the city. He needed sleep, some rest from the last twenty-four hours, although he knew none would come.

"Loren, I can—"

Loren shook his head, continuing for the silence of Portents. Without Soriya. Without Myers. And now without Pratchett. "Make a choice. Before it's too late for any of us."

CHAPTER TWENTY

John Pratchett never wanted the job. An inattentive, C student in high school, he never wanted anything really. Sports were an entertaining distraction but he was middling at best. No career path wowed him. No perfect dream, no great future waited for him.

His uncle changed that.

One night, flipping through channels, Pratchett caught his uncle on the news—an interview relating to an older case. His uncle spoke with such compassion, such grace about the city, about his time in the department. Pratchett sat in awe.

His uncle told tales of his work with each family visit. Most were used as deterrents. Don't do drugs, stay in school, and the like. But listening to him crack the case of a murdered young girl, four years after his retirement from the force? The dedication necessary to make it happen?

Pratchett made his decision the next day to join the academy after graduation.

He still suffered from a lack of ambition. Taking each day in stride was a lifestyle choice learned from a father stuck in a dead-end job and a mother who preferred to chide others than achieve anything of her own.

The work was good for him. He enjoyed the notoriety of the uniform, the usefulness of the job when connecting with the city. He preferred the dull roar of a patrol, the strange communion of the night and Portents. How it washed over him during his shift. How everything seemed so much clearer.

When his uncle approached him early in his career, Pratchett realized how little he actually understood the city—the true city. Harvey opened his eyes to Portents.

He stayed silent about it at work. He let the people around him believe his goofy grin told his whole story—a necessity to maintain the cover of their group. To do the work needed in the background.

To keep the city safe.

Now, he didn't know who he protected or served. Pratchett watched Loren depart the confines of the circle in front of the Franklin Center. Another hidden spot in Portents, the maze-like structure of the city offering a myriad number of which in the downtown area. Secrets hidden on top of secrets.

Like the image cradled in his grasp.

He wanted to tell Loren the truth. About the Circle. About the work being done. About Standish's involvement. And more. The guilt from years of secrets burdened him, especially with Loren.

Even at the darkest of times, when he was forced to pull him from Standish's bleeding body at the precinct and escort him from the building, Pratchett called him friend, a connection never earned. More guilt from the secret that infected his heart. He was no friend to Loren, not if the grizzled detective learned the truth of the choices he had already made.

Pratchett knew. Of course, he did. Working for his uncle, following orders, was one thing. But doing so without a thought behind them? That was something Pratchett never allowed. He quietly questioned everything within the Circle of Shadows.

The image crumpled between his fingers. The bodies of the dead, all recognized by the lanky officer of the Central Precinct. Their names. Their histories. The secrets they held. He knew them all and how they met their end. Not by his hand—not that it truly mattered. His inaction, his inability to convince Harvey of another way, made him no better than if he pulled the trigger himself.

He could have told Loren, should have told him something. But what would have changed? The dead were still dead. Each led back to the Circle. He had taken steps to make a difference, another secret on top of all the others. One he could have shared with the weary detective.

But he stayed silent.

Pratchett pulled out a lighter and flipped it open. It sparked with a single flick. The flame ran the length of the image, catching the corner. He held firm, and the mass grave was consumed by fire in a matter of moments. At the last second he dropped it, watching the secret burn to ash and memory.

Another mistake, but a necessary one. The Circle helped in their way. Pratchett did the same, trying to find a path out of the dark. He hoped Loren would see that before it was too late.

There was little chance of that, however. Loren would only see betrayal at the secret kept from him for so long—the same mistake, in fact, that set Pratchett on this path. He wanted to cry out, to catch up to his friend and spill his guts, to share it all. From that first mistake to the dead burning at his feet.

Instead, John Pratchett remained silent. Forever silent.

CHAPTER TWENTY-ONE

City Hall was once a shining beacon in the skyline of Portents. Before the obsidian tower at the center, it soared to the heavens and kept a watchful eye on the citizens below, a twelve-story decorated edifice updated multiple times to restore some of its former glory.

Glass elevators ran along the sides of the lobby, overlooking the city. A gift shop occupied two whole floors; tour groups constantly filtered along the non-stop traffic throughout the building.

Outside, four large flags waved at half-mast. The memorial service for Mayor Reginald Dunn was barely in the planning stages, yet the news conference confirming the man's brutal end brought a grand showing of support from people shocked by the loss of a man who promised so much.

If only he had the chance was the motto offered by his replacement, who was sworn in before the crowd. The goal of the speech—which was met with cheers for the man's ambition if not his track record—was to put the onus on Dunn's killer above all else. A woman everyone in Portents now knew thanks to every news station and publication in the county.

Soriya Greystone.

Afterward, those gathered paid tribute to the man by laying flowers outside the building. Prayers were spoken, family offered remembrances, and all made assurances that justice would be served.

Discussions continued in the charming corner office on the structure's seventh floor. Those called for the meeting sat, reflecting on the events of the day and the promises made by

Dunn's successor. She was the only one standing, peering out over the city.

"It was a nice ceremony," the newly installed interim mayor said, breaking the silence of the room. She left the cold of the window for that of a pristine cherry desk in the center of the room. "Muted, like the city."

Grumbles of confirmation passed between the pair across from her and she smiled at their hesitation.

"I'm sure you're wondering why I called you here."

They weren't, though the exclusion of the commissioner gave Wexler and Mathers pause. She would get to him soon enough, but for now she needed the two captains from the Central Precinct.

"We're working on it," Mathers said, sharp and upright. His spectacles glistened under the overhead lights. "Our chief suspect—"

"Has a name," she said. "Use it."

"Soriya Greystone, ma'am," Wexler started, shifting to the edge of her seat. "She used to consult with the department."

"So there should be a record of her somewhere? A place of business and a residence of some sort?"

Both shared a glance. Mathers cleared his throat. "Well, not exactly. It seems she wasn't cleared for the work in question."

"And we never paid her."

The mayor huffed. "She's a ghost then."

"For now."

"Damn right for now," she snapped. "Use whatever resources at your disposal. Portents is at a tipping point."

"Ma'am?"

"Something is coming, Captain Mathers." He straightened at the sound of his name, fixing his tie as she rounded the desk. "And I will need each of you to keep our city safe. Can I count on you?"

"Of course," Mathers replied.

Wexler inched from her chair to stand. "We'll find this Soriya Greystone woman, Mayor Winters."

"Thank you." The woman smiled. "And please, call me Karen."

Mathers stood, joining them at the door. Handshakes were offered, mumbled promises to appease the office and the woman behind the desk, all from Rufus Mathers as Wexler rang for the elevator rather than listen to his false bravado.

After they left Karen Winters laughed, slamming shut the door to her office. Soriya was in the wind, forces put into place to squeeze her out. She needed to understand how things went when alone in Portents. On the run. Surrounded on all sides by those once allied with her. A lesson her teacher never learned in time.

Karen hoped Soriya learned from her master's mistakes.

A test, however, was required. The city needed a wakeup call.

She reached for the bookshelf adorning the left hand wall of the office. When asked why the seventh floor out of every other option for the office of the mayor, the original occupant, Rudolph Hennessey, laughed and told reporters that seven was his lucky number.

He left out the real reason: the secrets built into the structure.

The shelves pulled away from the wall with the flick of an unseen notch along the frame. An alcove spread before her, one illuminated as she stepped deeper inside. Motion sensors were the latest addition, the sconces reacting to her presence with each click of her flats on the tile.

Hanging along the wall rested a long black cloak. She pulled it free and slipped the delicate fabric along her backside. Then she turned to the small display hidden behind the entrance. A white mask stared at her, the bottom half carved off by the actions of the black raven months earlier. She put it on, amber eyes peeking through. Her thin lips curled at the sight as she stood before the mirror in the small hidden room.

Karen Winters entered the alcove but it was the Luminary who exited. Her laughter boomed in the office, her hands spread in front of the window overlooking the city.

Her city.

Behind the obsidian tower, the moon displayed its brilliance, taking over for its fiery partner. Full and proud, the luminescent orb showered light for all to see. The Luminary grinned. She would miss the sight of it. But if Portents had to pay the price to finally see the ultimate truth, so be it.

"It's time."

CHAPTER TWENTY-TWO

Noah Jordan saw stars. Tiny dots filled his view, scattered across the clear night sky, a kaleidoscope of wonder. They blinked and shifted in and out of view, the dim radiance multiplied by hundreds of thousands of infinitesimal celestial bodies in the heavens. For a long moment he believed he would fall into space and take his place among them, forever lost.

The observation deck was empty. When the peak of Evans Tower shattered during the Night of the Lights, repair crews worked tirelessly to fix the glass structure at the heart of the city. The former office of one of the most powerful families in Portents fell by the wayside.

With no figurehead in place, the need for the space was no longer a requirement for the company. In fact, the negative press and the stigma of the events that occurred on the eighty-sixth floor of the obsidian tower made it clear to the surviving members that changes were in the best interest for everyone.

Instead of closing off the top floor of the gleaming spire, instead of boxing it off from the people so far down below, the Evans estate opened the space up to the public. The observation deck gave tourists a clear view of the entirety of Portents, a birds-eye vantage of every nook and cranny tucked in the shadows. From the docks to the east, the starting point of their history, to the coves spreading north, widening the reach of the burgeoning metropolis, all were welcome for a peek.

During the day.

At night, the place was restricted from use. Keeping with the rest of the structure, most of the railings, the flooring, the decorative lighting—all were built from material of deep blacks, the deck blending with the night sky.

Wind ripped through the structure, forcing Noah back a step. Down on the street there had been none, but so high up from ground level, the wind acted like a natural barrier, keeping him from the stark black railings surrounding the deck.

The moon rested overhead at its apex, lighting up the clear sky. So beautiful, so breathtaking against the dark. It filled Noah with light.

And doubt.

This was the wrong move. Part of him tried to fight it, tried to explain it to the Luminary, hoping for a chance to make a better choice. To find a different way forward. But just like everything else lately, it was a losing battle.

His need for answers dominated all other actions. His parents were dead, the void left filled with nothing but questions and the stone he found in the rubble of their home.

The Greystone fit along his palm and he squeezed it tight. If only it could speak, would the stone tell him the truth of his quest? Would it provide the answers to who killed his parents and why?

No. Only one person could provide that information. Only one person was willing to do that for him, asking little in return.

Just this. But was this really the end of his role? Another doubt. Maybe Gabe was right. Maybe they should walk away with what they had left and start over. Make a life. They had always been close, Noah doing everything in his power to take care of his younger brother and keep him safe. To provide a normal life.

Girls. School. Sports. Normal things. Normal problems. What was wrong with that?

Only it didn't solve the mystery keeping him restless, doing things he wasn't sure about in the first place.

He needed closure. If this small act helped, brought him closure, then so be it.

Noah stepped out on the deck and looked up into the night sky. He held the stone before him, wondering what secrets it held, what wonders he could find within.

And what nightmares it was about to unleash.

The light started to glow, will rushing from his chest, down his arms into the Greystone. He poured every doubt, every question, every ounce of anger and rage over the loss of his parents, feeding all to the stone.

The stone pulsed under his care, the light beaming brighter out over the city. The stars faded overhead. Winds whirled, spinning faster with each passing moment. Clouds formed above the city center, thick and black, and as if hidden in plain sight, they grew, spreading in deep circles. The moon blotted out in an instant, the growing cover stretching out to include the entire city.

Noah Jordan screamed.

The stone erupted with light, a single pulse splitting the sky as it sailed to the heavens. The clouds swelled from the effort. Lightning crashed, thunder booming from the thick layer of swirling storm. Like a vast vortex it spread, striking at the city from all sides. The pulse continued at its heart, a signal for all to see.

The long night had begun.

CHAPTER TWENTY-THREE

The signal was seen by all. Deep patches of black rolled in large sweeping circles, centered on the obsidian tower at the heart of Portents where a thin spotlight shot straight through the growing storm. Clouds swirled, thunder snapping the quiet. Lightning sheared rooftops, striking east then west before surrounding all. The storm was fierce, the wind rattling shutters and shattering thin panes of glass.

For most, it meant little. Another missed storm by the local meteorologists. Nothing out of the norm for their profession. Inclement weather was a part of nature, part of the world, and those who witnessed the storm took little interest in its origins or hidden meanings.

Others, however, did. The disappearance of the clear skies—starting with the center of the city and spreading over them like a black vortex—served as a warning. A sense of ill tidings at the night ahead. A threat on the horizon, rising quickly among them.

What that could be ranged from the spirits that returned with the Night of the Lights to the beasts that roamed Rose Riley Forest. Stories intended to spook children gained credence over the years. The unwritten rules came back to haunt the residents. From the downtown apartment high-rises to the rail yards to the west, the city sat in wait.

The actual meaning behind the signal was clear for its intended audience. It served as the beginning of something else entirely. A promise long in the making.

A call to arms.

David Kendrick stepped out on the balcony of his apartment, where his wife and children slept peacefully inside. He loved them, cherished the time spent together, but he was tired of the charade. It was necessary—the waiting, the need to hide—but the feeling sat in his gut, that need for more. That sensation stirred him awake. A sound from the pulse tucked behind the rolling thunder called him from his slumber.

The signal.

Across the way, others joined him in the darkness, staring up with wide eyes at the growing storm. Eyes of awareness and purpose. Dozens left their mundane lives, catching a brief glimpse at the larger picture painted before them by the maelstrom.

The same occurred downtown. From the bar scene, the few restaurants breaking tradition with the rules of the city, patrons and workers took to the street. It raged down the highways, filtering through the Knoll, racing up King's Lane and Lowtown. The smallest neighborhood felt the surge, as did those working diligently at the Central Precinct. Those the signal was meant for, at least. Snapped awake for the first time in ages. Called by a greater power.

Those chosen joined the chorus of thunder and lightning. Their cries grew, building block by block throughout the city. More than an answer to Noah Jordan's signal, more than a simple cry into the darkness.

The people of Portents were howling.

The change was sudden. David Kendrick and dozens like him fell to the ground, screaming. Claws grew from fingertips, paws replacing hands. Noses shifted to snouts, eyes widening and filling with black. Their clothes were shed, fur covering their bodies.

Where people fell to the ground, hounds rose up. Their howls echoed in answer to the signal, a pronouncement of the night ahead.

The Heads of Cerberus had returned.

PART TWO
THE FALL

CHAPTER TWENTY-FOUR

Screams filled the streets. The cry of innocents balanced against the lightning as the storm took hold. In the midst of the cacophony of terror, the Heads of Cerberus ran amok. The city was theirs and they intended to make it known—with as much blood as possible.

Commissioner Phillip Thorne knew it would end this way. His tenure as the top cop was plagued with murder and deceit. Infighting between his officers made the papers weekly, the discord sown spreading like wildfire to the populace. Murder, hate crimes, drugs, and the pettiest of misdemeanors covered his desk daily.

His wife stopped trying to be supportive. She took the bed at the end of the hall, once shared by them both, leaving him the pullout in the office. When sleep came—as it seldom did—his own snoring tended to wake him.

Not tonight. The storm took on his usual role, the lightning crashing around the stately domicile in the Riverfront district. Thorne stirred, his eyes heavy. His back ached and the paperwork of another day crashed to the ground from the wind gusting through the open window.

"Stupid," he muttered. He thought he closed it, could have sworn he did so before sitting to read through another update on the Dunn case. Reginald was a friend. Both propped up the other when the city turned to shit, an all too frequent occurrence of late.

Things were changing, falling apart right before their eyes. Even the wind sounded angrier, almost like it was howling.

Thorne left the office behind, his arthritic knees aching as he made his way down the hall. The bedroom door lay ajar, the light of the reading lamp visible.

"Helen?"

The bed was vacant, the sheets ripped and torn. Thorne rushed to the nightstand, the drawer shaking under his hand as it opened. His revolver fell to the ground. As he crouched to pick it up a growl filled the room.

Thorne turned, aghast. "Helen?"

"Not anymore."

Her nightgown lay in tatters over what was once her flesh. In its place rose fur of dark auburn. Twin black holes bore through him and she bared her fangs.

Thorne closed his eyes, recognizing the end as it arrived.

City officials fell by the dozen. Lawyers, council members, anyone of authority. They were the first targets, but not the last. Howls ranged from the northern coves to the western border of Tolliver's Grove. They rang out, cheering the return of the darkness. The beginning of the end.

For all but one.

She stood at the window, ruby lips curled. From her vantage at City Hall, the city burned bright around her. The fires started small, the aftermath of a murder in a Lowtown apartment complex. Another in a downtown high rise. A gas line failure up the Knoll blazed brightest, the storm giving it full exposure.

The city fell before her, the puppets pulled along by her strings in all directions. The citizens of Portents required a lesson and she intended to give them one they would never forget. One they would never be able to erase from their memories should they be one of the lucky few to see the morning light.

Karen Winters took a sip of merlot, savoring the dry nectar before placing the glass down on the sill. The dark light infiltrating the city blanketed everything she touched with blood and chaos.

The Luminary smiled, content to watch it all burn.

CHAPTER TWENTY-FIVE

It had been months since Soriya last stepped within the confines of the Bypass chamber. Hidden from view along the C-Line under the obsidian tower, the glowing orb of light floated majestically before her.

Along the surface, black streams flitted against its emerald green standard. Fluctuations grew, bursts of light whipping from the orb only to be contained by the four columns guarding the enigmatic artifact.

She tried to stay away, frightened by her lack of answers at the Greystone's changes. Her decision also allowed her to see the influence of the floating orb in the city—the doors opened and the threats released as stray flicks of light slipped away from the Bypass. It was almost as if the infinite was testing her, preparing her for what was coming.

The Greystone and the Bypass were two pieces of the same system, two sides of an unsolved equation. Both weapons in their own right, depending on the user. Depending on the question asked and the answer given.

Balance.

The key to everything, yet one Soriya never properly maintained. Between her failings to heed Mentor's lessons to her inability to keep Loren by her side, no stability existed in her life. Especially none with the object in the vast chamber.

She hoped being here would bring back some level of what she was missing. Connecting with the city, being in the light with her apartment, new contacts with the people she swore to protect was what she always dreamed. But it pulled at her, a normal life compared to the role meant for her. The connections were necessary—they grounded her in a way, but they also served as the distraction Mentor always warned her about.

How else could she explain the shadows among them? Mentor failed to recognize them as a threat, noting their appearances over the years, some dating as far back as a decade earlier. She needed to be better than her predecessor, to surpass her teacher, to keep Portents safe.

She picked at his notes, realizing what they meant, understanding the lengths the shadows had gone to maintain their secret. What did they want? Was it as simple as Noah Jordan believed? Were they killers, manipulators and blackmailers, trying to influence the city and everyone in it? Loren would never be party to that. He couldn't be. Not after all their work together.

But he walked away and Noah Jordan was here, his desire to work with her to find the answers. With him came the bonus of a Luminary, the last residing within the city limits.

It was too tempting. Too desirable to Soriya, who had lost so many over the last year: Vlad. Urg. Mentor. Loren, in a way, all over again. Gilgamesh too, forced to hide rather than be used as a pawn in an unseen game.

Soriya left the domicile, giving a small smile at the memories trapped in the space. This was home, and it always would be for her, no matter where she went. No matter what she experienced.

Stepping to the Bypass, Soriya pondered the correct path. The orb offered nothing in return. No shift in light, no great revelation. When Mentor sat before it, reaching out with his spirit to find truth in the unknown, there was always a chance he would never return. Looking beyond the veil, to all of time and space, held an array of risks. He almost lost himself more than once, mistakes of his prideful youth. The wrong questions asked, the incorrect answers sought. Over time he learned the cost of such questioning: that some truths were never meant to be discovered.

With the questions raging in her thoughts, the secrets buried from her own lost youth, Soriya was never allowed the attempt. A wise decision, though she failed to see it that way for so long. Like so many things in her life, she failed to understand until it was too late to appreciate the reasons behind them. Mentor kept her safe. Even with the secrets, the lies, all were meant to protect her.

Now he was gone.

She swiped at her eyes, desperately needing sleep. Thoughts pounded to the surface of her brain: the Luminary, her offer for assistance, the truth behind her claims of knowing Mentor so intimately... She wiped them away with the hope that rest would offer clarity.

Tromping steps above ended that hope. A wave of pounding feet raging in the tunnels of the C-Line caused small cracks to shower flakes of debris from the ceiling.

"What is that?" Soriya asked, stalking over to the metal staircase. She listened to the growing noise in the tunnels.

Holding her breath, she hesitated at the door. The sound roiled ahead, battering against the walls, the ground, and above. It rushed past the door, streaming deeper toward downtown.

Soriya opened the door, each act taking long seconds to avoid the scraping of metal or the creaking of old hinges. She snuck through the crack, closing the junction behind her.

Darkness surrounded her. The sound continued, shifting down the line for Evans Station. Her eyes noted the movement, bodies racing on all sides: From the walls to the ceiling to the ground, the wave shoved and rushed for the surface.

Her eyes, finally adjusted to the lack of light, widened when the figures came into focus. They were larger than human, covered in fur of deep browns and blacks.

More sounds joined the chorus. Snarls through fanged teeth. Growls echoed through the tunnel.

And howls filled the night.

The Heads of Cerberus.

There are more of us. So many of us.

"Not now. Why did it have to be now?"

CHAPTER TWENTY-SIX

The howling continued. At first, it was little more than a whisper on the wind, the cascading effect of a spring storm on the rise, but ever so slowly it changed. The intensity built, level by level, awakening everyone from their doldrums. From the sentries patrolling the property in the shadow of downtown Portents to those patrolling the interior of the forgotten Franklin Center, all were lost in the growing crescendo rising throughout the city.

Something had arrived.

Julian Harvey tried to ignore the sound. He huddled over the table in the large meeting hall, focusing on the maps before him instead of the storm awaiting them outside.

"We're seeing a flare-up over in Lowtown," Thomas said, pointing to the map. The tall, rugged ex-soldier loomed over his geriatric colleague, casting a shadow across the grid's interior. "Some freaky-ass illness among two blocks on the east side."

Harvey shook his head. "Freaky-ass is what we deal in, kid."

The man barely pushing thirty appreciated the admission. "True."

"The cause?" Harvey asked. Others made their way through the room, checking the premises every few minutes to maintain security. Everyone was on high alert.

Thomas stood upright, hands to the small of his back. "Some shaman by all accounts. Targeting a specific family. Reasons unknown."

Unknown. When it could be boiled down to only a reason being unknown, it was a win in their eyes. Everything about the terrain they dealt in, the subjects of their investigations during their time in Portents, stemmed from the unknown. Literature, both kept in-house and otherwise, only went so far. The real work took over from that, questioning everything, even that which seemed out of the realm of the possible.

"Alive or dead?"

Thomas cocked his head. "Like that is a question I thought I'd be answering after two tours in the Middle East."

Harvey nodded. "It is an adjustment."

"No, I know," Thomas said, relaxing beside the head of their circle. "Hey, I'm grateful to be here doing this. Keeps me…occupied."

Thomas Keating was ex-Special Forces, expertly trained and highly decorated. He served with distinction in Iraq and later in Afghanistan. Focused on the task, diligent in his mission, Thomas served a higher power. One that failed to come home with him.

He strayed, lost his way in the dark upon the end of his tour. There was booze. There were plenty of women, more often than not ending with bruises from the nightmares brought on by the drink. Jail time looked to be a certainty until Harvey came along. He was recruiting for a new mission, a way to serve again.

Thomas needed saving and now he saved those in need. Harvey relied on the young man for tactics as well as his love of classic cinema. When not in the field, the pair took to the theater in the basement of the Franklin Center. Disputes over the impact of Orson Welles and the cinematography of John Seitz. Harvey tried not to think of the man as a friend, tried to keep everyone related to the Circle as colleagues but they had grown to be more than that.

"Let's hope not too occupied." Harvey gave the man a slap on the back then returned to the map. "Now, the shaman?"

"Alive."

"Good," Harvey said. Alive meant more options. And less of a mess. "Smoke him out."

Thomas smiled. "Tracking down another relative as we speak."

Harvey nodded. "And the thing at the Walker Complex?"

"Sirens."

Harvey sighed. Once upon a time that term wouldn't have meant a damn thing. Now he knew exactly what was being referenced and hated everything about it. "Handled?"

"Two of the three."

"The other?"

Thomas took a sharp breath, his head low. "The Greystone."

Soriya. Not a day went by over the past week that she hadn't been involved in their operations. Mucking them up as usual, without any knowledge of their involvement. She was more active of late, using the city as her own personal playground without a care to the people around her. Or the delicate nature of their work.

"I could—"

Harvey waved him down. "Leave it for now."

"Right."

The former cop scanned the map, pausing north of the Allure marketplace. "Someone mentioned the Corridor earlier. Strange reports coming in?"

"Standish took it."

"He didn't mention it to me."

Thomas shrugged. "Said it wasn't a big thing. Probably some squatters scaring the locals."

"Wouldn't be the first time," Harvey muttered, recalling a visit to the neighborhood decades earlier with his former partner, Ruiz.

"Sir? Should I call him in?"

You have no idea who this man is, Harvey. Loren's warning repeated on him worse than the Cobb salad at dinner. Harvey knew Standish very well, prided himself on his selection of the man, of bringing him into the fold at just the right time. Standish was an asset, much like Thomas, only Harvey would never call the man a friend. He was useful. For now. "No. I'm sure he has it handled. Anything else?"

"No, just…" Thomas fell silent, allowing the howls to provide his answer. They were louder, growing in number.

"Tomorrow," Harvey said. He kept a smile, shrugging off the sound as background noise. They had heard plenty over the years in Portents. Great storms and greater enemies always pressing against the light. They always pulled them back into the dark. And they would again. *Tomorrow.* "Get some sleep."

Thomas hesitated for a moment and then nodded. He started for the lobby and the winding stairs to the upper levels of the massive estate. Harvey waited for his departure before returning to the winding map of Portents, and the threats waiting for them— both seen and unseen.

"You should take your own advice."

Harvey rolled the map, letting it fall into a neighboring chair. A cup of coffee took its place, the shaking hand of Bernice Caplan doing its best to keep from spilling. Harvey took the cup, steadying it for the nervous woman. "So should you." He took a sip as she sat beside him. He closed his eyes, letting the hot liquid settle over him before he put the cup back down. "Thank you."

"You keep pushing yourself, you're liable to—"

"How are you holding up, kid?" he interrupted, unwilling to hear her concerns, the same held by most. He was old, not stupid. Their view of the elderly wasn't something he hoped to change; he simply tired of hearing it after a long day.

She huffed, fixing the glasses to her face. "Okay. Well, not okay but…I should have been there, Harvey."

"You couldn't have done anything for him, Bernice."

"All the crap I gave that man…"

She wasn't the only one. Harvey berated the fallen mayor more often than praised him. Reginald Dunn served a purpose but at a cost, one continually questioned. His loss, however, hurt the organization overall. Harvey took Bernice's hand and squeezed. "All that crap, as you so put it, made him a better mayor. That's why you were there."

Bernice's lip curled as she wiped a tear from her eye. "I can't sleep, Harvey. I keep seeing him like that and now with this?"

The howls echoed in the grand hall. No closer, but louder. Definitely louder.

Harvey patted her hand. Standing, he helped her up. "Stay here tonight, kid. Grab a bed. Try to put it out of your mind."

"What is it, Harvey?" she asked, shivering at the rushing wind carrying the cries from outside. "What's coming this time?"

"I don't know," he said, escorting her to the lobby. "Not yet anyway. What I do know is we're safe here. *You* are safe here."

She left him at the base of the stairs with a nod. "Thank you."

"Get some sleep," he called after her, watching her reach the two guards on the landing. "We'll deal with it in the morning."

She stopped, her hand tight to the railing. "You'll find the monster that did this?"

"I'll find them all, kid. I promise."

Bernice Caplan fell into shadow, a troubled sleep ahead. Harvey circled back to the meeting hall. He reached for the cup of coffee and thought better. It would only serve to keep his already-swirling thoughts active long into the night.

His long-ago promise echoed in his mind. More than any other commitment, his quest to rid the city of the threats hidden in the shadows held weight. The vow kept him moving, kept him pushing harder, hoping for an answer—a way back into the light. Wondering if it was forever denied him due to the choices he'd been forced to make for so long.

None of this was what he wanted. He was a detective, law and order in his blood. Justice for all. How did justice serve creatures with no right to exist? How did you protect innocent people from monsters and beasts from their worst nightmares? Legends intent on destroying the sanctity of everything he spent a career building?

There was no right answer, no easy way out. Only the group he spent the last two decades building. A Circle of Shadows to combat the threats among them. A group with one thing in common more than any other.

Loss.

Now more than ever.

Four dead, all cherished and loyal members to the cause. There would be no more jokes from Dennis Carmichael over beers. No more policy arguments with Reginald Dunn. The emptiness of the hall disturbed Harvey more than he cared to admit. It carried more than the howling wind through its halls. It carried every loss, every death, every sacrifice for the betterment of Portents.

Harvey grazed the image of the city, Bethany Loren's photo depicting the stark beauty of the skyline. His tired eyes reflected against the frame, exhausted at the never-ending sacrifices to reach their goal.

He always wanted a life—a family. Work made it difficult but there was a time when he put effort on making that a reality. He had dreams of kids and a house in the suburbs, only to see them replaced with nightmares haunting his every thought. Young love fell silent; opportunities missed became those completely ignored in order to maintain focus on what now mattered.

Portents came first.

Now Harvey was eighty-two. His time for helping his city, for keeping his grand promise was running out. Who would stand in his place? What would become of his legacy? Ashes to ashes, the same as all who went before him. Forgotten and lost to history.

He refused to let that happen. To let his work fade away, to break the promise long since made. It had to end. The monsters, the nightmares, all of it.

Julian Harvey had to end it, to save everyone. Before it was too late.

CHAPTER TWENTY-SEVEN

Gabriel Jordan had done some extraordinarily dumb things in his sixteen years of life. There was sneaking into the girls' locker room after school hours in the hopes of catching the ladies basketball team in mid-change. He failed to take into account that their game was away. Or that the gym was being rented out to an elderly fitness class while their usual spot was sprayed for an outbreak of ticks.

If only he could forget that mistake…

There were others. Drinking at the behest of his best friend at the time, a growing "Dead Head," not that he had any idea what the hell that actually meant when the kid told him. Still didn't, not after they were caught by a random patrol. Drinking wasn't the dumb part of the evening. Drinking in plain sight of the street and a dozen neighbors? That took the prize.

Gabe learned from each one. What the exact lesson was he failed to articulate, but the fact that he never repeated the error meant he was capable of growth in some capacity. Yet for all the idiotic teenage nonsense committed in his short life, wandering the streets at night alone went above and beyond the definition of stupidity.

The decision stemmed from anger, as all moronic moves did. Another long day of sitting on his ass, watching mindless commercials mixed with even more mindless television. There was a two-hour window when *The Frighteners* was on cable so it wasn't a total loss, but beyond that?

Noah never called, never stopped to visit. He was gone all day—*work, my ass*—and by the time the moon rose Gabe was through with waiting. He left the hotel in a huff, jacket and ball cap in hand.

Portents was a ghost town. Shops were closed, even chain restaurants that offered 24/7 service in other cities shuttered for the night. A couple bars along the strip leading deeper into downtown had their lights on, but not for a sixteen-year-old kid.

Gabe tucked his head low, window shopping as he walked. With everything closed for the night he wondered what Noah could possibly be doing for work. What could keep him away from his brother, his single most important responsibility in the world? He knew the answer.

Noah was spiraling, lost in grief. Gabe loved his parents just as much, those first nights after the fire creeping up on him in fits of sobs and waking nightmares. Staying with the McCormicks down the street helped. He asked Noah to join him, to be around a loving family for support, but the older Jordan boy refused. He went it alone and continued to do so, unable to open up to Gabe except in sharp disagreement when questioned about their movements.

But why Portents? When they were in Santa Fe or wandering the beaches of Miami, Noah was still somewhat personable. He was hiding something but for the most part, his brother was around. Part of his world, doing his best to keep the pair together.

Not any longer.

The sky opened up, and the full moon above was blotted out in seconds by a swirl of thick clouds. Rain poured, lightning flashing from all sides of the city. Gabe squinted through the pouring rain, watching the thick, black wave of clouds grow from the middle and spread out.

"What the hell?"

He ran down the block, tucking under the overhang of an electronics store. The screens inside the display were blank, reflecting his saddened eyes and soaked frame. He buried his hands deeper into his pockets and sighed. This was not going well. He needed his brother back. He needed his life back.

The fact that he wished for school surprised him. To sit in a lunchroom surrounded by juvenile delinquents better known as friends, bitching about homework and the occasional awkward social event with the fairer sex, sounded like a dream come true—

one shattered as two figures loomed over his reflection in the window.

"You shouldn't be on the streets at night, kid," a voice grumbled.

He tried to stay calm, the surprise of their silent arrival frustrating him. He should have stayed in the hotel room, should have listened to Noah.

One of the men reached out for him and he knocked the hand away. "Buzz off."

"Look at the spine on this one," the other man said.

"I bet it tastes delicious," the first responded. Gabe blinked hard. The man's eyes shifted in the darkness from brown to black, growing in size.

"The young ones usually do."

Gabe ran, ripping away from the man's grip. Rain pelted from above, the wind slowing his movements but he pushed through it, rounding the corner for King's Lane.

The pair followed, their jeers echoing as they raced through the night. Gabe refused to slow, refused to stop for a second, making turn after turn deeper into the maze-like structure of the city. Until he slammed into a dead end.

"No," he exhaled. The two men stood at the mouth of the alley. "Guys? Listen, I don't—"

They silenced him. Not with words but with a howl. They cried into the night, their bodies snapping and contorting with their screams. Hands and feet turned to paws, fur covering them head to toe. The black eyes swallowed what little light remained and their fangs welcomed Gabe to the real Portents.

"What the hell are you?"

One snapped at the air, his thick, brown fur already matted down by the rain. Gabe fell out of reach, slamming into the fence barring his escape. Garbage piled next to him and he found a large wooden beam poking through the bags of filth.

"Down, boy," he yelled, slamming the makeshift weapon into the hound's snout. The beast snarled, salivating. Gabe knocked him back again with a blow. "I said down, boy!"

The second was on him before he could bring the beam back to block his attack. The hound's jaw snapped at the air. Gabe dropped the beam, fighting to push the beast away from his throat. It was getting closer, hot breath pouring over him.

"GABE!"

Noah stood at the mouth of the alley. The hound dropped its prey, joining his recovered brother as they padded toward the newcomer. Gabe wiped thick globs of saliva from his throat, shuffling through filth to stand.

"Noah?"

His brother was a man possessed. No longer the troubled, grief-stricken nineteen-year-old, Noah took action against the two beasts in their midst. Something small rested in his palm and he held it before him.

"Get down, Gabe! Now!"

Gabe dove into the trash as light grew along the surface of the rock in Noah's grasp.

Two sharp slices of air snapped in the alley. Gabe held his breath, unsure of what happened. Then the heads of the hounds fell beside their dead bodies, silent.

"How?" Gabe tried to ask. Noah rushed to his side, helping him to his feet. "What did you...? They were and then you and—"

"Take a breath, Gabe."

Gabe nodded, working to slow the break-dancing in his chest. He pointed to the object in Noah's hands, the light no longer present. "What the hell is that thing?"

"Nothing," Noah said, tucking it into his pocket before turning toward the street.

"Hey," Gabe called. "You've been carrying it since Mom and Dad..."

Noah never noticed Gabe when he held it in his hands. Never detected his brother keeping tabs on him in the aftermath of their shared loss. His older brother always thought Gabe was sleeping or focused on another crappy film, but he saw the wonder in Noah's eyes when it came to the rock he cradled so close.

Noah took it out once more. "I found it after the fire. In their room."

"A rock?"

"Much more than a rock, Gabe," Noah said. The two dead bodies at their feet attested to that.

"True," Gabe said. He held out his hand. "Let me—"

"Not on your life," Noah said. The stone fell into the pocket once more. "What the hell are you doing out here?"

"Looking for you," Gabe replied, exchanging sharp word for sharp word. "What is going on in this city?"

Noah's head fell to the blood-soaked concrete. "A wake-up call."

"Noah?"

"It doesn't matter. Keeping you safe is all that does." Noah reached for his brother and Gabe pulled away.

"Then why do you keep leaving me?" Gabe shouted. "And don't say work."

Noah peered around King's Lane, worry on his face. He shuffled his brother back into the alley. "There are things I have to do. For us. Always for us."

"For you," Gabe snapped. "You say us but you only mean yourself."

"That's not—"

"I want to go home, Noah."

"We don't..." Noah took a sharp breath. "Soon, Gabe. It's almost over. Come on."

His hand wrapped around Gabe's wrist and the younger brother snapped, "Let go of me."

"Gabe?"

"You don't get to play big brother whenever you feel like it. You're going back out there, aren't you?" Gabe shook loose from his brother's grasp and pointed to the dead beasts in the alley. "Even with these things out there?"

"I have to—"

"Work."

Noah sighed. Both started for the street. "It's not far."

"I know," Gabe said, unable to look at his brother.

"Go right to the hotel and stay inside," Noah said. "I'm going to make this right, Gabe. You'll see. For Mom and Dad. For everything. Trust me."

Noah rushed into the darkness of the city, leaving Gabe alone once more. Screams filled the air, coming from all directions. *A wake-up call,* Noah had said, the words terrifying the sixteen-year-old as much as his brother's killing blow.

Gabe watched Noah disappear before turning down the Knoll for King's Lane.

Trust me.

"I want to," Gabe whispered in the dark. "That's what scares me most."

CHAPTER TWENTY-EIGHT

"Dammit."

A bad night all around. Files needed updating, cases needed additional reports submitted. Wexler was up her ass about a dozen different things, all piling up around her. Samantha Myers was more than capable of handling each and every one of them as time permitted. But with each one came the inexorable sensation of him watching.

Loren was in the room even when he wasn't. Even when he wouldn't be again, most likely.

All because of her.

"Damn. It." She tossed the latest botched effort at work back on her desk and pushed away from the metal tabletop. Her chair rolled toward the window, weary eyes catching a glimpse of the moon before it disappeared behind a wall of clouds. Another dismal night in Portents.

No surprise there.

"What the hell did you do?" The same question followed by the same silence. The utter betrayal on Loren's face haunted her. She heard the cuffs closing on his wrists repeatedly. The clanging of the cell door, leaving Loren to rot the day away while she listened to cheers echo down the hall from Mathers' office.

She never should have followed him. At first it was meant to be protection. If Soriya was the killer, if she truly had unleashed the power of that damn stone on regular folk, Loren couldn't stop her on his own.

A nice excuse, for sure. It softened the blow. The argument was in her favor if that was the truth. But it wasn't—not by half. The truth lay elsewhere, in every secret communication from the past six months. From her recruitment to the city to the blackmail held over her, manipulating her every decision.

She allowed it to happen. Her arrogance at choosing the career, at trying to do the right thing for the only person that ever mattered to her in the world. For control, the lesson her father taught her repeatedly.

To no avail.

Control was lost, taken from her by someone she had never met, never seen face to face.

The phone blared on cue—not her office line with a lead on Soriya's whereabouts or a new case from Wexler, but the burner phone. It rang loudly from the center drawer of her desk. She opened the drawer, staring at the image she saved in her contacts. A blank face with a squiggly super-villain mustache and top hat, her latest masterpiece, and the only control she had when it came to the caller's identity.

She held the phone, watching the display continue to chime, beckoning for a reply. She opened the phone then quickly slammed it shut, dropping it in her pocket.

"Yeah," she muttered. "Screw you too."

Reports could wait, would *have* to wait. Instead of the next file on the stack, Myers grabbed her coffee cup and started for the hall.

The precinct was vacant. Considering the hour, the second floor should have been brimming with personnel. No matter how few civilians wandered the streets at night, the police always had plenty to keep themselves occupied.

Dunn's death was a logical reason for the lack of anyone on the floor. Patrols were stepped up, the APB for Soriya Greystone issued citywide. The death of the mayor tended to fast track the need for a suspect and an arrest. No one wanted the press to see the department's inability to close a case this important.

Not after Erikson.

Another mistake, one of many, thanks to the silenced cell phone resting at her side. Myers sighed, her pace brisk. Wexler's door was closed. Another surprise. The captain typically wandered the building, micromanaging the cases assigned to her team.

Did she miss a briefing during her self-recriminating? Where the hell was everyone?

Where was Loren? The same thought circled on her. Myers wanted to call, to check on him, knowing what a colossal error in judgment that would be. The hearing was scheduled for next week, the evidence stacked—*her* evidence—higher than the growing caseload on her desk. She had built up the small collection for months without his knowledge, damning the man she called partner. The man who saved her on more than one occasion in the short time they had known each other.

She growled in frustration, reaching for the coffee. She swallowed her doubts with the first swig of hot liquid, burning her tongue in the process. Heading back to her office, the elevator dinged. The doors opened and Alvaro stepped out.

Myers smiled. "I thought I was the only one here, Alvaro."

The friendly face was a welcome sight for the lonesome detective. She put the coffee down, moving for the elevator and the strangely silent member of the Major Crimes team.

"Please tell me there are drinks in our future," Myers continued. "I could use at least a dozen to wash away this—"

Alvaro tilted his head, his body contorted and shifting as he shuffled toward her. Myers struggled to laugh, confused at the joke.

"Alvaro?" She had known Alvaro since her arrival in the city. A man with a wife and three kids. A career cop, and a damn good one at that. He laughed and loved the world, bringing Myers to more than one happy hour and keeping her there with his charm and dozens of incriminating stories relating to their colleagues, including Mathers.

The figure before her wasn't Alvaro.

"What's going on?" she asked, backing away slowly.

The officer snarled and fell on all fours. Eyes turned black and fangs grew. Mangy brown fur covered everything, tattered clothes resting at his paws.

Myers held up her hands, shaking her head. "You've got other plans. It's cool."

An office door opened next to the pacing hound that was once Alvaro. Then another from the other side of the hall. Two more beasts joined the first, all salivating at the sight of Samantha Myers.

"Oh, shit."

CHAPTER TWENTY-NINE

Loren dreamed. He fought it, battled against the notion of closing his eyes, of finding rest, but his body succumbed as it always did. And he regretted it, as he always did.

Flowers swarmed across his field of vision. They covered the entire roof and spread across the ground like a lush meadow. Their smell was pungent.

Where once wonder and mystery sat in the dream, where once he felt at peace in its presence, now all he held was frustration. Loren tired of the dream and no longer wished to be the dreamer. He needed answers and sleep. He would have settled for the latter, knowing the former would never come.

"Greg."

Loren opened his eyes to the world of the dream and she was there, right in front of him instead of near the ledge.

"No," he said, falling into her deep blue eyes. Wishing they would stay, always wishing instead of acting.

"Greg." Beth smiled, her fingers grazing his arm. Her touch was warm and inviting. Behind her, the sun blazed, growing larger with each passing moment. "No more sunrises, Greg."

He took her hands and squeezed. "I can't do this anymore, Beth."

"I know," she said, her head bowed. She turned toward the light. "It's almost time. You have to make a choice."

Her words repeated on him. A knife twisted in his gut. Two choices—one life to save and one to lose. How could he make that decision? How could anyone?

"It doesn't have to be like this," Loren pleaded. "Tell me what I can do."

Beth shook her head. "You have to let her go. You can't save them both."

"I can try."

Her right hand ran along his cheek, her smile as bright as the sun above them. "That's why I love you. And always will."

He blinked and she was gone from his side—at the ledge. Loren reached out, caught in the growing vines on the roof.

"What am I supposed to do?"

"Live."

She fell into shadow, a scream filling the air. His scream.

Loren woke covered in sweat. He rolled from the couch, slamming against the side of the coffee table to the floor. Papers scattered from the table, surrounding him as he worked his way to his knees.

Reports. His so-called secret work, as Myers always said. What kept them apart, kept them from working together. What most likely drove her to follow him to confront Soriya and then to slap the cuffs on his wrists, which still ached but not as much as her betrayal.

"To hell with it," Loren grumbled, dropping the gathered reports and letting them scatter once more. His work had little effect. People were still dead, the acts of the Circle of Shadows still unpunished. He wanted nothing more than to tear down their cabal, throw a light on them for all to see, but he had no idea how far they went, how many were involved. If Dunn was a member, anyone could be part of their group, covering up secrets. And without the resources of the Central Precinct there was nothing he could do about it. Not on leave, not while waiting for his hearing. He needed to focus on saving his own ass for a change and not worry about the city.

Or Soriya.

She was being hunted now. Central's APB and the news about Dunn's death would spark a citywide manhunt. Soriya's photo was posted in stores and on street corners. There was no getting her out of it, not unless the real killer was found.

And did he really know she wasn't the killer? His own trust issues haunted him. He shuffled to the window, the rushing wind and driving rain helping cool his thoughts. He wiped the condensation off the leaky pane of glass then tucked his hair away to rest his sweating brow on the sash.

Where did the storm come from? He caught the weather report before dozing off and there was no mention of it. In fact, there was talk of a clear night and full view of a beautiful moon in the sky. Were they ever right about anything?

The rain paused, and the sound of screams rose up along the wind. Loren stared out at the street below. A young man raced down the block, pumping his legs with everything they were worth. Two men pursued.

No, not men. Loren blinked hard. The men wore no clothes and did not stand upright. Like giant dogs.

"What the hell?"

Loren grabbed his gun from the table and ran for the door. At the top of the stairs he paused, the lack of a coat or even socks causing his hesitation. One that could cost a life, Loren argued, rushing down to the street and out into the cold.

The kid, Loren saw once he was on the street, struggled to stay out of reach from the two enormous mutts clawing at him. He climbed over a dumpster and up to the lowered ladder of a fire escape.

"Keep back!" He knocked the closest beast away with a kick and the hound fell with a crash. The second slashed at the boy, whose hands slipped on the rain-slicked rung. The ground welcomed him, trash spreading from the impact. The hounds inched closer.

A shot echoed in the air. The hounds turned to see Loren in the middle of the street. "The kid said to back off. Now."

The hounds shared a glance, their black eyes widening with expectation. One snarled at him. "Loren..."

The detective rolled his eyes. "Oh, I love being popular in this city."

The beasts leaped at him and he let loose, firing two shots in rapid succession. They reached their targets and the hounds collapsed in a heap, the rain mixing with the blood in a dark stream flowing to the gutter.

Loren moved for the kid, who brushed garbage from his body. The teenager in the ball cap caught his approach, his response alerting Loren to the truth behind their situation. Two more hounds padded their way, the sight of their fallen brothers inciting howls.

"Crap," Loren muttered. He turned, pointing down the block. "Run, kid. Run!"

Loren caught up to him, pulling him along while firing wildly. They raced down King's Lane, the southern districts offering little in the way of coverage or escape. They ran full out to the end of the block, Loren pushing the young man along. Before making the turn, he stopped and spun around. His gun was already in place, his shots spaced perfectly.

Two more hounds joined their brothers in death.

"Behind you!"

Loren spun again, firing blind. One shot winged a hound but the other sailed wide. The first fell awkward, sliding along the slippery road past his targets. The second knocked the gun down but not out of Loren's grip, sending the detective flying.

Loren crashed against the ground, shaking away the effects of the blow. The boy punched the beast, screaming. The kid was going to get himself killed, though Loren was grateful for the seconds his ambitious assault offered.

Loren aimed and fired before the hound slashed the kid in two. The startled beast paused, blood soaking his chest. Then it fell in a heap against the street.

"Thanks," the boy gasped.

"Thank *you*."

"Now what?"

Snarls echoed from every direction. Loren peered for some respite, some refuge from the fight. He was down to his last few bullets.

Loren glimpsed a small alcove as the growling closed in on their position. He pointed, pulling the boy along. "In here."

"But—"

Loren forced him low, behind the parked van in the alcove. He shook his head, a finger to his lips. Paws pounced down the street, hesitating in front of the space. The beasts outside sniffed the air for their presence, although the rain muted their scent. The hounds passed their dead, one kicking the corpse against the side before they continued down the street.

Tough love.

"What are they?" the kid asked.

"Trouble," Loren whispered. He didn't have a better answer. After everything he had seen during his work with Soriya, he would have thought he would be better at this. The kid held tight to his torn sleeve. "How are you?"

"I'm fine."

Loren snickered, the answer familiar. The kid was strong, brave enough to face those beasts. "Let me take a look."

"I said I'm fine."

Loren nodded, backing off. "What are you doing out here alone?"

"My brother, he…"

"He's out in this?"

The kid shook his head, eyes wavering. "I should've listened. Stayed at the hotel."

"Hey," Loren said. "Not your fault, kid."

"Gabriel," the young man said. "Gabe."

"Gabe," Loren said, tucking his gun away. "I'm a cop."

"Loren," he said. "They called you Loren."

"Always wanted a fan club," Loren muttered. He inched closer to the kid and deeper into the shadows of the alcove. "I'll get you home. You have my word."

"But those screams? What about everyone else?"

They heard them over the pouring rain and the rolling thunder spreading in all directions. Loren shook his head.

"I don't know. And I wish to God I did."

CHAPTER THIRTY

"I should have told him."

Pratchett leaned against cold steel, which was refreshing even through his jacket. Vertical bars ran the length of the frame, a slit in the center open to receive food and other items when necessary. Each door down the long carpeted hallway was reconditioned in such a manner. For the safety of the city.

And the inmates held within.

Pratchett completed the construction himself. Every inch of the closed and forgotten orphanage had been updated to suit his needs. Alarms were positioned at every entrance, cameras set up at all angles to catch anyone trespassing or attempting to leave the premises. Every contingency anticipated, every threat foreseen.

Except his own guilt.

"I had the chance," Pratchett said, staring at the ceiling. It needed to be painted. Another project to keep the former orphanage in shape. "Hell, I've had nothing but chances for years and I never could. Never had the guts to even start the conversation. And each day that passes makes it that much worse. I just keep wearing the grin, muddling through each day. Going to work like it doesn't kill me inside."

The figure inside the makeshift cell rustled in the background, her breath slow and relaxed. Of all the inmates in the makeshift prison, she understood the reason behind it. She accepted her place in the first floor hall of Saint Helena's Orphanage, long since closed to the city.

Others resisted, their protests echoing throughout the four-floor structure. They sensed his presence and cursed his name. But their curses never compared to his own.

Pratchett pinched the bridge of his nose. Long nights at work and longer days here, working to make sure everything was taken care of, made sure those locked inside their cells had what they needed.

"Now this?"

His phone blared—the third call in the last hour. Work, of course. He was due at the precinct. His uncle needed him as well. Harvey expected news about Loren, worried that their operation was at risk now. Pratchett promised to take care of things.

He made too many promises of late.

Frankie turned out to be the third call. The one bright spot against the growing darkness of his life. Frankie Gibson, his girlfriend. Were they still called that at their age? Was that something only in adolescence? A joke they shared, despite the secrets he kept.

"My uncle isn't wrong," Pratchett continued, the figure in the cell shifting closer to the bars. "You're too dangerous to be out there. Hiding among us. Waiting for the other shoe to drop. But to kill, to slaughter so many?"

You have to make a choice. Before it's too late.

Loren was right. No matter what the Circle accomplished, no matter the good done for Portents, death was not the way.

Pratchett sighed. "Some were innocent. Not like me. Not like you. You get that, don't you?"

"Yes," the figure replied. Her hand squeezed through the bars, resting on his shoulder. Her presence once made his skin crawl, her voice sending him running from a room. Now Pratchett smiled, though his grin faded at the sounds emanating from outside.

Screams. So many crying out in terror.

"It's getting worse," Pratchett muttered. "No matter what secrets we bury. No matter what we hide in the shadows, it keeps getting worse."

Pratchett patted the hand on his shoulder and it fell away. He adjusted his uniform as he stood, straightening the badge pinned to his chest. It still meant something. He had to believe that.

"I have to tell him," Pratchett said. "He deserves the truth. And whatever judgment is out there for me, I'll take it."

The figure in the darkness of the cell nodded.

Pratchett gripped the bars. "Can I get you anything?"

"No," she answered. "No thank you, John."

"I appreciate you listening."

"Always."

Pratchett peered down the hall. Hands battered the bars on cells from the upper floors. He needed to check the security feeds to make sure everyone was secure. And he definitely needed to pick up some paint soon.

"I'll see you in the morning, Hady."

The former head coroner slipped deeper into her cell before the door closed. She remained silent, resigned to her fate, accepting the conclusion after so many died by her hand as the Charon. Pratchett helped her reach that conclusion, as he did with so many others lining the halls.

Screams echoed within and without. The pain and the horror fell squarely on Pratchett's shoulders as he started for the exit. A long night lay ahead, the darkness growing in Portents despite his efforts. Or because of them.

He was no longer sure.

"If the morning comes."

CHAPTER THIRTY-ONE

A bullet silenced Alvaro's snarling, dropping the hound in its tracks. Two more streaked over their fallen brother, slamming against the wall of the hallway on the second floor of the precinct.

Myers fired, unable to connect with either one as she pushed through the fire escape door. Down was an option, but letting the beasts out on the streets was unacceptable. She raced up instead, taking the steps two at a time. She rounded the first flight before the door ripped open, the hinges clawed off in a single swipe.

Black eyes screamed at her, damning her hesitation. Myers pumped her legs, taking the stairs quickly and shuffling across the third floor.

The emptiness of the Major Crimes department greeted her: a dartboard in the corner, an image of Henry Erikson at its bullseye—motivation to prevent another spree, though not enough, it seemed.

How did this happen? How far did it go? Her mind whirled with possibilities, each one darker than the last. If Alvaro could be a hound, who else stood at his side? How many cops were involved? And why did she get the feeling it didn't stop at the Central Precinct?

The door to her right burst open, a new player snarling a greeting.

"Dammit," Myers cursed. She fired at the swiping claw, the blow blasting the beast back into the office and silencing its cry for blood.

Her other two playmates made up ground in the act. They slashed at the air, closing the gap with each leap as she hurried for safety—not that she had any idea where such a magical place might be.

Heat sparked along her leg; blood sprayed as one of the hounds connected with a stray claw. Myers fell forward, struggling to spin with the motion. She held her gun out, locked between two shaking hands. Hitting the ground, her body skidded backward along the floor toward vacant desks and an empty coffee pot. She fired, screaming over their howling. Three then four shots, killing the pair.

She fought to breathe, her chest heaving. Blood pooled under her leg and she lifted it carefully from the floor. The gash was thick, running deep, three inches on her shin.

"Dammit."

Myers tried to stand, using the edge of the closest desk to bolster the act. She slipped in the stream of blood, her leg unable to carry her weight.

Falling back to the ground, Myers shifted away from the blood, effectively creating a second puddle. She tore at the sleeve of her shirt to create a tourniquet, wrapping it against the gaping wound. She squeezed the makeshift bandage into place, the pain enough to make her see stars for a brief moment.

She needed to move. Staying in the precinct was not an option, not one that had any chance of success if survival was the end goal.

A hound rounded the corner, hunger in its eyes. Myers took aim and fired, the bullet catching the beast just above the snout. It slid along the floor, crashing into the desks at her side.

Myers closed her eyes, slowing her breath. Then reality kicked in and her eyelids snapped open. She dislodged the clip from her sidearm, counting the diminishing bullets.

Three.

"Come on," she grumbled. "Kidding me with this shit?"

She slammed the clip back into place, filling the chamber. Someone else had to be in the building. Someone had to hear the shots fired or the screams. Someone other than the monsters roaming the halls. She held a hope where she deserved none—not after everything she had done. To Loren, more than anyone else, but there were others as well. Her manipulations. Her secrets.

This was earned many times over.

In answer, two more creatures slammed through office doors, racing for her. Her first shot missed but the second and third took the pair out long before they reached their kill. Myers pounded her head back against the desk holding her up.

"Damn, damn, damn." Sweat dripped along her brow, running over her eyes. Her heartbeat slowed as she took deep breaths, trying to find a way out.

A low growl brought her back. A hound, patient in its walk, salivated at the sight of her. He—or she, Myers couldn't tell any longer—savored the moment, edging closer to the wounded prey. Myers lifted her gun but the beast continued its approach, no fear entering its black orbs.

Myers pulled the trigger, a loud click showcasing her impotency. Her arm, exhausted from the strain, lowered. "Let's get this over with."

The hound inched closer, extending the kill for as long as possible. Its large fangs dripped pools of drool along her legs and up her heaving chest. She closed her eyes, holding back a scream. She refused to give the monster the satisfaction.

The creature sniffed at her, her hair blowing in the stiff breeze. Taking a deep breath, Myers opened her eyes to face her killer.

Finished with its playing, a lungful of her scent still caught in the beast's nostrils, the hound backed away. A grin spread as it padded toward the elevator.

"What?" Myers asked in astonishment. "What are you doing?"

She lifted the gun, another loud click escaping. She threw the useless weapon at the monster, the instrument of her frustration sailing over its head.

"Finish it!" she screamed. The creature continued, rounding the corner and disappearing from view. "Come back here and finish it, you bastard!"

Tears joined her sweat and the beast's thick drool. Myers slid to the floor, curling up against the cold tile soaked with her warm blood.

"Please just end it."

CHAPTER THIRTY-TWO

Soriya fought for hours. She leaped into the fray, joining the growing wave of hounds at Evans Station. Pedestrians screamed, the howls overtaking their cries for help. Soriya jumped into the mix, distracting the threat while the panicked crowd fled in horror.

Her arrival brought a recharged aggression, recognition in each and every black eye of the Heads of Cerberus.

"Greystone…" Her name echoed up the steps to the streets above where she met more of them.

The struggle flowed like a great dance. She knocked them back and more took over, forcing her to regroup. Rain poured from above, soaking her clothes and slowing her motion but she pressed on. Their fight began just after midnight and now the sky brightened in the distance. Still she fought on, exhausted with each blow against the roiling rage of the beasts.

If only there had been three, as she believed. The warnings of Russell Kerr confirmed her naïveté, but never in all her years would she have believed such a thing possible.

Why now? With everything working against her, with Loren pushing her away and the murder charges laid at her feet, why did this have to happen now? How did the darkness know when to squeeze and when to relent?

And why did she believe there was an actual answer to her questions?

A Circle of Shadows. The Heads of Cerberus. So many forces hidden in Portents, waiting to strike—and all at the same moment. When the city couldn't possibly handle anymore, when the people of Portents struggled to see the dawn of a new day, they preyed on them, burying their hope with endless darkness.

"Come on!" Soriya yelled, spitting out the rain with her bellow. The stone fell into her hand and she waited. All around her for the length of a city block, they came. From rooftops and alleyways. Out of windows and crashing through doors, they howled, surrounding the lone woman in the center of the chaos.

"Is that it?" she cried, a smile on her lips. Cuts and scratches lined her arms, legs, and back. Her clothes were in tatters from the struggle, yet she persisted, pulling the beasts closer. "A snarl here, a slash there, and you think you own this city?"

"It will be ours," one growled in return.

Soriya lifted the Greystone. "Like hell it will."

Light enveloped the block, a wave of concussive force blasting the threat away. Screams rose for a brief moment in the city and were silenced as awe took over.

People rushed to their windows at the sight of the luminescence growing from a single figure on the street. Parents cradled children close. Strangers huddled together, protecting each other from the shadows. All eyes fell on the lone figure in the street, blanketed in a warm light. Murmurs grew, identifying the woman wanted by the police, a woman standing alone against the nightmare rushing through their city. The single individual willing to stand against the evil, her light billowing across the block. The bright white faded from the stone she held and the darkness returned.

Soriya fell to her knees, her legs struggling to carry her in the aftermath. Everything went into her strike, one saved up during the melee. Her entire being led to this moment, to this fight. Years spent learning from the greatest teacher, the greatest father an orphan could ask for.

She refused to fail Mentor in this moment. Her moment. For her city. Always for Portents.

"You'll never have this city," she said, coughing for breath. She smiled, slowly rising back to her feet. She staggered, afraid she would fall once more but she stood. Her arms shook, her vision blurred, but Soriya remained standing.

The Heads of Cerberus returned with the darkness. At first, one at the end of the block, snarling and snapping its jaws at her. Then another at the opposite end, followed by a pair to the left and four more coming from the right.

Then the next wave crashed down from the sky.

Soriya stood her ground, never wavering. "I won't let you have it."

She ran to meet their charge head on, screaming defiance at their numbers, at their hate.

"Not you," she spat, punching the first in the face and knocking it back. She kicked out to her left, catching another. "Or you. Or any of you ugly bastards. Not while I'm here."

She drove them back, each strike placed perfectly to combat the swarm surrounding her. For the briefest of moments, victory was in sight. The sky lightened, the assault thinned, the howling silenced. She thought she could win, just as she always had in the past.

A claw sliced her left arm and she fell aside, her balance lost. The ribbon of Kali snapped to attention, whipping the hound away while retreating to bind the growing wound. It seared, cutting off the stream of blood caked to her skin.

Still, she fell, her next strike off center and missing the mark. The hounds pounced, knocking her further back.

"So go away," one snarled, slamming her in the side. Another threw an uppercut, one that collided with her chin and sent her soaring through the air. She shattered the front window of a nearby storefront, collapsing inside along the glass shards. New cuts adorned her body, her lip swollen with blood dripping down her chin.

"Never," she spat.

"It's over," the hounds shouted as one. They bounded for the store and the end of the Greystone menace.

"For you," a voice called from behind them. They turned and Soriya saw the young man standing in the middle of the street, tall and fierce, as if the world hadn't gone straight to Hell.

"Who?" a hound asked.

Noah Jordan extended the Greystone. Soriya's eyes widened and she dove for cover as a sigil beamed from the surface.

The world silenced, washed clean with the light from the stone. When Soriya opened her eyes again, Noah stood alone, holding out his hand for her.

She took it with a smile. "Took you long enough."

"You're welcome," he replied. She held tight to his side, glass covering her hands and feet. He lifted her out of the store. The Heads of Cerberus were gone.

Soriya laughed slightly, then slipped from his side to the ground.

"Holy," Noah exclaimed, rushing to catch her. "Soriya—"

Her smile remained and he followed her gaze to the sky above. The clouds overhead scattered, the storm diminished as if it had never been. Small streams of light broke through the cityscape.

"The sunrise…"

"Seems to be driving them off for now," Noah said. "You did it."

"My city," she said. "My job to—"

She fell once more and he caught her. "I've got you. I've got…"

The long night ended as darkness filled her vision.

CHAPTER THIRTY-THREE

Every morning began the same for Rufus Mathers. There was breakfast with his wife. Boxed or frozen, never freshly made. A quick bowl of cereal or a waffle heavily buttered and drowned in light syrup. A generous portion of coffee as a side dish and silence as their permanent guest.

Talking went out of style when the kids hit school age. Great dreams and proud parentage faded to routine. Passive aggressive questions about projects long since abandoned turned to thin glares shared over the morning news. Speaking was limited to what was necessary for the sake of hiding their dissatisfaction from the children. A deal on shoes, a better deal on chicken breasts at the local market, but never anything substantial.

Not for years—and especially not since his affair with Samantha Myers.

God-fearing was one description for his wife. Another was *loyal to a fault*. She knew of the affair—he was never good at keeping secrets. She said nothing, letting the silence eat at him until he informed her casually after the kids were asleep.

The couch welcomed him with open arms. Excuses of back problems, of excessive snoring, and many others offered the kids a reprieve from the domestic hell looming over them.

At least Mathers had work. A jaunt from his 2,500 square foot haven by the docks to the Central Precinct offered a more peaceful silence than the one at home. This morning, however, brought the stark realization that nightmares infected the city all around him and had for quite some time. Fires continued to burn along the main thoroughfares. Emergency crews put in extra hours after being forced to find shelter during the storm.

Mathers' own family slept peacefully through it all, leaving him to listen to the howls raging down the streets, wondering when they would crash through the front window. Wondering if he was meant to die in his boxers, alone on the couch that would serve as his final resting place. Wondering if he still loved his wife and if she did the same.

Work offered no solace. Murmurs rang through the halls. Stories of hounds in the dark, of the unnatural storm that blotted out the moon on a crystal clear night. All nothing more than fears to be swallowed to face the new day.

As he did every morning when he arrived.

The climb to the sixth floor was habit now. One going on five years, since his promotion to captain. He hated it, the feeling each step sent running up his spine. At the commissioner's beck and call like a mutt, a degenerate being called to question over everything that happened in a city spinning out of control.

Like it was his fault.

He hated the climb. He made it in the hope that he would be the one to call someday. That some other pissant would be the one to have to slave all day in the cramped office on the second floor and somehow claim jurisdiction over the acts of every lunatic within the city limits.

The usual greeting, that of Sandra Mueller—another lovely distraction—was mysteriously absent, as were the calls and busyness of the other dozen staffers on the sixth floor.

No one was around—the floor vacant and cold.

Mathers peered around the workspaces, expecting people to leap out at him with a laugh. He hated surprises almost as much as the trip up to the top floor. Nothing shifted. No one jumped out at him. Only emptiness throughout the hall.

Except for a single light from the commissioner's office. Mathers straightened his tie and entered the room. Instead of Thorne's burly frame looming over the desk under the dim light of the lamp, Mathers was shocked to see the slim figure of a woman.

"Mayor Winters?" he asked, inching closer. She stood before the window, back to the desk. Always looking out at the city. "I didn't expect... Did you ask to see me?"

Smoke rose in the distance. The mayor turned away with a smile. "I did. Rufus, right?"

"Yes."

"Karen, then," she said, offering her hand. He took it, curiosity leading him to the chair opposite the desk. "Please."

"Why are we meeting here, May—Karen?"

She fascinated him. Each word spoken carried a weight to it, every question asked setting loose a chain reaction for an answer. She was a beautiful woman by many standards, aged to perfection in his eyes, though he did his best to keep them locked on her own instead of the assets below.

"Do you know what a crucible is, Rufus?"

His brow furrowed. "A…a test. A rite of passage."

She nodded, turning back to the city. "Portents endured a crucible last night. An unbelievable horror most knew to be inevitable given what we've witnessed of late. The so-called Night of the Lights. The dozens slaughtered so indiscriminately only months ago. So much death, yet it continues.

"Crucibles are the ultimate test," Karen went on. "They forge us in fire, burning away those unable to stand, unable to find the strength to fight back and leave only the best of us. To make a difference for the future."

Stepping away from the window, Karen ran her fingers along her brow, pinching the bridge of her nose. She took a seat behind the desk, tired eyes straining at her guest.

"The commissioner is dead."

"What?" Mathers balked, almost tipping his chair over.

"One of the many fallen," she said. "We will grieve for them. We will honor those lost. When we can. Now is not the time for that, however. Now is the time to regroup, to prepare. Now is the time to stand."

Karen offered the leather chair once occupied by Thorne. "Are you ready to stand, Rufus?"

"Me?" His voice squeaked and he cleared his throat. "Why?"

"I understand if you don't want the position…"

"No, that's not…" he replied, moving for the chair on the other side of the desk. She grinned as he took it for a test drive. "But there are others and… Why me?"

"I've seen you, Rufus. Your ambition. Your potential. Your loyalty to the office and the city. Loyalty I will need in the days to come. I do not believe our long night is over. I fear it is only beginning. We will need to stand as one to protect Portents from the threats that circle us. Both from outside and especially those found within."

He followed her gaze, down her long arm to her delicately manicured nails painted red. They tapped against the work on the police commissioner's desk. His work, including the top file needed for the upcoming hearing of one of their own.

Greg Loren's hearing.

"I understand," he said with a grin. A problem child since the beginning. One who needed to be handled and now, finally, could.

"Good," Karen said, moving for the door. "One more thing, Rufus. A favor for a friend."

"A friend?"

She nodded. "Someone who helped me in my decision. An old colleague ready to do his part by your side."

"Who?"

Karen Winters ushered him inside, the man who had vouched so graciously for Mathers' rise to power. A man who served the department well before his unjust dismissal from the force. Another grievous act committed by Loren. One Mathers was happy to redress.

Robert Standish took the hand of the new commissioner and gave a firm shake. Then he sat in the chair across from him, propping his feet on the desk triumphantly.

"Ready to get to work, Commish?"

CHAPTER THIRTY-FOUR

When the morning dawned for Greg Loren, he breathed a sigh of relief. He traveled with Gabe across streets covered in shattered glass and the still burning husks of storefronts to get to the kid's waiting hotel. Not content to leave him at the door, Loren escorted the strong-willed teen to his suite, surprised at the size of the vast space occupied by two kids.

Loren asked about Gabe's brother who was nowhere to be seen, including his current profession to which no answer was offered—or could be offered. Whatever the problems at home, they were wearing down Gabe…and the night lost in the shadows, hiding from hounds, did little to help the matter. Strength could only carry the kid so far, though Gabriel Jordan had it to spare. Loren wished he had more to give his youthful companion, some advice or lesson he once learned.

Silence was all he had left.

Leaving the kid behind, Loren reached his apartment to find missed messages on his phone. He quickly changed his clothes, throwing buckets of water over his face and running a comb through his hair before heading out into the world once more. A meeting with the commissioner a week ahead of the scheduled hearing could mean any number of things. Reinstatement? A dropping of charges against him?

Reality sank in when he arrived at the Central Precinct. Cold stares glided his way from those left standing in the wreckage of the second floor. Loren stepped inside his office, opening the drawer to his desk for a stick of gum. He snapped it lightly between his teeth, then returned to the hall.

Doors rested along the wall, no longer attached to any hinges. Bodies were carted out in bags, some hidden under tarps. People rushed up and down floors, EMTs racing between the injured.

Myers was among them. Her leg was wrapped in a thick bandage. She winced with each touch, yelling at the EMT. A smile slipped on his face and she caught it, returning the glimmer of joy with sad eyes. A wordless apology passed the length of the hall between them and he turned away for the stairs, unwilling to hear any plea, unable to understand any possible explanation.

Near the elevator, Loren stopped. He spun back, scanning the crowd gathered at the far end of the hall. There had been a glimpse of someone he never expected—a large man with a well-developed gut. One who should never have been wearing a badge again yet displayed it proudly on his chest.

"Standish?"

Loren shook his head. He continued toward the elevator, pushing away the thought.

The doors opened with a ding and Loren entered the sixth floor. Never one to make the trek up, always content to send Myers or Wexler in his stead, Loren felt uncomfortable at the top of the Rath Building. More than his fear of heights, it was about feeling out of place. This was not where he belonged, the streets offering more for him.

"The commissioner is expecting me," Loren said to the woman at the front desk.

An eyebrow rose at his approach. He cleared his throat, tucking in his shirt. She waited then pointed to the office. "Go ahead."

"Thanks." A shave might have been appropriate. Hell, a new wardrobe would have been appropriate.

Loren knocked on the frame and turned the handle, stepping into the dimly lit office. He staggered back at the sight of the man behind the desk, who was gently polishing the clean surface.

"Mathers?" Loren exclaimed. "What the hell?"

Mathers sneered, offering a chair. "*Commissioner* Mathers to you, Loren."

Loren blinked hard, expecting to wake up in the hospital from a concussion or ten. He entered the room and closed the door, choosing to stand rather than join the man in his comfort.

"I can't believe this," Loren said, chewing rapidly on his gum.

"I honestly don't care what you believe, Loren," Mathers said. Excitement danced in his face, his eyes a brilliant blue behind his spotless spectacles. "Your badge and your gun. On the desk. Now."

"You smug son of a bitch," Loren snapped. "You think you can just—"

"Yes," Mathers replied, his words calm and collected. "I do."

"Without a hearing? Without a chance to defend myself? You think you have all the right answers here?"

"No. But I have the right questions. Questions the public doesn't need to hear after last night's tragedy."

"Like what?" Loren boomed, leaning on the clean desk. "Because I think you're full of—"

"Richard Crowne."

"What?" Loren asked, his voice barely audible.

"Thought you could hide his death?"

"What? No, I asked—"

He stopped. Myers. He asked Myers to call in Richard's death that night in front of the burned wreckage that was once his cabin. Loren left the scene, unable to think about the friend he had lost, his failure to pull the man back from the ledge. Another failure, another life lost.

He trusted Myers to back him up. She didn't.

"And the weapon used in his death?" An evidence bag dangled in his hand, the pistol immediately recognized by the faltering detective. Mathers beamed. "Yours, I believe."

"He shot himself," Loren said, all conviction lost behind his words. "Richard Crowne took his own life."

"With your gun?" Mathers asked. "How unfortunate…"

With my gun? How did he get my gun? "You have to listen to me."

"No," Mathers shook his head, smiling as he stood. "Be grateful I don't press the DA for a murder charge here."

"Why?" The answer arrived in quick succession. "Son of a bitch. You know I didn't do it."

"The convenience of having everything handed to me like this?" He scoffed. "There is little doubt in my mind that you're innocent. The courts would see to it eventually but that's the last thing I want. I sure as hell won't give you another chance to weasel your way back into this building. Your reckless behavior is no longer needed. Here or anywhere else."

"You can't—"

The commissioner pounded the desk. "The mayor is declaring a state of emergency in the city. Curfew is in effect. I have a city to protect and the authority to do so anyway I deem fit."

"You're being played," Loren said. The door opened behind him. Two officers waited to escort him. "Dammit, Mathers. You can't even see it."

"Oh, I see it very clearly, Loren. If it gets rid of you, I'll take it." Mathers loomed over him, triumphant. He held his hand out. "Your badge and your gun. *Now.*"

Myers' betrayal was complete. Loren removed his badge and tossed it on the desk with a clang. He dislodged the clip from his sidearm and slammed both beside the fallen badge. The commissioner salivated over them like prized jewels.

"I believe we're done here," Mathers said.

Loren shook his head. He pulled the wad of gum from his mouth and placed it on the sparkling tabletop of the desk. He mashed it deeper with his thumb, his eyes never leaving the newly appointed commissioner.

"*Now* we're done." Loren turned and headed for the door, leaving behind the Rath Building and his career as a detective.

CHAPTER THIRTY-FIVE

Myers sat at the bar in silence. She held the glass before her, swirling the thick brown liquid around the base before gulping it down. It joined the four beers and three shots from the last two hours. All rested in the hole where her heart should have been.

The solitude of the bar suited her. One of the few places brave enough to stay open in spite of the carnage ripping through the downtown streets only days earlier, McDuffie's was a final refuge for the forlorn detective. Her head ached, the wound down her leg burning at the slightest touch. The stitches held but it was only a matter of time before she screwed that up too.

Just as she had with everything else.

Loren was gone. She heard the news from an elated Mathers, who came to check on her injuries— and make a pass. *The damn prick.* Her evidence, from Loren's files with Soriya to the gun found at the final resting place of Richard Crowne, cemented his fate. She tried to warn him, tried to get him to trust her in the hope that she could do the same.

He never did. And she betrayed him for it.

Not that she had any choice in the matter.

She slammed a twenty on the bar in front of her, next to her empty glass. The bartender, Owen, stopped to pour another round. His eyes were red with sadness, smeared tears stuck to his cheeks. Myers peered around. No one else seemed to notice. Or care. Owen capped the bottle and she snapped her fingers.

"Leave it."

He hesitated but did so, the bottle clanging along the wood. He wiped his hands then his eyes, heading for the kitchen.

"Hey," she called. "Are you—?"

"He told you, didn't he?"

"Who?"

Owen leaned close, his head low. "Loren. He told you about Dominic?"

Myers recognized the name from the files she hacked. Dominic was one of the missing person's reports Loren was working on behind everyone's back. "Is he—?"

Owen nodded. "Can't believe it. I mean, he must have been, right? But to find him like that? I don't know how Loren—"

"He's good at his job," Myers replied, filling the glass more. *Or he was, at any rate.*

What the hell was she doing? The betrayal was one thing but to drown her guilt with booze? That was the ultimate loss of control. The antithesis of every lesson ingrained by her father. Control. Everything serving her world and no one else's.

Only she wasn't serving her own at all. Not really.

In answer, the phone rang. Never her official cell phone—no, work wouldn't need her. Not after what happened during the long night.

She flipped open her other phone. "What the hell do you want?"

She waited for the robotic voice to chime in her ear, her mysterious benefactor demanding anonymity. Instead, a deep voice replied. "To congratulate you on a job well done."

Myers' eyes snapped open, aware of her world for the first time that day. It was an actual voice on the line. A man's voice. It took her a moment to realize the joy on the other end of the line. "You can shove your congratulations up your ass. It's done."

"Upset about last night? Next time answer your phone."

"Were you involved?" Myers asked, dropping to a whisper as Owen made another sweep of the bar. "Did you know this was coming? Those damn…you know what? I don't want to know. It's done and so am I."

"I hope you'll reconsider." The threat was clear behind the words.

She shook them off. "I did what you asked. It's over."

"Detective…"

"Last time I ask," she snapped, downing her glass. "What do you want?"

"How about a drink?"

The phone nearly slipped from her hand. Slowly she turned to face the man standing behind her at the bar. A growing tooth-filled grin beamed at her through a fat lip and a swollen cheek. He was tall with a thriving waistline. But it wasn't all fat. She could see the muscle packed tight beneath his shirt. More than a shirt. His uniform.

With a badge pinned to his chest.

He let his presence wash over her for a long breath, closing his phone. He took the stool next to her.

"I know you," she muttered, trying to place the name.

"Robert Standish," he said. He held out his hand and it hung between them.

"Standish," she repeated. The man who ruined Loren's career the first time out. The man with more hate for Loren than Mathers. And the man controlling her every move since her arrival in Portents.

Robert Standish.

"I think we can do wonderful things together, Sammy." His hand fell away and he reached over the bar for a glass. Then he snagged the bottle and poured two shots, passing one over to Myers. She took it, watching her fate slip away with her control.

He clinked her glass, celebrating the day. "Cheers."

CHAPTER THIRTY-SIX

"This coffee is terrible," Loren muttered, struggling to finish the small cup.

"Don't drink it."

"I was thirsty." He moved for the fridge. "And you didn't offer anything else."

"I didn't offer coffee either. You poured it. In my mug."

Loren stared at the *#1 Dad* mug and shrugged. "Want me to wash it?"

Alejo Ruiz wiped his tired eyes and shook his head. "Are we really doing this right now?"

"I'm just saying that maybe you need a new coffee maker."

"It is new."

Loren sat down with the mug in hand. "With all the varieties out there now, how can a bad cup of coffee still exist in this day and age?"

"I happen to like it."

"Case closed, your honor."

"Greg."

Loren fell silent, unsure how to start. He came to Venture Cove with no plan—no grip on the situation at hand. All he had was time, more than ever before thanks to his removal from duty at the hands of Mathers.

Sleep would have been nice, a chance to bounce back with a fresh twelve hours of sack time. The couch disagreed. So did his dreams.

You can't save them both.

He couldn't save anyone now. Everything had been pulled away from him. Soriya. Myers. Pratchett. Harvey. Mathers. Wexler. Too many players, all with their own motivation. A Circle of Shadows. The four deaths, including Mayor Dunn. The hounds raging in the streets. How did they connect?

Ruiz didn't have an answer at first, letting Loren replay the last week for him. The captain kept his questions to a minimum, allowing the news to flow naturally. When Loren finished, Ruiz paused.

He broke his silence with a single thought. "Commissioner Mathers?"

"That's your takeaway here?" Loren asked, standing from the table. His chair clattered to the ground.

"Sorry," Ruiz said. He pulled back his salty hair, forcing his eyes wide. "But *Commissioner* Mathers?"

"Dammit, Ruiz." Loren lifted the chair, sliding it back into place. Sad eyes offered a silent apology that was quickly waved off by his friend. "Why now? What does it all mean?"

"You're too close to it. Take a step back. Soriya can—"

"Don't."

"What? She didn't kill those people, Greg. You know that."

Loren chuckled. "The fact that you can make that statement and I can't is laughable considering how you feel about her."

"Felt about her," Ruiz clarified. "So explain it to me."

He hesitated then reached into his pocket. The folded image slid across the table and the middle-aged captain looked it over carefully. "What's this? Your apartment?"

"The day Beth died."

"The day…?" Ruiz shook his head. "You think Soriya—?"

"I don't know," Loren yelled. He took a breath, quieting the storm inside. "Dammit, I don't know anything."

"Did you ask her?"

He tried. He came close while they hunted down what turned out to be a phoenix, pushing people to fulfill their dreams while literally burning them out. He was so angry, and still was, but the city needed them. Portents always took priority over their own desires.

"No."

"You should," Ruiz said. He took a sip of coffee, his satisfaction audible. Loren grimaced at the sound of lips smacking. Ruiz pushed the photo away. "Put this whole thing behind you once and for all. There is a reason, Greg."

"You sound so sure."

"You need her, she needs you. That's the way it's always been."

"Things change," Loren said, his head low.

"Not everything. Not the best things."

Ruiz peered down the hall at his resting family. His life, one built brick by brick through years of pain and sacrifice. Ruiz was happy, content with the world, his family by his side.

"Right now Soriya Greystone is the last thing I need," Loren said. "The last thing Portents needs. What it truly needs is you."

Ruiz blinked, surprised at the summation. He shook his head. "No."

"Just like that?"

"My family—"

Loren pocketed the image of Soriya. "Your family is not the issue here. *You* are."

"Hey," Ruiz snapped. "I almost lost this once. I won't let that happen again. Whatever the hell is going on will pass. It will be solved and Portents will continue as it always does."

"Until it doesn't," Loren huffed, running his hands through his unkempt hair. "I never thought I'd see it."

"What's that?" Anger welled in Ruiz's voice.

"You passing the buck."

"I'm not—"

"Not finished," Loren shot back. "You passing the buck out of fear."

"Greg…"

"You're afraid. I get it. You have a lot to lose. So do a lot of other people, Ruiz." Loren popped a stick of gum in his mouth and grabbed his jacket off the counter. Slipping it on, he reached for the door. "Maybe you aren't what we need. Not like this."

"Greg, wait…"

"Sorry to have bothered you."

He slammed the door behind him. The brisk morning wind forced him forward to the street and the city beyond. Ruiz couldn't help him. He was wrong to ask, wrong to force that sacrifice from a man who had given his all during his career.

It still angered him, but no more than the lack of answers everywhere he turned. Too many questions and none easily solved.

Except one.

Loren stopped at the corner, the photo back in his hands. Ruiz was right about one thing: It was time for the truth, no matter what came from it.

It was time to talk to Soriya once and for all.

CHAPTER THIRTY-SEVEN

Ruiz couldn't help Loren. That was what it boiled down to in his mind. Not from a lack of courage. Not from fear of what was happening to Portents, or a Circle of Shadows, or even Mathers sitting behind the commissioner's desk.

It was a promise he made. His family deserved to have top billing and everything he had done in the last six months stood as proof. His family thrived. Zoe came home on the weekends and the two talked for hours. He listened to Teresa's inane drama involving thirty people he'd never met, and she loved him for it. And Angela played catch with him in the backyard, at least for a few minutes before the time came for another tea party with her stuffed animals.

He was happy. Didn't Loren realize that? Couldn't he see this was how life was meant to be in the Ruiz home? That being pulled back into the nightmare enveloping Portents would wreck everything? And maybe this time Ruiz wouldn't be able to convince Michelle to take him back. What if something happened while he was away?

He'd never forgive himself.

Ruiz made the only choice available. The right one. The true one.

"Greg's not wrong."

All thought disappeared in the presence of his wife. "You heard?"

Michelle stood in the doorway to the kitchen, arms crossing her chest. Barely awake, and still she looked like she was put together by God himself. She pushed off the wall and joined him at the table.

"Everyone on the block heard."

"The kids?"

"Could sleep through the apocalypse if it came down to it," Michelle said, reaching for his hand.

"Not funny."

"Wasn't meant to be."

"How can you—?" Ruiz stopped, not wanting to argue.

"Go ahead, Alejo. Don't hold back on me. You didn't on Greg."

"We talked about this," Ruiz said. "My place is here with you and the kids."

She squeezed his hand. "It always will be. But right now there are other people who need you and I won't be selfish."

"I made a promise," he repeated.

"You kept that promise. Six months you've been hiding here, Alejo. That's long enough."

"I'm not hiding!" he yelled. The cup crashed against the counter, the handle splitting away and the rest dropping into the sink before shattering completely. "Dammit."

"Let me—"

"I've got it. I can do this."

Michelle shook her head, moving for the sink. "I know you can. You've been here, doing everything you can for this family. Being the dad, the husband, the protector, the homemaker. Everything we could possibly want, pushing yourself to fill every need in this house. Except your own."

"Michelle…"

She turned him away from the broken cup. "You kept your promise. You will always keep your promises because of who you are. The man I married."

"You don't know what's out there, Michelle. This thing Greg's talking about…" Ruiz closed his eyes. "Am I a coward for not wanting to face it? Am I really afraid for putting this house, our kids, you, first?"

"We're all scared, Alejo," Michelle replied, resting her head on his shoulder. "The whole damn city is terrified about what comes next."

"I'm supposed to protect you from this. But what if—?"

"You will. Like you always have."

He fought to smile, worried about the impact of their decision, about making the right choice and not being able to see one any longer. Being home, seeing the other side of a cop's life, the one that never truly came in a place like Portents was a dream come true. Was he wrong to hold on to it for every last second? To keep that dream alive as long as possible?

Michelle lifted his gaze from the floor, catching him with her deep brown eyes. "You listen to me, Alejo Ruiz. You are stuck with us and we are stuck with you. No matter what. We made our own promise."

"I know."

"They need you now," she continued. "Every family in Portents needs you now. Not just us. Portents needs your protection, Alejo. Are you going to just wait it out and hope for the best? Or are you going to stand up and defend us all?"

To serve and protect. Those words meant more to him once upon a time. They were his world. Portents was his world. Lifting the city out of the darkness, watching other families thrive and grow as his did. Seeing kids grow up to join him in his fight with the same pride, the same self-worth from being Portents born and raised.

Ruiz smiled and kissed her. "I love you."

Her hand against his chest warmed his heart under her delicate fingers. With the sound of waking children down the hall, Michelle smiled at their life and at her husband.

"I love you too," she said. "That's why you'll always do the right thing."

He nodded, looking out to the city, and wondered what the cost of that decision would be. For him. For Loren. For everyone.

CHAPTER THIRTY-EIGHT

Soriya woke in her apartment. The couch creaked under her weight, the fabric worn thin from age. She tried to sit up, her body screaming its resistance to no avail. The pillow at her back slid over the arm of the couch then tumbled to the floor. She moved to catch it, but the effort was too quick and sent her tumbling to the ground with a thud.

"Hey, what are you doing?" Noah asked, rushing into the room. He placed a glass of water on the end table, then reached for her.

She clambered back along the couch. "I'm fine."

"Looks that way." He held out the glass. "You talk in your sleep, by the way."

Soriya smiled, wincing as she shifted deeper into the couch. "So I've heard."

"You also drool."

"That one is new." She wiped the cool liquid from her lips. "How long?"

Noah peered toward the door to the balcony. Darkness had returned to the city. "Three days."

"Three..." She paused, putting the water down. Her hand shook and the glass tumbled over. Noah caught it as liquid ran down the table's length. She believed one day was lost after her struggle with the Heads of Cerberus, but three? What had she missed?

Soriya moved to stand, her legs miles away from her body.

"Hey," Noah shouted, holding her against the couch. Her eyes flared but he refused to relent. "Take it easy. You've been in and out. Barely able to take food before collapsing again. You need rest."

Footsteps rambled in from the kitchen. She peered at the newcomer to the room, a slightly shorter, more wild-eyed version of her rescuer.

"Here." A young teenager offered her a plate.

"Who are you?"

"My brother," Noah said with a grin. "Gabe."

He handed the plate to Soriya. She took a fierce bite of the sandwich, peanut butter and jelly—one of the few products always available in the apartment.

"Thank you," she said while chewing. "Both of you. Noah, if you hadn't—"

"It's all right. You'd have done the same."

Another bite, followed by a large sip of water, filled her empty stomach. Her body gurgled, joining the chorus of moans from the couch beneath her. Everything ached, everything screamed for a reprieve. Her body needed time to knit itself back together, the cuts adorning her dark skin scabbed over from her long nap.

"Three days," she repeated. "Have there been any—?"

Noah shook his head, standing at the door. "It's quiet. Like the city is holding its breath. And when it exhales?"

"All hell breaks loose."

You think there are only three? You're wrong. More will come... Russell Kerr's warning echoed in her thoughts. How could something like this come out of nowhere? How could they hide from her, biding their time? She was supposed to be better, supposed to fulfill her role and protect Portents and the Bypass from the monsters in the dark.

She should have known. The warning offered by Kerr a year earlier had been more than enough to start her investigation. But she didn't. Evans showed up and Mentor fell. Then the stone failed and Erikson unleashed the Charon on Portents. Now Loren? There was always something else, some distraction, exactly what they counted on to hide their movements.

"Cerberus."

"You know what this is?"

"The dog things?" Gabe chimed in, holding his arm. A bandage ran along his bicep, poking out from his shirt.

"*Gabe.*"

The younger Jordan shrugged. "What?"

Soriya nodded. "The Heads of Cerberus. I took three down awhile back."

"I thought there were only three?" Gabe asked, surprising both of them.

"I was hoping the same." Soriya finished the drink. Noah snatched the glass and the empty plate from her lap.

"Stay. I'll get more water."

"Thanks."

Soriya tried to shift, each movement a strain. The stone sat at her side, the pouch still in place along her belt. *Small favors.*

Gabe smiled, resting against the opposite wall. He rubbed at the back of his neck, unsure where to look or what to say, stopping and starting multiple times.

"I didn't realize Noah had a brother," Soriya said, offering an out from his predicament.

"He doesn't advertise it. Thinks he's protecting me." He picked at the bandage along his arm. The wound peeked out from the crumpled wrap, a thick scratch four inches long. "He's really protecting himself."

"Probably," Soriya said. "Sometimes we don't see it that way. We don't realize the hurt our secrets cause."

He stopped playing with the wound and stood, pacing the room. "He's been going out there. These last few days? I don't know where he goes or what he does. All I know is he keeps doing it. He keeps leaving me behind."

"That's not—"

"He's the only family I have," Gabe said. Fear and terror flared in his tired eyes. He needed his brother and Noah didn't realize, couldn't fathom Gabe's pain. Not with the idea of his parents' killer in the city.

Selfish thoughts raged in Soriya's mind. She hated the sensation, the need she carried for the young man with the Greystone. The Heads of Cerberus were in the city, killing indiscriminately without anyone to stand in their way. She needed Noah at her side to take them down, to find out what was going on in Portents.

Noah shuffled back from the kitchen, pausing at the entryway. "Anything interesting?"

Gabe looked to the balcony, slipping outside for some fresh air. Soriya shook her head, accepting the second round from his older brother.

"No." A low chiming sound rang out from the other room. "My phone?"

Noah's eyes widened. "Right. It's been going off for a couple hours now."

He returned with the beeping device. She unlocked the screen, thumbing through the piling number of missed notifications. All from the same person.

"Loren."

Gabe peered curiously into the room at the name, returning to the pair in the living room.

Noah went to ask his younger brother who waved him off without a word. "That guy that was arrested?"

"My partner," Soriya replied. "My friend. I should—"

"Rest. I can—"

She shook her head, reaching for his hand. He helped her to her feet, catching her as she fell forward. Balance would come soon—it would have to, or it would be a short trip for her. A wave of dizziness passed, her legs tingling but closer than they had felt minutes earlier.

She read the message again, repeated multiple times over the last four hours:

WE NEED TO TALK.

"Soriya—"

"I have to go." She smiled at her savior.

He shook his head. "You're still wanted for questioning, Soriya. The police—"

"Won't see me."

"You don't know that." Noah stopped her then let his hand fall away slowly. "You need my help. Together we can stop this. The Luminary can—"

"I'll be back soon."

"At least take me to the Bypass, Soriya," he pressed. "If it will help, give us some clue what these beasts want. We might be able to use it against them."

"Stay with your brother, Noah," Soriya answered softly. "The hounds can wait a while longer. Family is too important."

Hope filled Gabe's youthful eyes. Noah's, however, remained grim.

Soriya left for the bedroom, quickly returning with a bulky sweatshirt. She threw it on, the effort causing her to wince more than once. Noah stared through her, wanting better news, wanting more from her than she was willing to give. His brother needed him.

She grabbed the handle to the door and headed for the stairs. "We'll figure things out when I get back."

CHAPTER THIRTY-NINE

Unsteady steps carried the dark-skinned woman from the complex, her grip on the handrail much too tight. Pain wracked her body but she refused to slow, refused to pause and take a breath. Someone named Loren needed her and her first instinct was to run to help without a care to her own safety.

Yet Noah hesitated, standing with his hands in his pockets and not a damn place to go. He tried, multiple times, to join her. She needed him whether she recognized it or not, but she pushed back the request—she had pushed back every request, including the Bypass.

He needed to see it, needed to stand before it even for only a second. The answer was within, waiting for him to ask a simple question. Soriya refused him at every turn, unable to trust him even after saving her life.

How could she not understand how much he needed the truth?

Part of him understood her reasoning. He stood in the doorway to the apartment. Gabe's arms crossed his chest, his back leaning along the frame. Curious eyes caught his brother's before Noah left the stairs for the apartment.

Before he reached the door, another opened. Two heads ducked out, two young men close in age. Brothers not unlike the pair already occupying the hallway.

"Soriya?"

"She left," Noah said.

The younger one pushed ahead. "We wanted to ask her about something…"

"No, we didn't," the older brother said through gritted teeth. "We didn't."

"About the howling," his younger sibling whispered. "Remember, Davis?"

"Shut up, Kev," Davis snapped, pushing him back inside the apartment. "Good to meet you."

The door slammed. Gabe smiled wide and Noah shrugged, pushing past him.

"Nice kids."

Noah threw a disinterested shrug. Gabe closed the door behind him and the pair settled in the living room of the woman they had been doctoring for the last three days. Noah cleared the pillow and blanket from the couch, noticing the bloodstains along the side.

Gabe cleared his throat.

"What?" Noah sighed.

"You could have told me the truth."

"Huh?" Noah tossed the items into the bedroom and returned, wrinkles dotting his forehead.

"You and Soriya? Your so-called work?"

"What are you talking about?" Gabe's smile broadened. "We're not—"

"Seriously?"

"Yes, seriously."

Gabe rubbed his chin. "Can I—?"

"No," his older brother answered before letting out a low laugh. Noah ran his hand along the back of his neck, fingers digging deep. "Little brother of mine, that is way too much woman for you to handle."

"Says you. How many dates have you been on?"

"More than you, punk. Lizzie—"

Gabe cut him off. "No way. Lizzie Henderson does not count."

"Why not?"

"Hanging out in our basement doesn't count as a date."

Noah stepped over to the window and the waning light in the distance. He grinned. "Mom thought it did."

"That's right. She always stayed by the door."

"With a glass up to her ear to eavesdrop, like something out of an old cartoon." Noah's eyes flashed with memory. "I opened the door once and she almost fell down the steps. She tried to ground me for that."

"Then Dad walked by."

"'Game's on. Keep it down.'" Noah laughed, dropping the same stern look his old man wore when the Steelers were playing. "I haven't watched a game since…"

"We could," Gabe said. "Noah, we could if you—"

"Gabe." Noah faced the rising darkness outside. The hours passed too quickly—and with too much to do.

"No," Gabe said. "Where did you just go? Mom and Dad are gone. I can't lose you too."

"You won't. I'm trying to fix this. To make sense of everything."

"Not everything will. Doesn't mean you stop living, Noah."

Gabe wasn't wrong. Not everything made sense. Not with what he had been asked to do over the last two weeks. What started as simple revenge for the death of his parents against an organization operating in the shadows had broadened to something more.

The howling that terrified the city, from the old to the young including the two kids down the hall, was the start of his doubts. But there was more. Loren, the man Soriya worked with? He had heard people close to his benefactor discuss the detective and his downfall. All for the Greystone's supposed benefit, all to make her see the truth. All to win her over to their way of thinking.

Driving her to Noah and the Luminary was a lesson, a wedge to split her from her support circle. Like so many other facets of her life over the last few months. Noah knew little of the acts committed against the self-proclaimed protector of Portents, but they were in place.

Including his role in them. As well as how it was supposed to end.

He hated it. Looking around the young woman's apartment, he saw someone trying to make a life for herself. As he should have been. For his brother's sake.

But his parents' deaths hung over everything, the mystery that set a blaze to their former home, their former lives and cast them out into the darkness. The answers were here, in Portents. All within reach.

The Bypass. I have to see it. I have to know.

"I can't," Noah said, dashing any hope from his brother's face. "Not yet."

Noah fixed the couch cushions, flipping over two of them to hide the stains along the side. He flattened them out and reset the pillows along the sides. Grabbing his coat, Noah patted his brother on the shoulder and started for the door.

"Where are you going?"

Noah stopped. "To finish this."

"Noah?" Gabe called. He turned to face the teenager who was quickly growing into a man. "Walk away. We can do this. Together."

Be a family—everything they always wanted and never appreciated, not when they had it. Noah Jordan had been trying to do it right from the start by finding out the truth about his parents, closing the door to the past.

"Head back to the suite. Pack our bags, Gabe." He smiled to his brother. "I'll be there by the morning. I promise."

There was no more choice in the matter. Soriya pushed him to it, her inability to reach out and trust him completely. Only one last task remained. Then it would be over.

CHAPTER FORTY

Loren didn't know how much time passed. Not since his visit with Ruiz. Not since his last message to Soriya. He sat in the dark, the day slipping by without any care, without any need to do more than wait.

Everything was broken. Ruiz cowered in his home in the coves. Soriya was off the grid. Myers called—of course she did. Guilt had a way of eating at a person until they did the one thing they swore never to do. So she called him. He refused to answer, refused to acknowledge the message on his phone. Apologies could never replace what he lost.

She betrayed him. The Crowne affair, his case files with Soriya, and this latest disaster. Four dead and their murderer in the wind.

Or maybe it *was* Soriya and she was playing him. Everyone else had. Ruiz pulled Loren back into this world, away from his family, away from a life he could have built in Chicago. Myers destroyed what little he had been able to accomplish since his return, her every attempt to reach him nothing more than a chance to drive the knife deeper in his back.

And Soriya?

Everything screamed at her innocence. Including her own declarations in the alleyway. None of the pieces fit when she was placed in the center. They all scattered and distorted. Was that the remnants of the trust held for their friendship? The photo on the coffee table left every hope barren. The shadow in the window. Soriya on the day his wife fell. He had to know the truth. He had to know what secrets still existed between them.

Before he shattered completely.

"Loren?" a voice called from the door. A soft knock followed. It surprised him; the commonplace entrance was never Soriya Greystone's first choice. Or her second, typically.

"It's open."

She stepped inside, pulling back the hood of her sweatshirt. Her movements lacked their usual fluidity. She was hurt, the cuts more visible as she neared. "I came as fast as I could."

He clicked the lamp, the dim light a beacon in the apartment.

"Loren." Her smile returned, joy at seeing him. Always joy. One he failed to reciprocate for months. "Is everything—?"

"Sit down." He didn't look at her, eyeing the chair instead.

"I'm fine. Loren, what is—?"

"Do it," he snapped, bloodshot eyes cutting across the room. She joined him across the coffee table.

"I didn't kill those men," she said, concern in her voice. "You have to believe that."

He shook his head. "Why? Why should I believe any of it anymore?"

"Loren—"

"I lost my job, Soriya," he said, stopping her. "Because of you."

"I...I didn't..." She fell silent.

"I've lost everything because of you."

"That's not true," Soriya replied. "How can you even think that, Loren? After everything we've been through."

"That's exactly what we're here to learn!" Loren yelled, slamming his hand against the table. "The truth. Once and for all."

The photo glided across the table. "What's this?"

"You tell me."

She cocked an eyebrow, dropping the image against the table. "Me in your apartment? What does this have to with anything?"

"Everything!" Loren screamed, jumping to his feet. "The day this was taken, the day everything was taken from me..."

He turned away, leaving the table behind and the curious look from Soriya. He paused at the mantel, the dirt covering the mirror glossing over his reflection. Not that he would recognize the man looking back. Not anymore. Instead he lifted the single item not packed up in the spare room that once served as their office.

Their wedding photo.

"Beth," she called. "This is about Beth."

Everything was. Every reason for staying in Portents after her death. Every reason for returning after the Evans case. All in the hopes of solving her murder, of putting the past to rest. All in the hopes of building a new life.

A better tomorrow.

"Loren" Soriya said, standing close to the chair; leaning for support. "The city—"

"Can burn for all I care," he seethed. "You've hidden things and I've accepted it. But not this. Not anymore. Did you kill my wife?"

"What?"

He reached for her, pulling her close. His fingers dug into her arms, eyes flaring. "All secrets come to light. You told me that in your damn library. No more lies, Soriya. Tell me the truth!"

"I would never—"

He pushed her away, snatching the photo from the table to shove in her face. "This says differently!"

"This?" Soriya shook her head. "This doesn't mean anything, Loren."

"No," he said. He grabbed her arm and squeezed. "You don't get to dismiss it. She's dead and you were there. Don't deny it. You were there!"

"I wasn't!" With her free arm she slapped him, knocking him aside.

He staggered to keep upright, dropping his hold on her arm.

"I wasn't there in time!"

The cold light of his actions stalled him. He wiped at his cheek. "What?"

"Damn you, Loren," Soriya said. "Why do you think out of all the cops on the force, I reached out to you? Did you ever think about that?"

He hadn't. It never entered his thoughts. Her capture of the Kindly Killer was always an introduction, more a coincidence because of their crossed purposes, never anything more. He was wrong, unable to see the shared connection—one he never fathomed, never considered because he never knew the truth about Beth. He never knew a damned thing...

"She was my friend, Loren," Soriya said, lifting the image of his wedding off the mantel. Calloused fingers gently ran across the frame. "She was my friend and she needed me. But I was too late to save her."

CHAPTER FORTY-ONE

Seven Years Earlier

Soriya loved the city during the day. The flow of hundreds along every street, the constant buzzing that came from the citizens of Portents as they rushed from place to place. The connections made and those ignored, every moment lost or cherished depending on various circumstances. Call it fate, believe it to be happenstance—nothing was better than witnessing life all around her.

Allen Mason, however, proved the opposite was true. The owner of Atlas Books hated the city during the day. The endless questioning by ignorant people. The purposeless youth roaming mindlessly along the streets.

Soriya Greystone included.

She had been escorted from the property multiple times, her age and demeanor immediately drawing red flags. Yet she continued to return, always with facts on her side. Facts typically ignored by the burly manager, followed by threats to nonexistent parents and the police.

Atlas Books was a repository of useful information. Rare manuscripts were a specialty of the owner, originals dating back centuries lining the shelves for interested buyers. Or avid researchers. Soriya filled neither role yet her trips held merit.

Each year her training intensified, the obstacles growing to see how much she could handle. No matter the fresh scars, the broken limbs, the battered bruises that caused her once pristine, child-like skin to take the form of a rainbow, she refused to let the man down. Or let a valuable resource be taken from her due to her age.

She had a need, and the store met that need. Mentor's latest challenge proved to be quite the conundrum yet he stated it so plainly.

Capture a minotaur.

The phrase rolled off his tongue like he was ordering breakfast. Her initial attempts to complete her task met with limited success. She found the mythic beast and attempted to follow through on capturing it only to find herself in a cast or three from the exchange.

Talking things out with the minotaur was not an option—her fault. She led with her fists instead of her brain, though her drive and commitment to the task brought a grin to Mentor's face, more than making up for the pain of their battle.

Healed up and ready for another round, Soriya turned to Atlas Books for guidance. Mentor offered to assist in her studies of the creature, willing to take the burden from her bruised and battered body. It was the worst form of surrender in her mind and completely out of the question.

She entered the store during the midday rush, with people killing time during their lunch hour. Most were worthless when it came to shopping and Allen Mason was acutely aware of the situation. But he didn't care, making them almost invisible to his radar. Soriya followed a pair of women into the store, her hooded sweatshirt covering as much of her face as possible. Not the best disguise, but as it turned out, one was not needed. Mason was engaged with a guest at the counter, a young woman with blond hair, blue eyes and a smile that could win over the coldest fish in the sea.

"It's just for a day or two," the woman said. "I need—"

"To break the rules," Mason interrupted, his nose held high. "Like always. Beth, if it was anyone else I wouldn't even let you finish the sentence."

Beth scowled. "You *didn't* let me finish, Allen."

"Force of habit."

"Is that a yes?"

Mason sighed. "As long as you keep that boyfriend of yours—"

"Fiancé."

"What?"

Beth held out a finger with a gleaming ring locked in place. "Fiancé. So watch it."

Mason grumbled under his breath. "Well, you keep him away from my books. I keep finding coffee rings in them and I know it's him."

"Greg?" Beth asked with a laugh. "Never. He loves books too much."

"Uh-huh…"

Beth waited and an extensive tome slid across the counter to her waiting hand. "Thank you, Allen."

The young woman moved away from the register, tucking the manuscript decorated with glyphs under her arm. She checked her watch, staring at the ring for a long moment. A new addition to her finger, it brought another smile to her face.

"Writing a new book?"

The smile faded and she patted the text. "Something like that."

"A departure from your usual subjects."

"Just some background information," Beth said with a shrug. "You never know when you might need it."

"When referring to Hephaestus' hammer?" Mason replied with a laugh. His cheeks jiggled, his sweaty palms heavy on the counter. "Probably not anytime soon, I would imagine."

"Pays to be prepared," Beth said. "Thanks again."

Soriya listened from the stacks, focused on the woman's movements. On the way she held the manuscript and the worried look in her eyes. There were rumors of the hammer's presence in the city. And this woman, Beth, knew about it. Not for research purposes, though. No, Beth understood Portents in a way Soriya had not seen from many.

Before she realized, Soriya stood face to face with the woman she had been staring at for minutes. Beth moved through the stacks, peering along the aisle, the path suddenly barred by the teenager in the hooded sweatshirt.

"I'm sorry," Beth said, sneaking around her. "Please excuse me."

"My fault," Soriya said. "I was just looking for—"

"No problem," Beth answered, looking through the stacks. "I'll let you get to it."

"Actually," Soriya called before the blond exited the aisle. "I could use your help and I might be able to help you too."

"I don't—"

Soriya stepped up to her, removing the hood. "What do you know about minotaurs?"

Beth hesitated for a second, the question giving her pause. Then she smiled bright, intrigued at the discussion ahead.

CHAPTER FORTY-TWO

Soriya wiped a tear from her cheek. Memories flared, stories kept and buried for years from the man she trusted more than anyone else in her life. Each one brought a wave of pain and loss.

Loren stayed silent, unable to move. His chest rose and fell in sync with her words. His eyes never strayed, never flared. Through the two pale windows into his soul, Soriya witnessed the shattering occur beneath the surface.

"She was my friend. One I never deserved," Soriya whispered. "After her help tracking down the minotaur we worked together off and on. If I needed help and she wasn't around I would make little marks in her books and leave them out on the nightstand."

Soriya smiled. She reached into her pocket, causing Loren to tense on the couch. A sigh left her, fingers slowing to retrieve the item in her pocket. Her black marker. "Beth bought this for me. Silly, right? I used to mark up her books in pencil, all I had at the time, and she told me to go bold.

"It wasn't always monsters and murder with us. Sometimes we just met up for a meal and talked. It was rare. Mentor didn't really care for the idea. Shocker, I know. But for so long he was all I had. It was nice to have a friend."

Silence returned. Soriya wanted to reach out to Loren, whose hands clenched tight to his knees. Every word spoken was a dagger into their former partnership, the trust built over the last five years. One she initiated, the reason held secret. One secret too many for the detective.

She fought to find the right words. Everything she said was true; had always been true. But the omission threw doubt on anything she might say, any action she might take to sway him. Did he believe any of it anymore? Could he?

"We met a couple weeks before…" Soriya trailed off, glancing at the open window and the shadows of the city. "She was nervous. Something was bothering her. When I asked about it, she passed it off. Work, she said. Just work. Research into the city. Things like that. Beth told me she was working with others, like-minded souls who understood Portents. I figured it was more research nuts like her. When I would mention them, try to find out more, she changed the subject. Usually about you, but never about the group."

Soriya rested at the mantel, fingers stretched along the ledge. "I should have looked into it more," she said, swiping at the mirror in a thin streak. "I didn't."

She saw the change in Beth, the concern tucked behind her pristine smile. Over that last month, concern became fear. Beth passed it off as the stress of the job but Soriya, even at seventeen, knew better. But she didn't question, and her friend paid the price.

How could she explain that to him? To this man who became the embodiment of everything good in her life? Who brought joy to her lips with his mere presence? Who stood at her side in her darkest hours? How could he tell her she failed, that when he needed her the most, she wasn't there?

Soriya let out a long breath, turning to face her partner—to face the truth. "She called me that day. Something scared her. I was…distracted. Working. I don't know on what anymore. It didn't…it wasn't important after…

"The work always came first," she continued. "Even when it came to Beth."

Leaning over the coffee table, Soriya reached out and grabbed the photo of her in the window of the apartment. The shadow watching over the death of her friend. She turned it toward Loren, unable to look any longer.

"I was too late. When I showed up, when I finally made it here, you were already at her side. She was…she was gone."

The photo fell from her fingers, swooping through the air in a large wave as it glided to the floor. Both watched it hit the ground, the arc sweeping the divisive image under the table and out of sight.

"I should have told you," Soriya said. "I couldn't. The pain was always with you, a scab you picked on your own. You didn't need my help on your path of self-destruction."

Her hand fell over his, grazing his bruised knuckles. "I thought, I hoped, that if I kept you working—kept you thinking about other things—that you'd be able to let the past rest. Let her rest."

"You were wrong," Loren said. His hand knocked hers aside. He made his way to the window. The story ripped away the scar tissue built up over the last five years.

"Yes. I was." After Erikson she promised to make a change, to trust in him more, to not let things split them. Now they could begin again. They could put aside the past and face the threat currently plaguing Portents. Together.

"Loren…" she started, reaching for his shoulder.

He turned, his eyes flooded with tears. And anger on his lips. "Get out."

The words staggered her—the rage behind them. The sense of betrayal. Where she hoped for reconciliation there was nothing but hurt and hopelessness.

"We can work through this," she said. "We will work through this. Portents needs us now. Loren, *I* need you."

Loren shook his head, looking out into the black. "I don't need you. Not anymore."

"Please…"

"Get. Out." Loren hammered the frame of the window. There was no helping him. There was no hope left in Greg Loren. Only the past.

Soriya started for the door, her steps silent compared to the sobs of her former friend. Loren slid along the window to the floor, his face covered by his hands, broken and betrayed by the one supposed to save him.

Supposed to save them all.

"Just leave me alone…"

Soriya Greystone fled into the night, leaving the crumpled form of Greg Loren to his sadness.

CHAPTER FORTY-THREE

Noah Jordan paused at the base of the steps leading to the Courtyard. Rage boiled beneath the surface, his hands balled into fists along his sides. The Heads of Cerberus padded along the stairs, climbing the edifice of the modern building hiding the ancient structure within. They eyed him maliciously, salivating at his arrival.

Their numbers grew with each passing day, more joining the pack by the hour. Where they came from and who they were beneath the fur and the snarl meant nothing to Noah. Nor did it mean anything to their brethren. They came to conquer and had in a single act. They owned Portents whether the city had come to the realization or not. They merely waited for the final curtain to drop.

Something Noah dreaded, yet committed to long ago.

His promises caught up to him. Gabe's pleading eyes followed him from a distance but there was also the Luminary to consider. When she found him in the days following the death of his parents, he was a wreck. Gabe stayed with friends down the street, but Noah couldn't. He refused to leave the burned-out husk of a home, wandering through the devastation for some sign, some clue of what happened. He found the stone in his searching.

And Karen Winters found him.

She pulled him out of the darkness and offered him more than just hope. She offered the truth, something no one else could give him. An answer to the most important question left from the growing void of his parents' loss. There was no way he would let the chance at closure slip away.

Gabe wouldn't understand, so the conversation never happened. Noah moved them through different areas, distracting his younger brother while he waited for the call from the Luminary. Though she made the promise, other pieces needed positioning and he followed her lead.

He distracted himself with the stone, practicing away from Gabe and other onlookers. They traveled to Philadelphia and he unleashed the power on an out of control hydra. When the stone lit up for the first time, Noah dropped it, almost getting snatched by the six-headed monster in the process.

The more he put into the stone, the more it provided. Until he finally unlocked the potential within, using the stone without actually having it in hand. They were bonded, part of a single entity and the stone fed off his emotions, his strength but also his anger, to accomplish feats the young man never imagined possible.

All thanks to the Luminary. Her promises, her trust in him, gave him the will to continue in the shadows of his former life. He owed her much because of that act.

It was time to settle accounts.

The hounds made it easier to maintain his anger, to grow the doubts seeded by his own actions of the last few days. The guest within the Courtyard cemented those doubts into place.

Robert Standish, in full dress uniform, stood near the four pillars. His bruised sneer greeted the young man as he finished his dialogue with the Luminary. She listened to the man, continuing to carve into the base of the fourth and final pillar. Each rune had to be perfect, each character of dead and forgotten languages needed to be precise, and she diligently continued the effort despite the interruptions.

"You're sure?" the Luminary asked.

"They're making plans at the Franklin Center to strike as we speak," Standish confirmed.

"A distraction we do not need. Take care of it."

Standish nodded. "They won't even see us coming."

"Take as many as you need."

Satisfied at their deliberations, Standish departed. As he passed Noah, his elbow jutted out and knocked the young man away. He continued on his way like nothing happened. Noah brushed off the man's childlike behavior before heading toward his benefactor.

"I don't trust him."

Karen notched a final arc along the base, completing another character. She blew the dust from her work, wiping it clean.

"You shouldn't," she said, joining him in front of the pillars. "Robert Standish will betray us the first chance at a better opportunity. But he brought the shadows to light. Those responsible for the death of your parents."

That much was accurate. When the call came during their time in Miami, Noah was ready. What he had been unprepared for was the sound of a man's voice on the other end of the line. Standish, though crude and unable to make it a full sentence without a disparaging remark or three, told him the first name on the list. And the destination.

Portents.

En route, Gabe questioned everything. Noah remained silent, slowly receiving further instructions from Karen about the hotel and about the other objectives. Objectives like Soriya Greystone and how to draw her out, how to win her over to their cause.

The hounds were unexpected, never mentioned. Or the terror and death they would rain down upon Portents.

"What about my brother?"

Karen read his anger. "Noah."

He pointed toward the door. "Those dogs of yours almost killed him."

"A mistake."

"People are dead," he pressed. "Innocent people. That's not what I—"

"A necessity. To save Portents." She pulled him close, her words calm and slow, like their steps toward the pillars. "We are so close, Noah. You feel it too."

"I'm not sure. Soriya—"

"Ah, yes," the Luminary sighed. "And has the magnificent Soriya Greystone come around to our way of thinking?"

"She—"

"Refuses, doesn't she? The Bypass is her treasure and she hoards it from the world."

"Yes."

Karen nodded. "The Greystone failed this city. You see that, don't you? She holds the knowledge of the infinite, the secrets we both seek to share with the world. A better understanding, a new path out of the dark. Away from monsters and hounds and every unspeakable evil. A new golden age of enlightenment for humanity."

"But the cost?" All he wanted was the answer to a single question. "I don't think I can—"

"I've given you so much, Noah," Karen said. Her eyes were wide, drawing him in. "A clarity of purpose. To find out the truth about your parents, horribly lost before their time. Can anyone else offer you those answers? That peace of mind?"

"No."

"Trust me, Noah." Karen smiled. She lifted his chin and her cold stare softened. "As I trust you to do the right thing."

Noah took a deep breath and held it. She helped him escape the darkness when all seemed to be lost. She gave him purpose and strength to carry on. How could he not help her in the end?

He nodded and she patted his shoulder. "Excellent. I take it Soriya is back among the living?"

"Yes, she left to talk to her partner—"

"Loren." Karen turned for the door. "You heard?"

The hounds snarled at the entrance to the Courtyard, shooed for the streets in a single motion of her finger. She returned to the young man.

"You know what to do, don't you, Noah?"

Gabe would have to wait a little longer. His answers were close at hand. Only one last act and then closure. At last. "I do."

"Good." The Luminary beamed. She turned to the four pillars. "It ends tonight."

CHAPTER FORTY-FOUR

It was over. It stung—the weight of the decision, the fear of stepping out into the world without Loren at her side. She said her piece, told her tale, unburdened herself of the secrets she held for so long. Secrets that never impacted the way she felt about Loren or the work they accomplished in their time together.

Loren, however, let the past dominate all.

Soriya rushed into the night air, leaping from the fire escape for the rooftops. Any thought to her injuries faded behind the rush of wind in her hair and the pounding of her heart. She raced along the Knoll up King's Lane, pulling free the sweatshirt disguise and letting it fall behind her to feel the cool air along her arms. Downtown beckoned her, the stark shadows of the skyline surrounding the obsidian tower at her heart.

Each step took her further from Loren yet her thoughts remained with the man. His pain. His suffering. For so long she tried to help him deal with it. She carried him, and his dedication to their work lifted her to new heights.

No more.

It was time to move forward. The city needed her and she would not let it down. Her feelings for Loren and her nostalgia for the way things once were had to wait. The Heads of Cerberus were out there—their numbers too numerous, their power too great for her to handle. But only she was left to make a difference, to stand against them.

Except she wasn't.

Soriya paused on a rooftop overlooking the expressway that split the Knoll. Cars whizzed through, their glimpse of Portents fleeting as they headed for brighter destinations. So focused on

Loren, she nearly forgot Noah's offer. He had been there for her since the start of the affair, saving her from the growing horde of hounds infesting the shadows.

And the Luminary.

Who stands with you?

She never answered the question, unsure of what everyone felt. Now that was no longer in doubt, Loren's desire clear with his condemnation of her actions, of the secrets held. Nobody had her back.

"Freeze!"

Soriya almost slipped from the ledge of the building, the command shaking her from her thoughts. The sound of whipping wind swirled overhead, the bright beam of a spotlight shining on her.

"This is the police!" The voice boomed from the helicopter sweeping above.

Soriya spun, footsteps approaching on all sides. Shadows shifted, more officers took up position at adjacent buildings, cutting off escape routes.

So lost in thought she failed to see the danger ahead of time. So mired in her broken partnership, she neglected the true nature of her place in the city.

Wanted for murder. Four murders that culminated in the death of Mayor Dunn. The situation that ultimately led to Loren's dismissal, while trying to defend her from Myers.

"Hands in the air!"

Soriya stood, sensing laser sights roaming along her chest. With hands raised, she waited for their advance. Most stopped, instructions chirping in their ears as the helicopter overhead continued to swirl around in a broad circle over the building.

"Down on the ground. Get down on the ground," officers shouted over the snapping of the air. Their approach slowed to a crawl, nervous and wary. She lingered at the ledge, but refused to kneel.

"Get down on the—!"

She smiled and stepped back, dropping from the rooftop.

Tucking her arms tight to her chest she closed her eyes, feeling the ground rushing to greet her. The ribbon of Kali caught hold of an exhaust pipe and snapped like a bungee, releasing her on the street and into a full run in a fluid motion.

Patrol cars barred the street at either end. She ducked into the alley across the lane. Shots boomed, shattering the peace of the night. Concrete cracked, debris kicked up from the gunfire.

They followed her into the alley then silenced, no longer able to draw a bead on her position. Soriya continued to race into the night, twisting and turning deeper into the city.

Pursuit came from every direction, the police barking orders. Stray shots accompanied her, coming close to hitting their mark. Patrol cars screeched to a halt at each intersection. Their pistols added to the night's cacophony. Soriya failed to listen, focused on the next turn, the next escape route in her city's maze-like grid.

Three blocks faded in a blur, her legs pumping for all their worth despite her weariness. The Knoll fell away, Evans Tower within sight. The helicopter circled overhead, no longer able to keep up with her movements. The light centered on the wrong alleys, their pursuit hopelessly lost.

Soriya didn't stop. Not for minutes, her feet carrying her silently across a mile of cityscape. From the streets and alleys and back up to the rooftops with a clear view. Her heart pounded, sweat caked to her dark skin. She kept to the shadows, watching intently as coordination failed and the spotlight went out.

When silence returned to the city, Soriya let out a breath. It was all falling apart. Where once the city stood with her, helped her complete her work, now everyone sought her for questioning in a series of murders she had nothing to do with.

Even Loren.

If only he understood. If only there was another word spoken to heal the rift—but there wasn't and she couldn't. But she could save the city. With some help, the only help left to her.

Soriya moved for the edge of the rooftop. She paused, a shadow shuffling across the way. Then another. And another.

Soriya steadied herself, waiting for the police to besiege her once more. They must have ditched the helicopter to try and surprise her.

Only it wasn't the police at all.

Recognition came in the form of a snarl from behind. Soriya turned to see the figure step out of the darkness, grinning through its sharpened fangs. Lightning split the sky and she saw them all sifting among the rooftops of downtown Portents.

The Heads of Cerberus surrounded her.
Ready for a fight.

CHAPTER FORTY-FIVE

Loren cursed. Crumpled along the floor of his apartment he cursed everything. His weakness. His fear. His anger. He didn't know how long he had been sitting in the darkness, how long since he pushed Soriya away.

He cursed her failure. And the sadness at being discovered. The image of Soriya in the window filled his memory. Every word repeated on him. The secrets kept by his wife, by perfect Beth, friends with Soriya for as long as they had been married.

How could he not know? How had he not seen it hidden beneath the surface? Every late shift at work, every new book that never made it to publication? His constant questioning, insipid joking about secrets being kept from him—how could he not see the truth in his own suspicions?

And how could he blame Soriya for it all?

She tried to help him. For years, she offered herself up as a scapegoat, all with the hope of bringing him back from the edge. Every case worked was an opportunity to move beyond the pain that infected his memory. They worked well together. More than well.

They were partners.

And he threw it all away. Her sadness at his rage shook him from his tantrum on the floor. Loren fumbled to his feet, the windowpane sending chills up his arm. There was a way to check, a way to find the truth through all the lies.

He shuffled down the hall to the unused office. Boxes stacked near the doorway, ones meant to be transported to Chicago once upon a time. Boxes of Beth's books. Her writings and interests. His promise to read them kept him from tossing them away long ago.

He knocked away the lip of the first box, digging through the texts. He peered at each briefly, checking the pages for marks. The fifth offered a light at the end of his searching. A black dot marred stark white pages.

Loren pushed the box aside, flipping open the book. One of Beth's firsts, one she always went back to, or so it seemed from its prominent placement on her nightstand. He found what he was looking for on page 73.

A message from Soriya.

He continued to flip page after page, the rune littered throughout the text, along with dates and underlined passages. A coffee shop on Fifth. A diner along the Knoll. The rune signified Soriya's request, the image or text offering the details. All hidden from him.

The truth of Soriya's claims right before his eyes.

Loren dropped the book and moved for another. And another. His need for the whole story keeping him upright, pushing him forward.

Hours fell away. Eight books sat in a stack along the wall. Each offered correspondence between Soriya and his late wife. Each corroborated the story. For five years he trusted Soriya Greystone like no other.

Trust which dissipated from a single image. Soriya in the window of his apartment, plaguing his every thought. A photo offered by another trusted partner.

Myers.

She seeded doubt in his relationship with Soriya and used that doubt to cement the split. Every case offered an excuse to bring up the Greystone bearer, not to use as an asset, but to continue to rip their partnership asunder.

"Dammit." She played him and he didn't see it coming. The photo. The backup piece she must have stolen from him before Crowne used it to end his life. His files on Soriya, stolen and used against him. Everything to tear him down while also pulling away his support system. Leaving him vulnerable, leaving him without a friend in the world.

And he did the same to Soriya as a result.

He needed to find her. He needed to talk to her and resolve this.

But first there was Myers to question. Her actions led to this and they needed an explanation. She had to answer for what she had done to him.

Loren replaced his tear-stained shirt with a fresh one from the laundry basket. The face in the bathroom mirror was a stranger. Alert for the first time in days, Loren splashed a pool of water against his bristled cheeks.

He started for the door. A shadow loomed in the frame. Sunken eyes and reddened cheeks greeted Loren as the figure entered the apartment.

"Pratchett, what the hell?"

The lumbering officer closed the door behind him. "I couldn't wait any longer. I had to—"

Loren shook his head, moving for his coat. "If this is about the Circle, I can't right now. I have to—"

Pratchett's hand stopped Loren, locking on his arm. "It's about Beth."

"What?"

"It's my fault, Loren." Pratchett cleared his throat, his head dipping low. "I killed your wife."

CHAPTER FORTY-SIX

A paw slammed into her cheek, driving Soriya back. Her leap into the fray was charged, filled with screams of rage and anger. Her city turned against her, the world shifted and spun out of control.

But she could still fight.

The blow sent her reeling, the hounds quick to press their assault on all sides. She dodged the first, tossing the beast behind her and into three of its brethren. Another took advantage, knocking her in the ribs. The roof blurred and she fell, catching the ledge.

Jaws snapped at her and she let loose, the night air swirling. The ribbon down her left arm slipped free, shooting out for the balcony of an adjacent building. Soriya swung through the whipping wind. Claws shot out, slashing at the pink ribbon of Kali.

The life-saving tool forever at her side tore from the assault. Soriya's eyes widened.

She fell, blistering pain shooting up her left arm as the remaining strands went slack. The street greeted her and she rolled with the impact until coming to a halt against the brick edifice of a corner delicatessen.

She caressed the remnants of the ribbon, blistered and bloody fingers attempting to will the powerful instrument back to life. Nothing worked. No amount of prayer could bring it back. The pink strands slipped to the ground, lost and broken.

What little breathing room her jump afforded was wasted by her efforts. Her attackers joined her on the ground. They kept their distance, surrounding their prey. Her ribs screamed but she held back all agony, refusing to give the hounds the satisfaction. She spit blood on the wet pavement, watching it trail along the ground like a stream. Then she released the Greystone from the hand-woven pouch at her hip.

"You think this is your city?" she screamed into the growing crowd. Lights switched on in the apartments dotting the block, dark silhouettes appearing in the windows, watching the show. "Portents belongs to no one. You can't have it."

"A promise was made, Greystone," one of the hounds snarled. "You cannot stop the tide."

"I sure as hell can try," Soriya replied.

<

Light blanketed the block. Hounds struggled to clear the area before the earth rumbled around them. A gale force swept the street clear in all directions.

When the rune dimmed from the surface of the stone, Soriya stood alone in the street. She fought to breathe, the effort exhausting her further. The stone took power and will to drive its actions, and even after three days of rest she was still a long way from full strength.

Standing, she realized more lights beamed down the block. Dozens, possibly hundreds, of witnesses gathered in the dark to see the strange woman among them. Murmurs rang out from behind closed windows. The thrumming of glass, beating in rhythm like a great clap. A giant wave of acceptance washing from the depths of the block back to her for her efforts against the hounds.

One quickly evaporated by a cry of new arrivals.

"POLICE! FREEZE!"

Her pursuers had caught up. They raced from the adjacent alleys and from the stoops of buildings to surround her. She lowered the stone, tucking it at her hip, then knelt in the center of the street.

"You have to get out of here!" Soriya pleaded.

The officers continued to approach, sights locked on her from all sides, their entire focus on her and only her.

Just as the hounds returned.

The officers were unprepared, unaware of the danger. Howls ripped through the street, and lights turned off in the apartments above them, although the curtains rustled with onlookers' stares. Hounds blanketed the ground, padding down the block like an invading army. Others dove from above, surrounding the small force bent on arresting one woman.

"Run!" she cried.

The police opened fire, slaughtering the closest beasts. The next wave, however, was too quick, pressing too fast for the pistol-wielding officers to handle.

Three were gutted in an instant. The hounds showered in their blood, triumphant growls silencing the cheers of the people now terrified that they backed the losing side.

Another officer ran, tripping over his dead compatriots. The hounds swarmed, bloodlust in their black eyes.

"Get down!"

Lightning crashed, slicing through the row of creatures. Soriya snagged the officer's hand, pulling him to his feet. The act left her side screaming but she ignored it, driving him toward the nearest alley.

"Go," she shouted through labored breath.

"But you? What about—?"

"I'll be fine! Now go!"

The officer hesitated at the request. A claw latched on Soriya's leg and she kicked it away.

"Run, dammit!"

Hounds pounced at her, battering her on all sides. She kicked and punched, forcing them back, knocking them away with each blow. She struggled for space, for an inch. Instead, the world collapsed around her.

The officers were dead, including the one in the alley who didn't make it to the safety of the shadows. A hound gnawed at his flesh, savoring the kill. Stark terror filled the windows overhead.

Innocent bystanders hid, ducking out of sight and trembling at the brawl occurring on their streets.

Her streets. Her city. She had believed it so long.

She was wrong.

The stone fell against her palm, her left fist flailing to drive back the closest beasts. With nothing remaining, no strength left to bear against the Heads of Cerberus, Soriya poured her will, what spirit lingered within, feeding everything into the stone.

The hounds flew away, cries of pain at the sudden storm. Soriya collapsed from the effort, the stone skittering from her grasp across the concrete. She crawled for it, pulling herself along the bloodied ground. Over the dead and the dying, with nothing to offer either side of the equation.

Soriya picked up the Greystone and struggled to her feet. The hounds remained, their number growing. She could see them gathering for another strike from the rooftops above and down the block. There was no fighting them. Her body refused to cooperate; her city refused to assist. She was alone and she was too weak to continue.

There was only one option open to her, one never considered during her time as the Greystone, one never fathomed her entire life. Soriya Greystone ran away, rushing into the growing darkness of Portents.

Defeated.

CHAPTER FORTY-SEVEN

Five Years Earlier

Pratchett pulled the car in front of Gino's Italian Bistro and killed the engine. The heat was insufferable and returned immediately to the packed sedan. He stepped out, opening the back door for his passengers, their argument over the course of the trip silenced for the moment.

Bethany Loren carried a bag of books over her shoulder. She took Pratchett's hand and offered a gracious smile for the gentlemanly act. A curled lip was his greeting from his other guest, but one the six-foot-four tower of a man was accustomed to after so many years. Julian Harvey was a tough man to please.

"What are we doing here, Harvey?" Beth asked as the three headed into the restaurant.

"You'll see."

"Unc?" Pratchett called, holding the group at the entrance.

"Not now, Johnny," Harvey said. "Watch the door."

Pratchett nodded, holding back as they weaved into the restaurant. It was empty, not a single diner in the place despite the lunch crowd surging up and down the block. He had stopped here regularly during his shift, his route somehow always masterfully landing at the bistro just in time to pick up an order of fries and a meatball hoagie or two before closing. Just enough food to tide him over for the rest of his shift.

With the lock secured and the *Closed* sign visible for all, Pratchett wandered deeper into the dining area. Beth and Harvey continued for the back, the blond-haired researcher slowing her gait as the latter rushed to their business.

A man stood in the kitchen. Pratchett recognized him but not his bleeding companion kneeling on the floor. Or why Dennis Carmichael held a gun on him.

"What the hell is this?" Beth asked, catching sight of the gun and the battered man in the cheap suit.

Harvey pressed her ahead. "That's what we're here to figure out. You've been working on tracking down a… What did you call it?"

"Cerberus head," Beth said. "It's been commonly known that there are only three when in actuality there could potentially be thousands from what I've found in the—"

"Right." Harvey stopped her. "That's why you're here. The lore. The research."

"You're saying…?"

"He's one of them." Dennis nodded. He tightened the grip on the pistol, positioning it against the man's forehead. "I know it."

Harvey cleared his throat. "Unfortunately, we can't prove it. That's where you come in."

As the consummate researcher for their organization, Beth had been tasked with quite a bit. Research and study of some of the most bizarre topics ever broached. She did it without question, without hesitation. She loved it and Pratchett enjoyed listening to her work, hearing the theories of hidden histories spin from her lips.

Harvey never took her out in the field—that wasn't her place. She was meant to piece together mysteries and let the others take care of enacting any plan against the monsters hidden in the shadows of Portents. Until now.

"I don't understand," Beth said, locked on the bleeding man in the center of the kitchen. "Why are you doing this to him?"

"Please," the man begged. "I have a family. I have kids. I don't know what they—"

"Enough out of you."

The back of Carmichael's hand drove into the man's cheek, knocking him to the ground. Blood spilled from the man's swelling lips. He struggled to move, to roll away from his attacker. Carmichael was on top of him, pulling him upright.

"Let this man go." Beth stepped closer and Harvey cut her off, shaking his head. Her eyes flared with anger. "What the hell are you doing?"

Harvey took the fedora from his head, his brow covered in sweat. No matter the time of year, the man found an excuse to wear the hat. He laid it carefully on the counter beside them, then wiped his forehead clear.

"We're doing what we've always done with your research, kid," Harvey said in a calm, rational voice. Beth's reaction was anything but, shattering realism crashing against her idealism. "What? What did you think we were doing with your briefings on these freaks? On these monsters?"

They kept it from her, Pratchett included. When he was recruited by his uncle, one of the first approached during the early years of the Circle, he believed in what they were doing. He carried the same idealism. Stopping monsters before they hurt people.

How that happened, what was done to the beasts, never entered the equation. Part of Pratchett knew the truth, knew what they were doing, but the greater portion—his dedication to his uncle and to his city—outweighed the moral question of their actions. Saving Portents from itself was all that mattered in the end.

Beth wasn't so sure.

"I thought... I don't..." She backed away. "Not this, Harvey. Definitely not this."

"Is he one of them? These Heads of Cerberus?"

"I don't know."

"I'm not!" the man yelled. He shuffled closer to the pair. Carmichael's hand locked on his shoulder and held him in place with a squeeze. "Whatever the hell that is, I'm not! I'm a car salesman!"

"Bad one too." Carmichael grinned. "Almost sold me a new Buick at cost."

"I needed the sale!"

"Let him go, Harvey," Beth whispered to her companion. "This isn't right. Let him go."

Pratchett had seen the shift over the years. From a need to protect, to a desire to eradicate. The ends justified the means as Harvey took less care for the knowledge behind a threat and more for the means to end each one. He watched his uncle's eyes go cold against the losing battle they faced, refusing to back down, refusing to give in. He admired that determination for so long.

And cowered before it, afraid of the man's wrath.

"Let him go?" Harvey shot back. "So he can change into one of these pooches and kill people? That's what he will do, Beth. That's what these monsters are doing to Portents. We can stop him here. We're the only ones that can stop them before it gets worse."

"I won't…" Beth started, staggering for the door. "I don't even know how!"

"I can always give it the old college try." Carmichael cocked the hammer back on his gun.

"No, please," the man cried. "Let me go!"

"Down boy," Carmichael chided, squeezing tighter to his shoulder. "Stay—"

The man leapt from his position and drove into Carmichael. The dishwasher, surprised by the blow, lost his footing. He staggered back, the gun swinging wide. A shot rang out and a ceiling tile shattered from the impact.

Beth ducked for cover from the blast. Harvey went for his sidearm, spinning to greet the fleeing man but it was too late. He was out of the kitchen and heading for the front door.

The man snarled, his teeth sharpening and growing like the fur springing out over his skin. Fangs snapped the bindings around his wrists, claws stretching out of his fingertips. He howled in the vacant dining room, racing toward freedom.

And the waiting John Pratchett.

The officer raised his sidearm and fired. The hound reeled, crashing into the nearest table. He did not get up again.

Pratchett lowered his gun, his heart pounding. Harvey grinned from the kitchen. Carmichael cheered at the act. The officer couldn't care less about their reactions. All he saw was the hurt in Bethany Loren's eyes.

The fear that grew in her deep blue orbs.

"Oh, God." She rushed to the creature's side, trying to find a pulse. Standing away in defeat, she shook her head. "What did you…? John, what did you do?"

"He was a monster, Beth."

"No," she said, moving for the door. Unable to look at him, unable to heed his words. "He wasn't the monster here."

"Beth?"

She ran out of the restaurant, her bag of books slapping her back with each step.

CHAPTER FORTY-EIGHT

"It was too much for her," Pratchett said, his cheek stinging from tears. "To see her work used to kill. She left."

Loren appeared ready to collapse. He squeezed his coat, choking the life out of the inanimate fabric. "You followed her."

He nodded. "My uncle had to make sure the circle was closed. Secure. He trusted me to handle it."

"To *handle* it." Loren shook his head, wiping away the streams running down his thick beard. "To handle it?"

He dropped the coat and charged for Pratchett. The towering officer stood unflinching and absorbed the initial blow to the gut. He fell to his knees, the angered detective looming over him. Loren unbuckled Pratchett's holster and yanked out his sidearm. He chambered the next round, leveling the pistol at the reeling Pratchett.

"And you just went ahead and handled it!"

"No," Pratchett said. "Of course not. Beth was my friend. I only came to talk. If Beth could be reasoned with—to keep the Circle and its work secret—there would be no need for Harvey to send someone else."

"You're not that stupid, Pratchett." Loren's bloodshot eyes needled at the officer before him.

"I know. A naive thought. But an honest one. Not that it mattered."

Pratchett peered toward the open door and the hallway beyond. No longer seeing the darkness in the space, but the blazing light from the summer sun filling the room. The stinging heat saturated the air, sweat covering his brow.

"She ran when I arrived," Pratchett said, each word slow and lost in memory to that day five years earlier. "Pushed right through me when I came inside to talk. Clocked me in the leg, if you can believe that."

He tried to laugh, rubbing his leg. Loren pressed him without a word, his patience ebbing.

"I don't blame her," he continued. "Not for any of it. How could I? The murder was too fresh in her mind. She was rattled, frightened and not thinking straight. She ran, taking the stairs to the roof, probably worried I didn't come alone."

"Did you?"

"What?

"Were you alone, Pratchett?" Loren asked. "There had to be someone else, anyone else. Tell me the truth."

"I am. I wish I wasn't. I wish I hadn't come, that it would have been anyone else. Maybe if it had, maybe if she hadn't seen me earlier that day she wouldn't have run. Maybe things would have been different." Pratchett blinked and the lights of the past vanished. "But she ran and I—"

"And you followed again." Loren words condemned him. He deserved each one.

"I wasn't ready, didn't consider the chance at a struggle." His head lowered. He moved slow, hands always visible for the man looming over him, and wiped away tears.

"She jumped me on the roof. Came out of nowhere as soon as I opened the door." He took a breath. "I was surprised, stunned. She was screaming, so angry over everything. I couldn't hear her, couldn't see her, not with the sun overhead. Like it filled the whole damn sky. So blinding."

The gun wavered in Loren's hand. "What... What did you do, Pratchett?"

"I..." He hesitated.

"Tell me!"

"I lashed out," he whispered. "On instinct, survival skills, whatever... I pushed her. Dammit, Loren, I pushed her so hard."

Blond hair soared, blotting out the sun. Beth's body floated in the sky like an angel. Pratchett closed his eyes against the sight but she remained, always in the back of his mind.

"The ledge was…" Pratchett choked back tears, each raging like a riptide. "She couldn't stop and I couldn't reach her. Not before…she fell. Loren, she fell so far."

In his mind's eye, the towering officer watched her fall, like the city swallowed her. Pratchett collapsed against the ledge and wept over her fallen figure, the same tears flowing down his cheeks five years later.

"I waited until the emergency crews arrived and filtered out through the crowd," Pratchett said in a quiet voice. "You were…you were with her by then. You never saw me."

"Who else?"

"I told you…"

"Not then." Loren fought to stay upright. The gun threatened to slip from his sweaty grasp. "When you left. Someone else was there. They took a photo. Who was it?"

"I don't…" Pratchett stopped. His eyes squeezed tight, and he felt the sun blazing overhead and the heat soaking through his shirt. He slipped into the crowd, just another officer working the scene. It was a busy day. The Knoll's usual patrols were caught in traffic but there was one officer there faster than the rest. Pratchett's eyes snapped open. "Oh, God. It was—"

"Standish."

"How did you—?"

Loren shook his head. "Doesn't matter."

"He was taking photos of the scene," Pratchett said. "I never…I never thought about it before. Why was he—?"

"Not important," Loren snapped. "Not now."

Pratchett understood. "It wasn't supposed to happen, Loren. She was my friend. And you? You were too. You are. I've tried to tell you, wanted to, but I couldn't."

"You took her from me, Pratchett." The gun clicked, Loren's finger tight against the trigger.

"I did," Pratchett replied, staring down the barrel. His eyes dried; his vision cleared. He didn't want to miss this moment. "And I've tried to reconcile what happened. I have. But if this settles my tab I will gladly pay it."

The gun shook, Loren's eyes deep red against the shadows of the apartment. The world outside faded. There were only the two of them, two men lost to the past, trying to find their way out.

Pratchett made his peace, the guilt lifted from his chest. For too long it weighed on him, the loss of someone so perfect, someone so good in the world, when there was so much evil. Pratchett grabbed hold of the barrel and steadied the weapon along his forehead.

"It's okay, Loren," he whispered. "I deserve it. I do."

"Beth…"

Loren screamed and the gun fell away. The widower collapsed, his knees slamming against the hardwood floor. Silence was all he had left, his vacant stare trying to make sense of the great truth finally known.

Pratchett slowly stood, afraid to reach out for the man he called friend. He hadn't earned the right to call him that in a long time. But he would again.

"I can't bring her back, Loren. But I'll fix this. I'll fix everything."

He didn't know how, didn't know the way back into the light, but he knew where to start.

CHAPTER FORTY-NINE

Nothing worked. Forty-eight hours into what should have been the pinnacle of Rufus Mathers' career and not a damn thing worked out for him.

The meeting with the precinct captains went as expected: horribly. Infighting, screams, and blustering turned to fisticuffs for some. Tensions were high enough with what occurred during the long night, with so many officers and officials dead or missing. To be handed a new commissioner, one with Mathers' short list of credentials—at least compared to his contemporaries—was a tipping point.

It took hours for the anger to pass. Promises were made to keep the peace and bring everyone back to the table. And none came from Mathers. Every compromise, every entreaty to make things work came from Robert Standish, and through him, Karen Winters.

That was the first moment of impotence in a two-day window full of them. Patrols were updated. Reports were modified. The chain of command was reworked and refined for better coordination, all coming from the top, from Mathers' office.

Or so he thought.

"Dammit," he cursed, slapping the paperwork off the corner of his desk. It spread like a wave across the floor, leaving only the report crumpled under his fingers to suffer further wrath. He should have been consulted, should have been involved in every decision relating to the department.

"These things take time," Standish offered after their initial meeting, feet on his desk. "Don't worry, Rufus. She'll take care of you. It pays to have friends in high places. I've always said that."

Mathers understood the message. Dreams of setting policy, of making real change in the city he swore to protect—one where he raised a family, where he practiced his faith—were dashed in an instant. He was a figurehead. A puppet.

Not the hero of the story at all.

That needed to change.

Mathers stormed out of the office, starting for the elevator. The mayor would see him; Standish sure as hell would too. His voice would be heard. It was time to take a stand.

A light beamed from the conference room at the end of the floor. Hesitating at the elevator, Mathers let the doors close. A lithe shadow passed against the glass of the conference room entrance.

Winters.

Mathers cleared his throat and straightened his tie. He pounded along the hall, making his presence known before twisting the knob hard to enter the room.

"This is my conference room," he proclaimed. He left the door open, rounding the table.

Winters nearly laughed, holding it back to a sly grin at his arrival. "One I gave you, Rufus. Try to remember that."

Mathers slammed the crumpled report on the table. "You're diverting patrols in my name."

She nodded. "Better allocating resources. For the city."

"Ignoring incident reports. Ignoring eyewitness statements. Tip line calls," Mathers yelled. "Everything we've received places the Corridor at the center of this. We could squeeze out whatever this nightmare is. Instead, you've pulled everyone away from the area. Why?"

The heart of the matter. The one that kept Mathers locked in his office for the scant hours of his so-called reign over law enforcement in Portents. Calls were made to his family. Terse words, never a congratulations from his wife, but one from his kids, which was comforting. His wife, however, wondered what it truly meant for them. The same question he asked.

"Why are you doing this, Karen?"

"Are you questioning my resolve to protect Portents, Rufus?"

"From what exactly?"

"From itself, of course." Her eyes sparked, cold yet vibrant.

Mathers moved closer, reaching out. "You asked me to protect this city, Karen. You are impeding that effort. If I have to—"

"Watch your next step, Rufus," Karen replied, ignoring his mounting anger for the view outside. The roar of downtown. The thrumming of the raging storm. "Protecting the city? You think too small. Keeping them in the dark has led to this impasse. Protection is not the answer."

"Then what is?" he asked, keeping his distance. "What the hell do you want?"

She looked back with wide eyes blazing. She knew. This was her doing: the long night, so many dead, his rise to power—all her plan. For how long? How far back did it go? How did this end?

"No," Mathers said, shaking the unanswered thoughts away. "I thought I could do this, thought I could finally make a difference, but that's not why I'm here, is it?"

"Perceptive," Karen said. "Standish always said so."

The elevator dinged, the doors sliding open. Wexler exited, heading straight for them. Mathers grinned.

"Perceptive enough to know it's over for you," Mathers said, his confidence brimming now with backup approaching. "I'll see you charged for your part in whatever the hell is going on out there."

Wexler stood in the doorway, hesitating to enter. Curious looks spread between the three of them, Mathers waving her inside.

"Arrest this woman," Mathers demanded, pointing at the mayor. Wexler pinched the bridge of her nose. "Wexler?"

"That won't be necessary, Rufus."

"What are you—?"

"The poor dear has a headache," Karen mused. She sidled beside Wexler, patting her on the shoulder. "You should take care of that, shouldn't you?"

Wexler grinned. "Yes, ma'am."

"Wexler?"

Karen sauntered down the hall, offering a wave before reaching the elevator. "I'm sorry you couldn't see things my way, Rufus. Everyone else will."

Mathers raced for the door. She couldn't be allowed to leave. Too many questions needed to be brought to light. For the sake of the city, his job, his career. He was supposed to be the hero of the story.

A hand stopped him. "Wexler, what are you doing?"

Her eyes shifted to black. She nudged him, her hand pressed lightly against his chest. The small act sent him soaring over the conference room table, crashing into two chairs. He rolled, slamming into the wall. Mathers struggled to his feet.

"Wexler?"

Wexler was gone. In her place was a hound. It snarled and snapped at the air, its mangy fur and enormous paws inching for the trapped commissioner.

Hungry as hell.

CHAPTER FIFTY

Pratchett drove for hours. He circled the Knoll at first, catching Loren leaving his apartment. He followed him at a distance until the suspicious detective ducked out of sight on his way south—for what reason he didn't know, though he noted the glint of his sidearm tucked in Loren's belt.

He should have taken it back, should have insisted on it, but the damage was done. He couldn't demand anything from the man, not after everything he stole from Loren. One mistake, shattering the lives of everyone connected to the event. Still shattering them with each thread pulled, and each secret brought to light.

Closure was an ideal outcome. Putting the past away and moving forward, building instead of tearing down.

It was the reason Pratchett left Loren to his task as the towering officer headed downtown. The city was loud, painful cries ringing in the night. Portents was in as much agony as those left within her borders, those not smart enough to flee after the long night.

Those who still held out hope for the dawn.

He parked outside the roundabout in front of the Franklin Center. When Harvey first brought him to the reclusive headquarters of the secretive group, he believed his uncle was playing him for a fool. The way most of his family treated him, from his parents—not the most ambitious folks on their own—to his cousins, all following in their parents' footsteps rather than striking out on their own.

Instead, Harvey welcomed him with open arms. He showed him the world as it truly was, the hidden threats always on the periphery. Days of wonder had followed. Unbelievable sights—it was the stuff kids dreamed of when they played with their action figures, blasting each other with pretend ray guns.

Pratchett loved the work and the group that grew with each passing day. A secret on top of a secret, helping people without ever needing the credit. Without being seen or heard—unlike the ramblings of a certain police captain who craved the spotlight.

Beth made it better. She taught him about the city, showed him the truth behind Portents and the Franklin Center itself. Hidden alcoves, passageways locked by random triggers built along the walls and tucked under photographs. A remnant from a bygone era.

Like Beth herself.

One he took from the world.

Pratchett sat in the driver's seat staring out into the darkness. He held tight to a small golden key, the lock to Saint Helena's Orphanage. Another mistake buried under good intentions? He no longer knew. Regardless, it was time to end it, time to work to take back their city.

Loren offered him a second chance. By refusing to give in to grief and rage, to pull the trigger in the hope for vengeance against his wife's killer, Loren opened the way for Pratchett to fix things. To find a better way. He intended to keep that promise.

The key fell into his pocket and he stepped into the cool rain. Howling echoed over the rooftops, scattered beams of light cutting through the fierce storm. Clouds rested over the city, unwilling to relent.

The door to the center lay open a crack. A thick streak of blood ran the length of the light oak, marking the property. A hand caught in the frame kept it from closing.

"What happened?"

Slow steps turned to a trot, and Pratchett suddenly wished he kept his sidearm after all. He recognized the dead woman in the doorway. A recent recruit. Dennis Carmichael's wife, still grieving from the loss of her husband. *Hannah. Her name was Hannah.*

Deep scratches spread across her abdomen. Her eyes stared up to the ceiling, terror resting in her final moments. Pratchett shook his head. He had seen enough death to last a lifetime. Crouching over her, he closed Hannah's eyes and entered the Franklin Center.

Another body dangled over the railing to the second floor overlooking the foyer. The man's neck had a bite taken out of it, blood dripping steadily along the banister down to the carpet.

Pratchett fought the urge to vomit. Dozens of bodies scattered across the room, bloodstained and already decaying. A massacre against a Circle of Shadows kept hidden from the public for so long.

"Uncle?" Pratchett called. He scanned each of the fallen, waiting for any remnant of hope to fade with the recognition of his uncle as one of the dead. He couldn't find him. Not among the operations crew decapitated along the left wall. Not among the translators holding their innards to the right. Not even at the table where six sat with their throats slashed open.

No bullet holes dotted the wall. No great battle where the forces of good struggled against the dark. Brutal and efficient, a slaughtering of men and women without remorse. The Circle was broken, shattered, and it didn't stand a damn chance at the end.

"Unc?"

Pratchett couldn't see him. He searched the first floor, from the offices to the off-limit passageways. Harvey could have ducked inside, waited out the struggle with some of the others, before finding a way to escape.

Julian Harvey was like that. After years of ridicule and shame for his lackluster ambitions, Pratchett remained devoted to his uncle. Always working to make him proud, to do something to earn his respect.

No one was found in the hallways, the locked passageways tucked out of sight. Not a soul. The only thing Pratchett found was Harvey's fedora, bloodstains along the rim.

He picked the hat up and dusted it off, but was unable to wipe the rim clean. Pratchett's chest heaved then tightened. He rubbed his neck, peering around the hall for some sign, some way to find his missing uncle.

Hoping, still hoping, he was somehow safe from the nightmare that surrounded him.

"Please," Pratchett whispered, staring at the hat for guidance. "Where are you?"

"Dead," a voice called from the shadows of the lobby. "They're all dead, John."

She stepped out of the darkness. Her clothes were stained red, yet she appeared perfectly preserved. Snapping a stick of gum between her teeth, the young woman ran her hands through her pink hair.

"Frankie?"

"It's me, John," she said, reaching out for him.

He ran to her, pulling her close. Her heart raced, matching his own. Confused, he stepped back from their embrace.

"What are you doing here?"

He never told her. He wanted to, but he never had the chance to explain about the Circle, about what he was doing when he couldn't be with her. Their time together had been brief but he enjoyed every second of it, having someone to laugh with when there was so much to cry about. "Frankie?"

"I'm sorry you had to see this," she said, scanning the hall of bodies. "Sorry it had to be this way."

"What are you—?"

She kissed him, her lips warm and moist. They filled him with light and his heart slowed, his body relaxed.

A sharp pain sliced along his chest and he pulled away. Blood dripped from Frankie's fingertips, only they were no longer the painted fake nails she typically wore.

They were claws.

Black eyes locked on him as he fell, clutching the gaping wound along his chest. She licked the blood running the length of her hand, savoring every drop. Pratchett collapsed to the floor. His vision blurred, the room darkening. "Frankie…"

"She promised us the city, John," Frankie said as he struggled for breath. "Portents is ours now. There's no room for shadows anymore."

CHAPTER FIFTY-ONE

Her footing gave way on the metal stairwell and Soriya fell. Instinctively, her arms flew up to protect her face as she slammed against the steps. The ground rushed up and she collapsed at the base of the stairs in a heap.

Everything hurt. It wasn't the cuts running down her arms or across her back, nor was it the gash down her left leg and cracked ribs on her right side. Her insides felt like they had been boiled, raging deeper than any fire blazing above in Portents over the last few days.

The culmination of her injuries took hold, keeping her on the floor of the Bypass Chamber. Unable to rest. Unable to think. Her world was lost.

The Heads of Cerberus won. Portents was theirs.

Soriya crawled, inching across the cold concrete. Her body failed to respond with each attempt to stand. Her legs were dead weights, the race to escape the hounds taking every last ounce of strength. The final fall shattered what remained.

Her spirit crumbled, tears mixing with the blood and sweat of her battle. Her failure was absolute. There was no one to console her, no one to stand by her side and lift her back into the light. She was alone.

Except for the glowing orb before her. The Bypass hummed, sending a wave of light over the room. Soriya clawed at the ground, pulling her tired and broken body inch by inch toward the floating crossroad to infinity. With the stone at her hip there was a chance, a small glimmer of a way out of the dark. *If* she could reach the Bypass, if she could ask the right question and make the correct offer.

Each pull sent waves of agony up her arms. She screamed, the pain echoing through the forty-foot chamber. The distance was too great, the pressure too much for her weary frame. And she collapsed.

"Hey," a voice whispered. "Take it easy. Try to—"

A hand wrapped around her arm, and a sting of pain caused her to flinch. As she rolled from the assistance the figure stood over her, his eyes glowing in the light of the Bypass.

"Noah?"

"I'm sorry," Noah said. "I followed you."

"It's…" She stopped, her breath lost as he helped her stand. He carried her burden, letting her collapse against his side, her arm wrapped over his shoulders. "Thank you."

"You're welcome." He smiled. Then he turned to the glowing orb in the center. "Is that…?"

The same awe rested on his face as all who faced the infinite. Past and future, all spreading out behind the veil of the sphere of light.

She nodded. "The Bypass."

"Incredible."

"And dangerous," she replied. Staggered steps inched closer to the glowing orb. Noah helped her along, his eyes never leaving the object at the heart of the city. "That's why it has to be kept safe."

"Hoarded away, you mean."

"Noah?"

He slipped her arm from his shoulders. She maintained her footing for a brief moment before sliding to her knees. Her legs, unable to hold her weight, tucked under her as the young man paced the chamber.

His warm smile, the look of sincerity that woke her from her three-day slumber, faded. His hand reached out to the Bypass but he continued to keep his distance, feeling its presence rather than touch it directly.

"All the answers are in there. Right there. Yet you lock them away under the guise of protection."

"It's more than that," Soriya said. "I can show you. But the Heads of Cerberus… Portents needs us. Together, we can—"

"We?" Noah interrupted. "I don't think so."

"What do you mean?" Her hand reached for him and he slapped it away.

"This was never what I wanted," Noah said, staring deeper into the glowing orb. "None of this. But I needed the truth. I had to know what happened to them and she knew how to find the answer."

"Noah?"

"She was right too, you know? She said you wouldn't give it freely. That you wouldn't share the knowledge contained within."

"It isn't mine to share."

"Spare me the sanctimonious crap, Soriya. You dress it up as a lesson, a code, to make it seem more righteous when it's nothing more than the selfish whims of a child." Noah's eyes glowed against the light of the Bypass. "We had to draw you out. Turn them all against you. Make you see it doesn't work alone."

"The deaths," Soriya whispered. "It was *you*."

"They murdered my parents! Of course I killed them!"

"You don't know that, Noah. She…the Luminary is using you."

"She's the only one telling the truth! The only one willing to help me!" Noah raged, fists tight to his sides. "I had to do this. I had no choice."

"Let me help, Noah. Together we can stop Cerberus."

He loomed over her. "Who do you think sent the hounds after you in the first place?"

Her Greystone fell into her waiting hand and she brought it to bear against her betrayer. Every movement was delayed, her speed diminished from the constant struggle. Noah kicked the stone from her grasp, the weapon skidding across the room toward the domicile tucked in the corner.

"Don't."

"You bastard," she snapped.

He waited as she struggled to stand. Her fists flailed through the air, her body unwilling to assist. The back of his hand connected against her cheek, driving her to the ground.

"I said, don't."

She spit blood to the concrete floor. "You don't understand, Noah. The Bypass—"

"You're right," he said. He stared at the orb, spinning brighter and brighter with each turn. Small flecks of black filled the surface, sparking in long strings toward the pillars locking them in place. "But I will. Everyone will."

Light grew along the surface of his stone.

"Wait!"

"No." His fist crashed down on her, knocking her down. His kick sent her reeling, her cracked ribs screaming from the blow.

"Please…"

Her words held no sway. She could do nothing but watch as the light formed on the young man's Greystone. He let go of the weapon and it spun before him in sync with the Bypass.

Around the chamber, bright specks of white showered down. Characters and runes sparked along the four pillars locking the Bypass in place beneath the heart of Portents.

The Bypass shook, the infinite raging against its prison. The orb spun faster, the black overtaking the majestic green that fluttered through its surface. Waves shot out, snapping against the brightening pillars as more runes unlocked from the ceiling to the base of each column of white marble.

"Noah…"

"Stop," he called, awestruck by the object in front of him. "Stop trying to fight this. It's over."

In the span of a second, before her final plea left her, the Bypass screamed then fell silent. The room, once bright as the sun, fell into darkness. The only remaining light came from his stone, which faded as he turned from the empty chamber that once held Soriya's entire world.

Her purpose was to protect the Bypass. Her reason for being, the years of lessons from Mentor, all centered on holding the line to keep the infinite from abuse. Her failure was complete.

Noah Jordan stood over her, the stone before him. Light grew along the surface but she no longer saw it. All she saw were the shadows in his eyes, the black holes once so bright in her mind. In the end his voice carried her away.

"It's over."

PART THREE
THE CHOICE

CHAPTER FIFTY-TWO

The chisel worked against the stone, rounding out the etching. A breath cleared the remaining debris from the symbol carved in place. The woman behind the work paused to observe the result.

It was finished. Each of the four pillars stood majestically, identical to another set hidden beneath the city. Perfect replicas to recreate the power held in the four columns of the Bypass chamber.

Tonight. The dawn approached, the city's last. Afterward, there would be no need for light in Portents. The Heads of Cerberus would take what belonged to them and she would do the same.

Noah Jordan's arrival at the Courtyard confirmed her suspicions. The Luminary, cloak and mask in hand, spread her arms triumphantly at her achievement. Yet Noah's face drooped, the constant doubts of the last week wearing on the proud and excited Karen Winters.

"It's done," Noah said, his head low. There was no joy in the task, just a boy finishing a chore he found distasteful.

"Show me," Karen said. She lowered the mask and cloak, and relief filled Noah's face.

"The pillars?"

"Perfectly replicated," she replied, grazing the closest with her fingertips. She held out her hand, eyes flaring. "No more stalling, Noah."

Noah removed the stone from his pocket. Her smile widened, the excitement growing like the swirling wind in the microcosm environment of the Courtyard.

Circling the pillars, Noah's stone began to react with each. Though at his side, the surface brightened with each pass. The stars shifted overhead, more illuminating as the seconds ticked by.

The ground started to shake. The pillars shifted but remained intact, the buildings surrounding them struggled against the shuffling of earth but held. Noah took a deep breath, returning to the center of the street before the intricately carved columns of white.

The stone soared from his hands, spinning slowly at first then quickening with each rotation. The light grew, shifting and changing, bringing a response beaming from the pillars.

They came fast, thrumming deeper with every successive iteration. The four columns began as separate entities, a different character unmasked along the breadth of the carvings. From four original markings a fifth appeared on the stone and the weapon's stark white light spread to the columns until all stood united.

In the blink of an eye it appeared. Glowing green light floated just off the cracked street. A perfect sphere of energy, a heavenly body contained on the earthly plane by the four illuminated columns.

The Bypass was home.

Karen clapped. "Incredible."

She had never before witnessed such beauty. Years of hassling Christopher for a glimpse, a chance to study the object of her every desire, the answer to her every question, brought her nothing but emptiness. His growing distance, especially after the closure of the library, strained their relationship to the breaking point.

None of this would have been necessary if he had shared access to the floating orb in the first place. The point was moot, however; the task finally complete. The Bypass was hers—and with it, every secret imaginable, waiting to be unlocked and shared with the world.

The ground quaked. Rubble shattered from the neighboring buildings as black sparks shot from the pristine sphere. The columns fought to contain the screams of the Bypass as more darkness infiltrated the surface.

"Wait," she muttered, racing to the young man's side. "What's happening?"

Fear struck Noah's eyes, both wide to the growing tremors of the place. He held the stone before him, squeezing tight. "Give it a minute. The barrier—"

"Will hold," Karen barked. She was exact with her carvings. She was precise with the setup, one duplicated to the detail from texts shuttered in the Library of the Luminaries.

She found them in the final days of the library. The meetings were daily regarding the group's future, the doubt about their presence in the city and the impact they held for the world at large too great to continue. Disbanding was all but inevitable, their fear overpowering all sense, bringing about the closure of the repository of knowledge.

Karen struggled with that course. The luminaries were her life and had been for decades. But they were a weak bunch, unable to look past their own knowledge to unlock the greater secrets of the universe. Of *every* universe. Only she understood the potential of such information.

The books were tucked behind a stack, forever buried at the back of the fifth floor, a rarely used section of the structure. She wandered for hours, running her fingers along the rare manuscripts. They fell from the pile, calling to her, begging her to act.

The world held its breath, the tremors growing. For a second, Karen Winters thought all had been for nothing. That her efforts brought her to an ending instead of the beginning she imagined.

Then the shaking settled. The pillars held. The sparks of light dimmed, the black thickening but remaining.

"There," Noah sighed with relief.

Karen smiled. "After so long. To have it here after everything…"

"I did as you asked," Noah snapped. His eyes were heavy. "Soriya…she trusted me."

"And you trusted her to make the right choice," Karen said. "She didn't."

He turned away, unable to look in her direction. Instead, he focused on the Bypass. Their goal in reach. "You promised me answers."

"And you promised me unfettered access to the Bypass."

Noah hesitated, lost in the sight of the glowing sphere before them. She understood the look: He was seduced by the power inside, which held the truth about everything from the dawn of time to its final breath. It was all available to them.

He ran his fingers along the surface of the stone, his prized possession since finding it in the aftermath of his parents' tragic demise. The one thing holding him together in his unending search for answers.

He handed the Greystone to her. "I never wanted this. Any of it. The murders. The lies. All to know the truth about my parents."

"A truth that will set you free," she said, cradling the object. She rubbed the stone, feeling its warmth run up her arms. She tucked it in her pocket, focusing on the boy. "I would never deny you that."

"Don't you need the stone?" Noah asked.

She shook her head and stepped behind him with glee. Lost in the Bypass, he searched along its luminescent surface for the answer.

"You see the truth is your parents died as they lived," she said. "Unnoticed, insignificant little specks taking up space in the universe."

"What?"

Her hands snatched the sides of his head. "The truth, dear Noah, is that when it came down to it, no one—not the police, not their colleagues, nor their friends—gave a damn."

"Stop. What are you—?"

She squeezed harder, strength channeling through her. "And neither did I when I ended their miserable existence."

"You—?"

A loud snap crunched under her hands, his neck twisting to finality. Noah Jordan's body collapsed, his eyes lost in terror at the answer truly realized at last. She stepped over his fallen figure, wiping her hands clean, as she inched toward the Bypass and her destiny.

"Enjoy your freedom, Noah Jordan."

CHAPTER FIFTY-THREE

Samantha Myers moaned with displeasure upon entering her apartment. She dropped her keys on a small table near the door, which promptly closed behind her, then slipped her jacket off, letting it fall to the floor. Exhaustion filled her frame from another long shift.

Not that her guest cared. When she moved for the bed on the far side of the one room loft, Greg Loren cocked the hammer of the gun.

"What was it?" he asked from the shadows of the apartment.

Myers jumped back, hand to her sidearm. She stopped at the sight of him, sitting on the edge of her easy chair. "Shit, Loren. I almost—"

"What does he have on you?" he asked again. His night had been draining from the revelations by Soriya and Pratchett. He'd reached closure on the topic. Now it was time for answers of a different sort, a way to make things right for everyone. To fix things, as Pratchett said.

"Who?" Myers answered. She started for the couch and he shook his head, using Pratchett's pilfered weapon to direct her to the far side of the room.

"Standish."

"I—"

The gun inched out of the shadows. "Think very carefully, Myers. Think about those next words."

Myers sighed, pulling back her hair to tie it off. She paced the length of the room before falling on the edge of the bed. "My father."

"He's dead," Loren snapped, losing patience. "Heart attack, six years ago."

She smiled. "Breaking into my personnel file? I'd feel proud if not for the gun on me."

"You'll get used to it."

He had no choice. He couldn't trust her answers. His search to find them on his own came up empty, though. Myers had no family, no real history except the academy and her time in New York. Those mistakes led to her dismissal and her sudden and unexpected arrival in Portents at the Central Precinct.

"Gee thanks," Myers muttered. "And no, he's not. My father, my real father, is very much alive. Kenneth Myers is my father."

Loren failed to recognize the name, his only response being silence.

"A criminal, Loren. A killer," Myers said. "Standish found him in the system. Witness Protection. Being a Cro-Magnon douche, he pieced together the link to me."

"He brought you to Portents. His connection to Mathers opened the door to the Central Precinct."

"And then my connection to Mathers..." Myers stopped. Loren's brow furrowed, a question on his lips. She stopped him there. "Don't ask. It's not worth getting into now."

Realization settled over him. *Her and Mathers?* "Or ever."

"Standish wanted you. He hates you."

"The feeling's mutual."

"I screwed up. Back in New York," Myers said. "You read the reports, I'm sure."

"Yes." Her misjudgment led to the deaths of four women and her suspect. She didn't believe he would be armed. Never thought for a second there was any risk.

"I needed this shot. To protect my old man from other bastards like Standish."

"You knew he was alive."

"I did." Myers pushed off the bed. She shuffled toward the balcony and looked out at the pink hues of morning spreading against the fading night. "He gave me a chance to live free and clear of his mistakes. I hated him for it, for leaving me for so long, until I realized what he was actually giving me, the thing he always tried to give me: control. Control over my own destiny, instead of at the whim of some suit with a badge—looking out for their own interests.

"I had to keep him safe," she continued, closing her eyes. "I thought I could outmaneuver Standish. I was wrong."

"You did what he wanted."

The end of his career. The evidence stolen from his office, the files about his work with Soriya. His gun. Richard Crowne. All for Robert Standish.

Always Standish.

"Loren, I…"

"Stop. You betrayed me."

"I had to!" she yelled. "What was I supposed to do?"

"Tell me the damn truth," Loren replied. "I was your partner."

"And what about you and your missing person's cases?"

"You…" Loren stopped. She told him she wouldn't hack his files, wouldn't pry into what she called his *super-secret work*. Always a term of endearment, or so he believed. But then, he believed her about pretty much everything—and that ended well for him, didn't it? "Of course you knew."

"You never trusted me. Those people—"

"Are dead!" Loren shouted, stopping her cold. "Because of Standish."

"What?"

"He killed them. Dozens stacked atop each other like refuse."

"No…"

"You have a gift for protecting the wrong people, Myers."

Her head lowered, her hands to her hips as she took long, steady breaths. "Dammit."

He studied her, wondering if the reaction was genuine. What involvement, if any, did she have in Standish's Circle of Shadows. "Is it over? I've been dismissed. The city is in lockdown. Mathers is in the top spot. Sounds like a win for Standish so…is it over?"

Myers huffed. "Of course it isn't! He's a cop now!" She caught his quiet stare. "You saw him?"

He was at the station that day, Loren's last day. Standish earned his shield as Loren's was taken away. There was no coincidence behind the move. And Mathers? Ruiz was right to doubt the man's appointment. Someone played them, moving people around the board like chess pieces. And Standish stood at the center, twirling his invisible mustache like a damn second-rate villain.

"Mathers legitimized the bastard," Myers grumbled, pulling open the balcony door and letting in a wave of fresh air. "Standish could turn on me in a second and with what I did to Rufus… All I ever wanted was control. Of my world. Of my own damn life." She sighed. "Now no one has any." Birds chirped to welcome the new day. A small smirk grew across her face. "At least I have the sunrise."

"What?"

She turned to him, the light from the morning sun starting to hit the sky. "He approached me after your meeting with Mathers. Standish expected friendship, an understanding. God knows what else. I told him to shove it. I told him I'm done, Loren. And if he tried anything, if he even thought about it, I'd go to Mathers, to the DA, the press. Damn the consequences."

Loren understood the consequences well enough. He had been on the receiving end of them both now and over a year earlier when he was suspended because of Standish's manipulations. A small part of him wanted to comfort Myers, to put the gun away and hope they could move forward, but he remained silent, letting her stare out over the city.

"I just wanted one more sunrise," Myers said, smiling at the light streaming over her. "My dad and I used to have this little place on the Upper East Side in New York. Noisy neighborhood no matter the hour. Except at sunrise. Then it was silent. Peaceful. It's all I have left from that time besides his love of gardening."

Loren didn't notice them at first, the plants beside the door on both sides. Potted plants on the ground, smaller ones on shelving units. Lilies covered the frame, spreading out and reaching for the light approaching with the dawn.

"No," Loren whispered.

"Loren?"

He dropped the gun, jumping to his feet. He ran toward Myers, seeing everything at last. "No more sunrises."

"What are—?"

The light. The flowers spread across the landscape. Everything sharpened behind his eyes. Including the red dot along Myers' chest.

"Down! Now!"

Loren tackled her to the ground. Shots rang out overhead, shattering the glass from the balcony door. Plaster and paint fell from the walls, showering over them. Loren tucked lower to the ground, covering the stunned Myers.

The sound faded as quickly as it began. Myers opened her eyes. Loren shuffled the glass from his back, while keeping her protected.

"How the hell—?"

"No more sunrises, Myers."

Loren rolled off her and scrambled deeper into the apartment away from the door. Myers followed and he helped her to her feet.

"You think it was—?"

"Standish," Loren said with a nod. "Guess he didn't like your choice."

Loren returned to the chair, retrieving his gun and his jacket. He started for the door, his mind working overtime.

"Where are you going?" Myers called. She was no longer the tough-as-nails, shoot-from-the-cuff detective he had come to know. She was the little girl protecting her daddy from a mistake neither could outrun.

"To make a better one," Loren said. "Shouldn't you?"

He closed the door behind her, starting for the stairs. He raced for the city. *One has to die.* Beth's warning repeated on him. A warning he refused to accept.

I can save them both. I have to.

I have to save Soriya.

CHAPTER FIFTY-FOUR

Soriya was alive.

She knew this only from the pain swelling with each breath, which spread down her arms and legs, raging anywhere and everywhere at the same time. She fought to roll over, to open her eyes from the darkness washing over her.

Only her eyes weren't closed—the darkness was the Bypass chamber. The great light was gone, stolen from her, taken against her every protest. Noah Jordan took it and seemed poised to take her life.

Why didn't he?

Her fingers dug into the concrete, and she forced her body to its knees. Her screams filled the vast space hidden beneath the city. Each breath burned in her lungs, each inch an endless array of agony.

She didn't know how long it took, how long the trial endured. It faded the moment her hand grasped the edge of the domicile, locking tight to the door to Mentor's room. She shuffled inside to the corner and the waiting fireplace.

Working through the darkness, Soriya found the matches on the shelf above the unit and struck one. Flames sparked along the wood and warmth washed over her, melting away the pain and the dismal dregs of defeat.

She leaned along the wall, afraid to sit, afraid to lie down upon the bed. There was no guarantee she would be able to stand again. The crackling of the wood inside the pit, however, brought her a level of comfort she had not reached in months.

Long winter days were spent before the fire, she and her teacher. Their lessons were sparse, the conversation changing to experiences as the years passed. He would relay old adversaries he'd faced and she would inform him of her current struggles. He always knew ahead of time about them. Mentor always knew everything about her.

And she knew little. Even now, she knew so little.

Noah lied. He was the killer all along, taking the lives of four men. All to draw the authorities' attention to Soriya. To split her from those she allied herself with, her trusted friends. To isolate her. To manipulate her. And in the end, betray her. All for a single goal: the Bypass. The time spent pulling at her heart, driving her toward his cause, his search for the truth about his parents and the truth behind a Circle of Shadows infecting Portents was only a means to an end. When she failed to jump at the chance to work with him, he devised a new plan.

The Heads of Cerberus.

Their terror in the streets was a distraction, a test, and she failed. All her efforts went toward a fight that didn't matter, the true threat hidden behind a kind smile and a similar backstory.

The Bypass was the cost of her mistake. The one thing she swore never to lose, never to stop fighting for, no matter the challenge faced. Gilgamesh warned her. He told her something was coming and if the glowing light of the infinite fell…

"Dammit," she muttered.

Gilgamesh wasn't the only warning she'd received. The etching against the ground in the Courtyard beside the black feather of her friend, Kok'Kol, stirred in her. Another sign of what was to come, one found within the small bedroom of her deceased teacher.

It marked the spine of a journal resting on the extensive bookshelves along the right hand wall. The brown leather canvas was graffitied in several areas in black, the most profound image matching the rune left by the raven for her to find.

She pulled the journal from the shelf, flipping through pages in the firelight. Noah may have been the instrument of her failure, the tool used to steal the Bypass and unleash the hounds on the city.

However, he remained a pawn in unfolding events. The true manipulator, the dark light foreseen several times over during the past year, pulled his strings.

The Luminary.

Mentor knew her all right. The journal documented every meeting, every meal shared, and every conversation between the two of them. Her reactions to questions asked and his own to hers. All recorded. A failsafe Mentor believed to be required when it came to the woman named Karen Winters.

Photos littered the pages, taped into place next to notes. Images documenting the woman's movements dating back years. Concerns rose after the shuttering of the Library of the Luminaries. Where the other members departed for parts unknown, Karen remained.

Out of them all, she reached out to Mentor to establish a relationship. To spark a connection when there had been none before. He allowed it, but as the notes confirmed, he was skeptical of her motives.

With good reason. In the years that followed, dozens of pictures and news articles marked her rise in public life, especially in political circles. Each appointment, each position earned through bitter elections or outright shady practices—though never identified by a public deluged by scandals on the left and right— every change sparked new concerns in Mentor.

His notes questioned everything, tracking her through the city. It was never enough for him to act on his suspicions, though. Or, at least, never having the chance to act.

Their meetings ended years ago. He cut ties with her, as he did with the rest of the world. Karen Winters turned into yet another secret kept from Soriya. A final nail in the coffin of their relationship that now threatened Portents.

Soriya closed the journal, grazing her fingers over the cover. Mentor held all the answers as he always did. But he was gone, and relying on him was no longer an option. Loren was lost to her, as was everyone else she once counted on. She had to stand and fight on her own.

Her shuffling feet carried her to the edge of the domicile. In the fading firelight she found the small object resting on the ground. The Greystone.

Noah had made his first mistake by letting her live. Leaving the Greystone was the second. Soriya picked up the stone and took a sharp breath. The stone hummed, warmer than the glowing embers of the fire at her back. Her body ached, her limbs threatening to lock up rather than work with her. She needed more time, the one thing no longer available for her.

The Heads of Cerberus. The Luminary. Even Noah Jordan. All had to be stopped. Now.

And only Soriya Greystone could stand against them.

CHAPTER FIFTY-FIVE

It took hours for Myers to leave her apartment. Hours spent hiding away from the shattered peace of her balcony. Glass remained scattered along the ground, holes buried in the wall behind her bed and stretching the length of the room.

She earned it. From Loren's breaking and entering to Standish's reprisal at her refusal to continue their work, she earned the ire of all around her.

Part of her hoped Loren would stay, would help her in the aftermath. They could mend their friendship and track Standish down. Work together as they once had, like those times had been a lifetime ago rather than a matter of days.

Instead she went alone. Once back in the streets, she tried to find her would-be assassin. Every hole was considered, every seedy bar searched to no avail. A day of disappointment left her with the fading light as nothing more than a reminder of her constant failures.

No more sunrises.

She believed it. Loren's condemnation, the anger in his eyes. But also his compassion. No matter his hatred of her, no matter what Myers had done to him, he still saved her from Standish's revenge. He had offered one last chance to make things right.

To make a better choice.

She didn't know how, or if such an act was possible. Not after everything, all the lies and the betrayal. When Myers entered the Central Precinct, it was more out of habit than anything else. Why she bothered, with so much going on in the city, she didn't know— but there was nowhere else for her to go.

The parking structure was full. No patrol cars raced through the streets, the general flow of traffic in and out of the Rath Building nonexistent. No one worked the door; no one monitored the holding area.

When the elevator opened on the second floor, she realized why. Officers lined the hall, flooding the entire floor in both directions. Dozens upon dozens. Beat cops mixed with detectives. Policemen from Major Crimes muttered to those from Homicide. Secretaries and support staff joined in the chaos, their speeches muted to desk sergeants and janitors alike.

Fear resided in their eyes. Not in a few, not in the young or the old, but in them all. Fear *owned* them. In the way they stood, in the way their voices quieted as Myers passed through. Fear controlled their actions—or, point of fact, their inaction.

Stories ran like water between the formed cliques. Homes burned or trashed. Landmarks shattered and destroyed—like the statue in front of the Rath Building and the stained glass windows at Saint Sebastian's Church. Hounds. Images of Alvaro's change caused Myers' body to shake and her wounded leg to pulse with pain when she walked.

Myers stood in the center of the chaos at the precinct and closed her eyes. She took it all in, feeling every ounce of terror rising from the crowd. There was no direction in them, no orders raining down from on high to motivate them. There was only the fear locking them in place. As it had for her for so long.

Make a better choice…

"Enough!" Her shout was lost in the murmurs of the crowd. She clenched her fists, her leg screaming in pain as she climbed on the closest desk. "I said, ENOUGH!"

Murmurs stretched back before falling silent at the sight of Myers standing over them. It took her a moment to realize their eyes were on her. So many eyes looking to her.

"Got it out of your system?" she asked. Curious stares followed and she pushed through them. "Good."

She took a deep breath. The fear remained. Without and within.

"I get it," she started, her words slow yet growing louder. "I get the fear, the terror. It's what everyone in the city is fighting through right now. They are cowering in their homes with their families— husbands, wives, children—praying tonight isn't their last night on this earth."

They made the same prayers, the officers along the hall. Some played with rings on their fingers, others clutched tight to a necklace, a cross, or other reminder of home. They stood at work instead of with those at home, pondering their decision.

"But prayers aren't enough," Myers affirmed. "Hope is not enough. They need protection. They need to feel safe, that the shadows will recede and the light will return."

Doubt rested in their eyes: doubts about her words, about her in general. They heard about Loren, about Standish and what she had done. They knew everything.

"They need us," Myers continued. "Now more than ever. Portents is asking you to fight for her. I…I am asking you to fight with me."

Myers paused, the silence unnerving her. She held her breath, waiting and hoping for an answer.

Then the grumbling returned, the murmurs growing like a wave. Doubt swelled in her chest—the fear of what was out there, of what awaited them and their families. Hopelessness took hold. Her words weren't enough. She wasn't enough.

"I'll fight with you," a voice boomed at the end of the hall.

Alejo Ruiz stepped out from the elevator, passing each person, their eyes locked on him as he traveled the length of the corridor. In an instant the doubt within her faded and the fear muted, tucked behind a wall of something that hadn't been present for days.

Hope.

Myers clambered down from the desk to greet him. Her hand extended and he took it with a hard shake and a satisfied grin.

"Captain," she said.

He nodded, a silent word of thanks in his eyes. Then he turned to the watching crowd surrounding them.

"Who's with us?"

The cheers of the Central Precinct echoed through the Rath Building.

CHAPTER FIFTY-SIX

Getting a cab was impossible. Buses had stopped service two days earlier. Storefronts were shuttered, banks closed, and most essential services ran on autopilot. The term *ghost town* didn't do Portents justice but it was the closest viable description for the vacant city blocks.

Fires continued to burn. The larger ones were contained but smaller, more abrupt disruptions sparked along the outskirts. They served as reminders of the terror from the long night barely in the rearview.

Loren left the marketplace on Allure, disappointed it matched the rest of the downtown area. Empty. Closed. Even the Cobbler's Den that served their needs in their search for Henry Erikson was gated from entry. *Too bad*, thought Loren. *I could really use some new shoes.*

Allure was the second strike against his ever widening search for Soriya Greystone. The Library of the Luminaries was first on the list, the closest to his residence on the Knoll.

Loren pulled up his collar, tightening his jacket around him as he shuffled across another street. His searching offered no end, no great clarity in tracking Soriya, but he refused to quit. His dreams spoke to his resolve. One didn't have to die. Not if he found her. Not if he saved her.

"Give me a damn sign, Soriya," Loren grumbled, rain falling in his eyes though he continued to peer up at the gray skyline. It worked in the past, hunting for a random lightning strike or an out of place flash of light. But there was nothing. "Come on. Where are you?"

He wiped at his thickening beard, shoes splashing water from the growing puddle taking over the street. Hours of searching yet he felt more refreshed than he had in months. Having the clear path, putting the questions of Beth to rest, woke him from the unending dream that plagued his every night. Now he knew what it meant and what he was meant to do with it.

A patrol car rounded the corner. Loren, surprised by the presence so close to the coves, stepped into the street to wave it down. The driver, one he quickly recognized from Central as Danvers, was busy arguing with his partner, Sloane. The co-pilot slapped the driver's shoulder, pointing to the street and the obstacle in the lane.

"WHOA!"

Danvers slammed on the brakes. "Holy…"

The car screeched to a halt, water kicking up and covering Loren's pants. His sneakers, filled with dirty rainwater, squeaked with his each step to the side of the vehicle.

"Sorry, guys."

"Loren?" Sloane asked, hand to his chest.

Danvers leaned on the steering wheel, shifting to park. "Hey. We heard what happened and—"

"It's fine," Loren said. "Thanks. What are you two doing here of all places?"

Sloane whacked Danvers on the shoulder again, offering the soaked former detective a nod. "My question exactly. See?"

"I do see," Danvers snapped, knocking the man's hand away. "I also see a hand that is getting broken if it doesn't leave my personal space."

Sloane sniggered, his fingers inching around an increasingly annoyed Danvers. "How about now? Huh? How about now?"

"I swear to God…"

Loren tapped the side of the car. "Guys?"

"Right," Sloane said, settling in his seat.

Danvers leaned closer. "Orders from on high."

"Mathers?"

Sloane shook his head in disbelief, one shared by his partner. "Like that guy knows anything. All the shit we've been hearing about activity in the Corridor and we've all been pulled from there."

"The Corridor?"

Danvers smacked Sloane's shoulder. "They finally called us back for some big meeting."

"Thanks, guys." Loren patted the roof of the patrol. He started down the street, the rain increasing.

"Loren? What…?" Sloane tried to ask, sticking his head out the passenger window.

"No problem, Loren," Danvers shouted. "Weirdo."

Loren stopped to wave, the patrol drifting along the road until turning for the expressway. The former detective grinned at the continued argument of the pair, then started east. The light faded above, the gray slowly darkening.

"The Corridor," Loren muttered. His walk transitioned to a trot and then a full run as the rain continued to pelt from above. "I'm coming, Soriya. I'm coming."

CHAPTER FIFTY-SEVEN

Electricity sparked along the second floor of the Central Precinct. Not from the overhead lights or the random lamps on the desks in the bullpen of the detective bureau. It came in the eyes of the gathered crowd. It came in their cheers, in their growing energy at the order being given.

He needed them and they needed him—the work, the job, protecting Portents. Everything built from the words of Samantha Myers to the organization stemming from Captain Alejo Ruiz.

"Let's move it, people," Ruiz called to the gathering.

Dozens rushed down the hall, others moving for the phones. Coordinating the effort took each and every one of them but there were no questions, no doubts about his intentions. Each was only grateful at the sense of direction, at having someone at the head of the table, the role he had tried to maintain for years without success thanks to the efforts of his superiors and colleagues.

The phones blared, confirming new directives and shifting priorities. The energy from each passing patrolman, the determination of each officer raced through the returned captain. Recharged and ready for the fight. Myers waited patiently at his side and he smiled.

"It was a good speech."

"That no one believed."

Ruiz shook his head. "I did."

She chuckled, turning to the rushing feet of the officers around them. "And they believe in you. So do I, Ruiz. I—"

"Leave it."

"What?" she asked, tracking his stare. He didn't blink, didn't flinch.

"Leave it for now."

"Loren told you."

"Myers…"

"Right," she said. The pair listened to the work surrounding them, the effort unlike any they had seen before. Myers fought back a laugh. "Can you imagine Mathers trying to organize this many people?"

He could. Ruiz could also imagine how poorly the effort would go for the man. While Ruiz didn't feel inspirational in the least, he realized Mathers' pandering only worked with a camera crew and a makeup artist. Still, he was surprised at the lack of questions coming from the sixth floor.

"Where is Mathers?"

For a glory hog and a need for the spotlight, to not have him in full view was too strange. Ruiz started for the elevator, accepting the pats of camaraderie from those around him, the quiet whispers of hope from the others on the floor. For all his confidence, there were still too many variables in the way, too many things that could go wrong.

Myers followed close behind, wincing but never complaining about the pain from her leg. The pair quietly traveled to the top floor. Somehow, even after everything, she managed to surprise him. Out of all the people in the precinct, to see her stand in an attempt to unite for the betterment of the city—especially knowing what she had done to Loren—he never would have imagined she would be at the center of the resistance.

"My God." Bloodstains on the carpet greeted them. Ruiz ran the length of the lobby for the conference room at the far end, stopping short of the doorway.

Mathers' body was barely recognizable. If not for his suit, shredded to tatters, and his glasses cracked and torn from his bloodied face, Ruiz wouldn't have been able to ID the man he worked with for years.

"Rufus," Myers whispered, covering her mouth.

Ruiz moved from the body, stepping in front of her. "You don't have to be here, Myers. I know what he—"

"It's okay," she said, shaking her head. "I'm okay."

Ruiz peered around. "No one saw anything? Heard anything?"

"These monsters can look human. They can be anyone."

His hands fell to his hips. "Feeling better about our chances with every second."

"How, Ruiz?" Myers asked, her eyes locked on the man she shared a bed with for a time. "How the hell are we going to stop this?"

"I have an idea." The elevator doors closed and a young woman with blond hair and dark eyes moved toward them at a brisk pace. An officer crashed through the door to the left of the elevator, trying to catch up to the new arrival.

"Sorry, sir," the officer yelled. "She ran past—"

"It's fine," Ruiz said. The woman, seemingly no older than Zoe, wore a hooded sweatshirt and jeans. Nothing special. Nothing unique, yet her bold eyes screamed a different story. "Who are you?"

"My name is Thel."

Myers huffed. "Her name is Thel. She'll take it from here, Ruiz."

"Myers…" Ruiz tossed her a glare.

"Sorry."

Thel stared them down, unafraid. "Someone recently gave me a second chance. A chance to make a difference, a better life for myself. For everyone. I owe it to her to try."

"That's very generous of you but I don't see how—"

A melody erupted, Thel's voice carrying across the floor. It rose with her song, the gentle musing pulling at the officer watching from the elevator doors. He walked forward, his eyes vacant with the movement.

"What—?" Myers started to ask, mirroring Ruiz's many questions.

Then the officer ripped open his shirt, dancing to the beat of her song. The tattered clothing fell by his feet, his belt joining it. His eyes showed no sign of concern or control. Thel owned him.

He danced without a care in the world, caution to the wind. There was only Thel and her song, driving him on. His pants joined the growing pile on the floor. Standing in only his boxers, the officer moved for the final piece of clothing.

"Okay," Ruiz said. The song continued, and the kid's fingers reached for his boxers. "OKAY!"

The song ended. The officer shook his head, looking around. His eyes widened at the uniform at his feet.

"What the hell?" he muttered, embarrassed glances toward his superior as he gathered his clothing up along with his wits and ran for the stairs.

"I think we could have waited another second or two," Myers said with a smile. Ruiz tossed her a sharp look. "What?"

"You're with us, Thel. Welcome to the fight."

"Wait," Myers said. "That's it? A contestant from *The Voice* and a couple hundred uniforms?"

She wasn't wrong. The odds were against them. They knew nothing of the hounds, including the numbers they faced. Those were questions once asked of Loren and Soriya, but they weren't with them, couldn't be with them. They had their own fight ahead.

"I might be able to help those odds." A voice rang out, scratchy and soft, from the elevator. Myers' face went white and Ruiz's jaw dropped.

Pratchett slipped from the wall that held him upright. As he sunk to the carpet, Myers saw that blood covered his shirt, running in streams down his pants. The tourniquet was soaked through, the cuts beneath visible.

"Pratchett!" she cried. She ran to his side, immediately applying pressure to his wounds. He smiled at her, his eyes hazy and fading.

Ruiz stayed close, giving her time, letting her work to stop the bleeding. But there was too much. Pratchett fought to smile, his breath caught in his throat.

"You were right about Frankie…"

"Pratchett," Ruiz choked. "You hold on. You hear me?"

"It's okay, Captain." The stalwart officer of the Central Precinct shook his head. A golden key fell from his hand. "The orphanage. Everything you need is at Saint Helena's."

Myers held him close. "Pratchett, don't you dare…"

His hand grazed her cheek. "I'll miss you too, Myers." His breath slowed, his chest struggling to rise. His skin was pale and sweat poured along his brow. "Myers?"

"I'm here, Pratchett… John. I'm here."

He smiled. "Kick some ass for me."

His head fell back, eyes staring blankly at the ceiling.

"John!" Myers shook his body, hand tight over his wound. "JOHN!"

She howled, tears streaming down her cheeks. Ruiz's hand fell to her shoulder. The key gleamed in his hand, the final gift of

Officer John Pratchett. And with it, one last hope against the darkness invading Portents.

CHAPTER FIFTY-EIGHT

Ruiz offered a quiet and reserved Thel a bottle of water. She took the beverage, twisting off the cap and enjoyed a satisfying sip. Though young in appearance, her steely resolve was that of someone who had experienced much in life—and survived to tell the tale.

They needed survivors like her for the fight ahead.

They took up positions in the center of Heaven's Gate Park. A small bunker, vehicles strategically placed to give them cover from the streets, acted as the command center of the entire operation. Three officers remained in the cars, working the radios and offering any change in direction as well as status updates for Ruiz every few minutes.

Coordination like this was years in the making, not typically the hours they had to pull everything together. Time was not on their side though, and the officers of Portents did what they could to make the impossible a reality. One last time.

For one last stand.

The plan was sound. The waiting game was over. If the police were all that stood in the way of the hounds taking the city, then they would make their presence known. All thirteen precincts were pulled in one by one, shifting resources and bringing everything to bear at the park.

Just shy of 800 acres, Heaven's Gate Park offered natural cover with various tree lines and three ponds scattered across the grounds. Snipers took to the trees. Barricades blocked the entrances. Officers patrolled in groups, while others stayed low and out of sight as a second defense for their uniformed brothers and sisters.

Bringing everyone together was only a first step. Spreading the word took caution. So did handing over their plans to the enemy.

"I don't like this," Myers grumbled, pacing through the command bunker.

"So you've said," Ruiz said. Thel nodded another thanks for the water and the captain joined Myers at the perimeter. "Is everything ready?"

"Eyes are on every entrance. Wexler's heard what we wanted her to hear."

Wexler. His replacement at Central. When he took his leave she came highly recommended by his superiors and others outside his purview. Now he wished he knew who those people were so he could wring their necks. Wexler was one of the hounds the whole time, unnoticed by all.

Internal security feeds picked up her assault of Rufus Mathers on the sixth floor. While no one else caught the act firsthand, the cameras locked on to Wexler's change and her vicious slaughter of the newly-appointed commissioner. Mathers didn't stand a chance—not that he had the means to combat a hound. He had never even reached for his sidearm. The act was over too quickly. Too brutally.

Myers left the room rather than watch, but Ruiz stayed. He noted every gory detail, his anger rising at not being there. Loren was right: He was selfish and stupid, letting fear for his family drive him instead of worrying about all the other families that needed him.

Wexler's involvement wasn't the end of the revelations. Mathers argued with another person in the conference room before the end, one who blissfully grinned at the evisceration of Rufus Mathers. A puppet master on both sides and one the city put its faith in during its darkest hour.

Karen Winters. The mayor of Portents.

"You couldn't have known." Myers' words were soft along the night air, the wind sweeping along them and causing the trees to rustle with anticipation. "About Wexler. About any of it, you couldn't—"

"I know," Ruiz replied, not believing his own words for a second. "What else?"

"The last of the boys from the First are rolling in from the north now. We're all here. If that means anything."

"It does, Myers. It does. What about the others?" She turned away, staring deeper into the darkness. "Myers?"

"They're ready," she whispered. "Waiting on you."

Ruiz nodded. "Shouldn't be long now."

Myers huffed. "Every cop in the city."

"They want us? They have to come get us."

"Ruiz?" Myers lowered her voice, inching away from the rest in the bunker. "About Loren…"

"We don't have to do this, Myers."

"We do, actually. I was wrong. Protecting the past is a surefire way of destroying the future. I'll hand in my badge when this is over."

Ruiz laughed. Myers immediately crossed her arms over her chest.

"What's so funny?"

"When this is over," Ruiz said, still smiling, "I expect you to buy the first round." His hand fell on her shoulder. "Our past doesn't define us. And we sure as hell each have one. The present gives us a chance to make it right again, Myers. Each moment. Each choice. I know you'll make the right one."

He had more to say—angry words. She betrayed Loren, a man who stood for everything good in the city. A broken man who lost more than anyone could give back because of his work. And Ruiz was justified in taking it out on the young detective. Tonight, however, wasn't about blame, much as he wanted to compound it on his own shoulders for Mathers' death, for not being here when he was needed.

Because he was here, standing up against the darkness, against the worst threat the city had ever seen. And he wasn't backing down. Not tonight.

A car door slammed. An officer rushed to their side, panic in his eyes.

"Sir?" he panted. "We're picking up—"

It broke through, echoing in the air. The sound shattered the quiet rustling of the trees. It took away the last moments of peace from the faces of the men and women surrounding the bunker. One, then two, then dozens, filling the air.

"Gunfire."

"They're here." Ruiz nodded, rushing for the center. He pulled out his sidearm, thumbing the hammer back as he waved to the others around him. "Now or never, people. We stand or Portents falls."

CHAPTER FIFTY-NINE

"They're everywhere!"

Hounds ripped through the front defenses, taking over the barricades at each of the four entrances to the park. They pounced over the tall walls circling the grounds, surrounding the lines on two fronts.

Those backing up the first responders did their best to compensate. They littered the earth with bodies, shots ringing out from every direction to defend the center. Screams raked the freshly-trimmed lawn. Ruiz wondered who fell, if he knew them, if someone was at home waiting for their call.

And how many more would join them before the end.

"Danvers!" Ruiz bellowed over the gunfire. The officer's head tilted, his eyes never leaving the forest. "To the east. Bolster the Sixth. Myers—"

She turned, crying out, "RUIZ!"

Her pistol leveled on him then rose above his head, a single shot taking out a leaping hound. It howled as the bullet struck. Ruiz dove to avoid a collision, the creature slamming against him, driving him to the ground. The beast continued to roll from the impact, skidding to a halt in the command bunker before dying.

Ruiz struggled to breathe, the heavy weight on his chest pushing the air from his body. Myers rushed to his side, "Ruiz, are you—?"

"Thanks, but…" His eyes flared, his gun rising on instinct. He fired, the bullet blowing her hair on the right as it passed. The shot connected with another hound falling before it struck the distracted detective.

"Holy shit," Myers muttered, helping Ruiz out from under the dead creature.

"Stay focused, Myers."

The bunker was collapsing on all sides. The hounds pushed hard from the initial strike at the entrances to Heaven's Gate Park, plowing through the weak resistance offered by every man and woman in uniform that remained in Portents. They slaughtered mercilessly, not caring to defend their own.

Danvers cried out to the east, the Sixth no longer responding to the radiomen in the patrol vehicles bolstering the bunker. Sloane raced to follow, refusing to leave his friend behind. He managed four steps before falling to a wave of craven beasts.

"I think they're close enough," Myers cried over the shots.

Ruiz scanned the perimeter of the bunker awash with furry creatures he never thought he would see. He could have said the same for anything over the last year. From the crimson eyes of Nathaniel Evans to the Charon that almost took Loren from the world and so many others.

They rushed on all sides, the men and women at his side faltering. Their hope diminished like the lights above.

"Are they?" he asked, both turning to the young woman in the hooded sweatshirt.

Thel stood, once confident eyes wavering. "I don't—"

"Now or never, Thel," Ruiz said, hand reaching for her. She took it and nodded.

"Cover your ears."

Ruiz screamed to the radiomen still able to call out the play. "Earplugs, people. Now!"

Thel took a deep breath and let loose her voice on Heaven's Gate Park. The melody shook the bodies of those closest to her, Ruiz struggling to stay upright even with earplugs in place. Myers pulled him along, fighting for cover as the hounds continued to pound through the inadequate barricades.

They howled in a battle for dominance and Thel battered them back, her song more powerful, more tried and true from her centuries as a siren. The beasts slowed; their growling turning to whimpering. Their rage-filled eyes softened and their tongues panted for more.

"She's doing it," Ruiz said. "She's actually doing it."

Officers swarmed the hounds, lost to the sound of the woman's voice carrying over the entire park through the radio system put into place. They picked them off, working to take out the beasts that had slaughtered so many.

Those closest reverted during the song, the melody at a fever pitch. Their human forms collapsed in the grass as uniforms rushed to cuff them and cart them to the vans lining the perimeter.

"She did it," Myers said, her smile bright and bold. "Thel, you—"

No one saw the hound until it was too late. How the creature managed to make it so far without falling victim to the siren's serenade was explained by the beast's one missing ear and a scar over the other. The wounds of war saved the creature from their plan.

No one could save Thel from the hound's. It leaped into the bunker from behind the siren and swiped across her back. Myers knocked Thel aside after the initial strike and unloaded her clip into the beast. Myers continued to scream at the fallen creature, Ruiz crouching low to pull the wounded woman close.

Blood streamed from Thel's back, the scratches deep and thick. "I've got you," Ruiz said, panicked eyes searching for help. "I've got you."

"Tell her," Thel whispered. "Tell the Greystone I earned this chance."

Ruiz nodded, looking up to see a stunned Myers. "The Greystone?"

"Tell her, please?"

Myers joined them on the ground, holding the woman's hand. "I'll tell her. I will."

An EMT rushed through the bunker, overwhelmed at the bodies on the ground. Ruiz called out, "Over here! Hurry!"

Thel's eyes were closed when the man reached them. Bandages fell to the ground, Myers assisting the EMT to stop the flow of blood.

"How bad?"

"Sir? I don't—"

"Answer him," Myers snapped. "Is she—?"

"Let me work," the EMT yelled. "Just let me work."

The sound of gunfire and howling returned to the park. The next wave arrived, working their way closer with each passing moment. Ruiz pulled Myers deeper into the bunker.

"We need to regroup."

Myers shook her head. "Let them loose, Ruiz."

"Sam," Ruiz shot back, his eyes heavy. Thel was still breathing; the EMT was doing what he could. She gave them hope. They had to do the same. "We can still—"

Myers grabbed his arm and pointed to the bodies scattered on the ground. "Do it, Ruiz. Do it now."

He fell to the back wall of the bunker and the shadows shifting in the darkness. He offered a silent prayer, looking to the heavens before falling back to earth.

"You heard her," Ruiz said to the shadows. "God forgive us if we're wrong."

"You're not," Hady Ronne replied. "Trust us, Alejo."

She led the charge, her eyes fading into black chasms. The Charon bellowed for death, the horrors hidden in the depths of Saint Helena's Orphanage by Pratchett, crying out for vengeance as they met the Heads of Cerberus with the fate of Portents hanging in the balance.

CHAPTER SIXTY

When they approached Saint Helena's Orphanage, Ruiz took the lead. He unlocked the door to the abandoned four-story construction near the city limits and entered without fear. The chants and screams echoed down the halls, each cell adding to the chorus. Time was not on their side. The coordination of the thirteen precincts took every available man and woman to put into motion.

At the orphanage they stopped near the entrance by the first cell. Hady Ronne called to Ruiz from the shadows; he answered. The words of childhood friends passed, the memories of her actions as the Charon—the force behind the slaughter of dozens months earlier—forgotten as Ruiz pitched their proposition to the masses incarcerated by John Pratchett.

Freedom was their reward to take, either by helping or not. The chains came off and the decision remained their own without coercion. Hady was the first to sign up, scores joining at her approval.

They turned the tide. Myers felt it the second Hady's mask fell away and her true nature took hold. The detective tried to fight the chill running along her soul, one she almost lost at the hands of the former head coroner, but let it come in order to watch her work on the hounds surrounding the bunker.

They fell as quickly as they arrived. The Charon led the assault, followed closely by the others. A female wolf, a shape shifter with a predilection for clowns, four guys wearing jackal faces and tunics, and more, pouring from the shadows of Heaven's Gate Park. A regular carnival ride and one the citizens of Portents unknowingly counted on to save their collective asses.

Ruiz threw orders out where he could as the fight pulled away from him. The EMT continued to work on Thel, the siren fighting for breath. Officers stood side by side with the monsters hidden from their view since the beginning of Portents.

Myers, however, was looking elsewhere. She desired other prey and found him rushing from the Rath Building toward his car parked on Main. "Standish…"

She started for the road, peering back to Ruiz. He tracked her gaze. "Go."

She didn't need to hear anything else. Breaking into a full run, Myers departed the bunker, ducking through hounds battling monsters for dominion over Portents. Shots blew past her.

Standish's gut bounced with each step for the rusted out sedan parked at the end of the block. A bullet sliced through his left leg and he cried out, falling to the sidewalk beside his car.

"That's far enough," Myers yelled, gun trained on the squirming man.

"You're kidding, right?" he remarked, seething at the slightest touch. "You? Of all the—" The sound of thunder roiled again, a bullet through his right leg this time. "You bitch!"

"I've been called worse," Myers said with a shrug. "It's over."

"For you, it is," Standish said, spitting at her. "And your old man."

Her finger tightened against the trigger. Her heart pounded in her chest. The mere mention of her father took away the control he always tried to give her in every situation. He was the best man in her life. The one she gave up everything for, to keep him safe from those in the world like Standish.

"That's it," Standish sneered. "The killer instinct. He taught you that."

"Myers." Ruiz called from down the block, gun at his side. "Don't."

"She won't, Alejo," Standish said, drawing out the captain's name syllable by syllable. "She'd miss me too much."

"I'll get over it."

"Then he'll know. The real you. That's right, Alejo. You have no idea who Samantha Myers is, do you?" Standish's smile grew with each word. Sweat poured down his brow, the shock from the two gaping wounds taking hold. He cocked his head to the waiting sedan. "The glove box. Check it out, Alejo."

"What is it?" Ruiz moved for the car, heading to the passenger side. He opened the door and then the glove box, a small thumb drive falling into his waiting hand.

"Ruiz…"

Standish grinned. "The truth. The truth about her and her old man. Their crimes. Their murders. Dates. Associates. Everything."

"I walked away from that life."

"No one walks away from their past," Standish replied.

Myers wanted to pull the trigger. She wanted to take away his control, to take away his damn smile. A hand fell over the barrel of her gun, lowering the weapon. Ruiz nodded and she took a step back, then he turned to Standish.

"You're wrong," he said to the bleeding man. Dropping the drive to the ground, Ruiz lifted his boot and stomped the device, smashing it in two. "I do know who Samantha Myers is."

"You stupid…"

A pair of cuffs dangled from Ruiz's fingers. "She's a cop. One of the best."

Myers smiled, taking the cuffs and moving for Standish.

"It will come out," he said. "You think I'm the only one who knows?"

Myers lifted him to his feet, cries of pain widening her grin. The cuffs slammed against his wrist and this time there was no guilt over the act as there had been with Loren. This was the right move, the better choice. The one she should have made a long time ago.

"You have the right to remain silent…"

"They'll come for him," Standish said. "They'll come for *you*. No one outruns their past."

"I'm done running."

"She never has to again," Ruiz confirmed, tucking away his sidearm. "Oh, and Standish?"

"What?" Standish growled, turning to face his former superior. Ruiz's fist connected with his cheek. Standish spun with the blow, slamming head first into the side of the sedan before crashing against the sidewalk.

Ruiz shook his fist, standing over the unconscious man. "She told you to shut the hell up."

"I can't believe it's over," Myers whispered.

In more ways than one. Standish would get his day in court, after a brief stay at the hospital to patch up his wounds. But beyond that, his time in Portents was over.

The same could be said for the hounds. The Heads of Cerberus were overpowered during their distraction with Standish. Cheers flew throughout the park, relief from the officers and monsters at their side rushing up to the treetops and spreading to the neighborhoods beyond.

"It is over, isn't it?" Myers asked.

"Not yet." They both knew it didn't start and end with the hounds. They were being directed, brought here by a woman with her fingers at their controls.

Karen Winters.

She manipulated the hounds on one end and the police on the other, with Mathers as her lapdog. The reports gathered over the last few days were clear as to the location of their next destination. Exactly where Soriya and Loren would be to put an end to things.

The Corridor.

Ruiz ran toward the parking structure, keys jangling in his hand. He stopped in the center of the street, looking back at Myers.

"Coming, Detective?"

Reinforcements exited the park, happy to escort the bleeding heap at her feet to his final destination. She still had work to do.

"Yes, sir."

CHAPTER SIXTY-ONE

Soriya pushed away the outside world. She lowered the volume on the screams raging downtown, caught up in the swell of violence filling the streets of Portents. The rain, another distraction, cleansed her from the blood and sweat covering her like a second skin. With the Greystone at her side Soriya journeyed into the bitter wind and biting rain, unafraid and unwilling to back down.

She didn't have to wait long for what she was looking for. From both sides of the Corridor they arrived—the Heads of Cerberus. They padded along from the homes and the abandoned businesses alike. Steam rose from their flaring nostrils. Their black eyes swallowed the glow offered from dimming streetlights running the length of the forlorn district. They saw everything clearly—the object of their hunt, their final retribution close at hand.

They lined up before her, each one taking an imaginary number. They paced the width of the street, eyes never leaving her. She did the same, the Courtyard locked in her mind.

On the far side of the growing number of hounds.

Howls rang out, a cry for blood. One Soriya returned in kind, screaming as she raced toward them. Her body cursed every inch, but refused to halt, refused to slow down. It was now or never, with the fate of everyone and everything on the line.

The first hound flew back from her assault, her fist catching the craven beast against the jaw. Four of its brethren jumped in as replacement fodder only to meet the glowing light of the Greystone in return.

The stone pulsed in her hand. If the connection remained it meant the Bypass was still accessible. Not lost as previously imagined. Moved. Shifted. For the Luminary.

Another wave soared through the air, the growing whirlwind offering her a breath and a glimpse of the Courtyard. Still in the distance. Still so far out of reach.

The thought spurred her forward, keeping her striving toward her goal. For every strike against her, Soriya paid the hounds back with ten of her own. She kicked, punched, and screamed her way through fur as black as night and hate that could envelop the kindest soul.

None would stop her, none could. She danced through the rain, leaping over flailing claws. A precision instrument, the weapon she was always meant to be, the one she always struggled to reconcile herself with, for fear of losing any hope at humanity. But there was a greater need.

The Bypass wasn't safe. It wasn't contained. It was loose in the city and vulnerable to the Luminary's slightest whim. The consequences of the dark light's actions were too great, too numerous to imagine.

"It ends tonight," she yelled over the growls of her opponents.

Fire erupted along the closest three beasts, spreading out in an ever-widening circle to the next wave and the next. Howls turned to cries, the rain helping to mute the pain but not enough.

Soriya pressed the attack, knocking each hound away with a punch, a kick, or a combination of the two. Her limbs caught their own blows, bleeding from numerous scratches and gashes. Never enough to halt her progress. Never enough to stop her.

Her chest heaved. Blood dotted the street around her, dripping from her fingertips, from her lips, and down her legs. The world spun and her with it, struggling to see through the pounding rain.

Only to find more waiting.

They clawed their way down from the buildings, racing to surround the desperate woman looking for a reprieve. Looking for hope.

"Well?" she bellowed. "Let's get this over with."

A snap of air answered her call. The hounds spun around, confusion in the air. The lead beast stumbled, blood running from the small hole in his temple. He fell, slamming against the wet concrete. Then another snap, another body brought low. Two more in quick succession before all turned to face the newcomer to the field.

Greg Loren smiled, a fresh clip primed and ready. "Sorry I'm late."

CHAPTER SIXTY-TWO

"Loren."

He ducked under the swipe of the closest hound and Soriya decked the creature. The beast flew aside, crashing to the pavement. Loren's grin grew wide. "Thanks."

"Loren, you didn't—"

He shook his head, firing at the pack raging toward them. "Don't get sappy on me now, Soriya."

"Wouldn't dream of it." She squeezed the stone tighter, feeling strength surge through her arms. Leaping deeper among the beasts, she cleared a path for Loren, who followed as he unleashed hell in rapid fire. "Glad you could make it."

"Want to tell me the score?" he asked.

"We need to get to the Courtyard. Now."

A wave of hounds cut off their progress. "I'm open to suggestions."

"Make for the closest yard!" she shouted, raising the stone.

Blinding light sent the hounds scattering. The pair jumped over the fence of an abandoned home. Soriya landed beside him, peering back as the hounds struggled to regroup. The light faded, but their confusion remained. The rain muted their scent enough to buy them a moment.

The yard was small, the grass becoming mud from the storm. Water ran in a large stream to the street, the same as the other homes along the abandoned housing project. The home was empty, the windows shattered on all sides. A small, wooden picnic table rested next to the fence, forgotten over time.

"Found your killer," she whispered, her back to the fence.

"You usually do."

"He has a Greystone," Soriya said, catching her partner's surprise. "I should have seen it right away but I didn't. He took the Bypass."

"Took it? How does someone do that?" She cocked her eyebrow and he rolled his eyes. "Right. Like there's a damn manual for that stone."

"He's working with a Luminary. All of this—the hounds, your dismissal, *everything*—has been her doing."

"A secret librarian? Don't I feel special."

"You should."

"Soriya…"

"Don't get sappy on me now, Loren." She flashed a smile, patting his arm softly.

Loren nodded, peering toward the masses approaching from the street. "Have a plan?"

"We do it together," she replied.

"We are," Loren said. He took her hand, helping her to her feet. "We always will."

Soriya jumped over the fence, crouching low along the sidewalk. The hounds snarled and grinned at her arrival, blood staining their fangs. She extended the Greystone before her.

A bright light exploded from the surface. This time, however, the hounds were prepared, shielding their eyes in time. When the light faded, they were ready.

Their target, however, was gone. In her place stood Loren who took aim, unloading an entire clip in seconds. The front line fell without a fight, and the second wave was barely able to defend themselves before they joined their comrades on the blood-soaked street.

A fresh clip clicked loudly in the pistol and Loren cocked the hammer back.

"Well?" he called. "I don't have all day."

The remaining hounds rushed toward him, rage in their black eyes. Loren smiled, lowering the weapon. A crack of thunder boomed down the block. Wind swirled around them, the storm intensifying with each beat of his heart. He continued to wait, letting them race toward him. When they reached the edge of the street, Loren jumped atop the rickety picnic table in the backyard of the abandoned property.

"Now, Soriya!"

The light from the stone gave away her position on a nearby roof. It reflected her joy, the sigil burning bright for all to see.

Lightning ripped from the skies. The water from the storm soaked the ground beneath the feet of the Heads of Cerberus. All paused, terror awakening them to their situation. Electricity surged through them, smoke rising from singed fur. Dozens fell in an instant.

Loren returned to the ground, leaping over the fence for the quiet street.

Soriya joined him from the shadows across the way. "Risky move, Loren."

"I learned from the best," Loren said.

Snarls echoed from the end of the street. Stragglers to the party, four hounds bounded for their position.

"I've got this," Loren said. "Go," he yelled, opening fire. "I'm right behind you!"

The Courtyard stretched out before her, the double bronze doors open. Soriya ran up the steps, stopping at the doorway into the microcosm environment hidden within. The Bypass hovered in the middle of the street, flitting sparks of light at the four makeshift pillars holding it in place. The Luminary stood in front of the orb, a

Greystone held high above her. A black cloak wrapped around her like a blanket. Her white mask covered her eyes and nose, but didn't hide the smirk across her face.

"Welcome, Greystone," the Luminary beckoned.

Soriya entered the Courtyard, her stone blazing. "This ends now."

CHAPTER SIXTY-THREE

"Noah…"

As Mentor did for Soriya, the Luminary offered Noah a second chance at life. Then she took it all away. His body lay in the street at the feet of the woman known as Karen Winters, his neck twisted, his eyes staring at the shifting stars overhead. A quick end.

Soriya intended to return the favor.

"He begged for the truth," the Luminary said. "I gave it to him."

"It was you." Soriya circled the arena, stone at the ready. "You killed his parents."

"They had the stone and chose not to play ball." She shrugged.

"You manipulated him."

"And so many others," the Luminary sneered. "Who do you think offered Nathaniel Evans a way back? Who handed Henry Erikson that special little coin and sent him on his way? All failures, but they served their purpose."

"And so did Noah?"

"It was always going to end like this for the poor boy. There was no going back. I'm sure you of all people understand."

Soriya shook her head, refusing to believe differently, hating that the doubt existed. She saw his anger, noted the building rage from the death of his parents. Noah Jordan killed four men out of vengeance. The road back would have been difficult but not impossible.

If only he realized the truth, as Soriya did now. "The Bypass. That's what this was always about."

"Your label is so mundane. So human." The Luminary laughed. "This is ultimate knowledge. All those years tinkering, hoarding in that godforsaken library? And for what? Trinkets compared to what the infinite holds beyond the veil."

Soriya stepped forward. "You can't keep the Bypass here."

The pillars shook, snaps of black flitting from the surface of the Bypass and crashing against the invisible box keeping the floating orb in place.

"There's too much power inside. It's not safe," Soriya added.

"The barrier will hold. I've followed the instructions to the letter," the Luminary said, hand to her chest with pride. "I am nothing if not a faithful student."

"And a lunatic."

She shook her head. "This fight is unnecessary, Soriya. You're weak. You can barely stand, you're so exhausted from Cerberus."

"You offered them the city."

"For the chance at saving the world!" the Luminary yelled. "Any world. All worlds. The Bypass opens the door to anything. Think of the potential. Think of what we can offer the future! Portents? Was there ever a chance in hell at saving this damned place?"

"Always," Soriya said. "As long as I'm still here. As long as someone is willing to fight monsters like them. And people like you."

"Open your eyes, Soriya," the masked woman said, eyes flaring beneath the stark white covering. "I have no desire to see you dead. Not when you could stand with me."

"Never."

Soriya vaulted at the cloaked figure, a driving fist in front of her. The Luminary swiftly dodged the blow, unleashing her own against the Greystone bearer's exposed side. Her ribs screamed beneath the surface, Soriya's body dropping to the ground. She held tight to her chest, fighting for air.

The Luminary towered over her. "We're the same, Soriya. We seek the truth. Our purpose. Our destiny. That stone you bear, don't you want to know what it is? To find out what the Bypass truly is? We can find the answers together."

Soriya knocked the Luminary away, a weak punch sailing wide of her target. The Luminary pushed her aside and she fell. The cloaked woman crouched before her, holding her face, nails digging into her flesh.

"Dammit, Soriya," she seethed. "Don't you want to know the truth? All those secrets Christopher kept from you. About your parents—"

"My parents are dead. They died in a car accident."

The Luminary dropped her and stood. Joy spread across her face in a thick grin. "Is that what he told you?"

The cloaked figure soared back, crashing into the side of the nearest pillar. Her mask cracked, manic eyes blazing. Shards of rubble broke from the brick edifice next to the column and the Luminary rolled out of the way. Her cloak failed to clear the way and she tore the bottom loose from her back.

Soriya's breath was labored, each movement an unending wave of pain. Soriya struggled to stand, let alone fight for her life. The Luminary was refreshed, triumphant, blocking her blow for blow before landing her own. Soriya fell to her knees, blood dripping from her lips.

"Perhaps I was wrong about you, Soriya. An error in judgment I intend to rectify."

The stone extended from the Luminary's slim frame, light pouring into the surface. Soriya didn't blink, didn't turn away, refusing to give the Luminary any satisfaction in the end.

"Do it already."

"As you wish. Goodb—"

Amber eyes lit up, her jaw agape. The Luminary staggered forward, the stone slipping from her hand. It rolled away, spinning around the falling figure of Karen Winters before rattling to the ground beside her.

A hunting knife jutted from her back, blood soaking the blade.

Soriya stared at the fading light in the woman's eyes, lost to the sight of the Bypass before her. Her ultimate treasure forever out of reach.

The Luminary stilled, never achieving the knowledge she sought. Including the name of the man who killed her.

"Who the hell are you?" Soriya asked, her breathing little more than a wheeze.

He stood silent for a long moment. Then the elderly man bent low to retrieve the fallen stone. He cradled the weapon, eyeing the enigmatic tool.

"Shut it down."

Soriya shook her head. "Doesn't work like that."

"It damn well better, kid." Pain filled the old man's eyes; the strain in his step was obvious. He was hurt, a visible gash hidden beneath his blood-stained hair. "It's time to end this, Greystone."

"You're with them," Soriya said. "You and your Circle of Shadows."

"Julian Harvey," the man announced. She didn't recognize the name. The threat, however, was clear as he removed a pistol and took aim. "I have to thank you for the distraction, kid. I didn't think I'd ever get in here."

"The Bypass—"

"Is a danger to everyone in Portents. If those beasts in the street weren't enough of an indicator light for you, this bitch should have been."

"She saw it her way. You see it yours. Doesn't mean either one of you are right."

"Doesn't matter if I'm right. I came to do one thing: save this city. I'm doing that with or without you."

"There is good and definitely a ton of evil locked in there as well. Take one away and you take both sides with it. I won't let that happen."

"Not your choice. And that's a damn small price to pay in my book, kid." Harvey cocked the hammer of the gun. "Sorry you couldn't see it that way."

CHAPTER SIXTY-FOUR

The remaining four hounds fell from afar without a snarl or moan. The wind shifted, the rain lessened. Quiet stretched along the Corridor with Greg Loren at the center. Ejecting the spent shell, Loren lowered his sidearm. The ground was marred by puddles tinted red. Bodies of the fallen Heads of Cerberus rested along the two wide lanes.

He did it. He wasn't too late. His wife's warnings were wrong.

He took to the steps, never straying from the center, even though the threats of the old crone and the tiger were shattered at the base on each side. *There is always a third path.* Soriya's lessons resonated in his mind. The better way he sought for so long was finally clear to him.

At the apex of the steps he felt a drip from above. Thicker than water, saliva clumped against his shoulder and Loren nearly tumbled down the wide stairs. He peered up, tufts of fur blotting out the light. Black eyes flashed, hungry for fresh meat.

"Of course it's you, Loren," the hound ground out. "Always interfering. Always where you're not wanted. It's enough to give someone a migraine."

"*Wexler?*"

She snapped at the air, leaping for the scrambling detective. Loren stumbled, slipping down the steps. Breath left him and the gun scattered along the ground. Loren jumped for the weapon, Wexler cutting him off.

She swiped at him, searing heat rising from his arm as the skin peeled away like the rind from an orange. "You should have known better. Should have stayed curled up on your couch, broken and alone."

"There was nothing on television," Loren answered. He held tight to his arm, reeling back from her pounding paws.

"Always with the jokes."

"Man needs a fallback career," he said. The marble base of the stairs met his back. He tried to shuffle around, but Wexler's claws blocked his escape on either side. She towered over him, snapping her jaws. He shot his elbow up, knocking her head back. Leveraging his knees against her gut, he flipped her into the stonework.

Scurrying along the ground, Loren found his gun. Wexler recovered, howling in rage. She bounded for him, leaping into the air. Loren spun and fired, the sound like thunder in his ears to match the pounding of his heart.

Wexler fell to the side and didn't move.

"Guess I won't count on a reference from you." Loren's chest heaved; his arm screamed in pain but he fought for his feet. He rushed for the entrance to the Courtyard.

The Bypass floated along the main thoroughfare. The glowing orb of green light hovered mere feet above the ground, spiraling quickly against the pillars carved into neighboring buildings. Each was inscribed with hundreds of etchings and runes of various forgotten languages.

The pillars sparked and cracked with each subtle impact from the glowing sphere. A thrumming reverberated against the street. Loren reached for a nearby guidepost to keep steady. The world within the world was collapsing and no one was doing anything about it.

The cause stood before the columns containing the Bypass. Julian Harvey loomed over a dead woman wrapped in a tattered cloak. Twin torches emblazoned the shoulders—the mark matching the entrance to both the Courtyard and the Library of the Luminaries. A large hunting knife jutted from her back, blood spreading in all directions. The retired detective aimed his sidearm at the only living person left in the Courtyard.

Soriya.

Gashes marred her dark skin. Blood coated her like a shield, dripping from her fingers and streaming from dozens of cuts on her arms and legs. She was beaten and broken from the struggle, unable to stand.

Unable to act against Julian Harvey's weapon.

"Harvey," Loren tried to say, stumbling toward them.

The elderly man caught Loren's approach in the corner of his eye and smiled.

"Don't," Loren cried, running at them.

The hammer snapped, the gun booming in the Courtyard as it fired—twice.

"NO!"

Soriya remained still for a long moment then fell to her side. Beth's warnings echoed in his mind, all hope suddenly lost.

CHAPTER SIXTY-FIVE

Loren hurried to Soriya's side. Her eyes fluttered, her body spasming. He pulled her close, dropping his gun to the side. He held her tight, bringing her body under his control. The bullets passed through—a good thing—but in conjunction with the constant beatings of the last few days, she appeared to be one giant wound.

One that would not heal. Not quickly enough. Not before the end.

"Loren." Her eyes caught his, a hand grazing his cheek.

Loren fought back tears. "Hold on. I've got you, Soriya. I've got you."

Applying pressure on the wounds did little to stem the effect. He had nothing to offer, no way to save her. Not from this.

"Hey," she whispered, noticing his panic. "It's okay."

"I'm sorry," he said. "I'm so damn sorry. I should have—"

"I'm glad you're here." She wiped away his tears. "Always here when it matters."

He fought to smile, threading his fingers between hers. "Wouldn't want to be anywhere else."

"Touching." Julian Harvey held a gun in one hand and a Greystone in the other.

"Damn you, Harvey," Loren snapped. He kept Soriya's shaking frame close, her cold sweat mixing with the blood spreading beneath. "You and your circle are—"

"Dead," Harvey replied. "Slaughtered like so many others. Because of the monsters you protected in this city. Safeguarded in places like this. And what happened?" Harvey turned away from them, raising the stone at the floating orb of light. "Never again. I won't let it happen again."

"You don't know what you're doing," Soriya said, struggling to sit up. She fell aside, a coughing fit spitting blood into her hand.

"I'm closing this door. And every other door."

"It doesn't work like that," Soriya pleaded. "You can't—"

"You had your chance, kid," Harvey said over the snapping wisps of light flitting from the surface of the Bypass. "This has to be done. For everyone. I'm keeping my city safe."

"By killing," Loren said. "You're no better than those monsters out there."

"I'm human."

"Humanity is defined by our actions. You killed innocent people."

"Monsters! Myths and legends that have no place in this world. Who—"

"Who did nothing but live and thrive side by side with us," Loren shouted back. Dominic. Urg. Vlad. Dozens upon dozens of interactions with the people, human or otherwise, that made up Portents. The true city. "With us, Harvey. Not against us. People we called neighbors and friends."

"Doesn't change who they were."

"No. It changed who *you* were. A damn cop, Harvey. Justice, not vengeance."

He could feel her eyes on him, her fading brown orbs, catching every word. She fought to breathe, struggled to hold on with each passing moment, but stayed with him. She funneled her strength through him, feeding him the courage to take a stand against this little man with a skewed vision of how the city worked—missing the point completely.

"Where do you draw the line?" Loren asked. "When does it end?"

"Right here. Right now."

"And then what?" Blank eyes stared back. Loren pressed ahead, unafraid of the gun in Harvey's hand. Unafraid of anything except losing the woman cradled in his arms. "You hunt down the rest? When they're gone, who do you turn to next? The common criminals, the thugs? Those who disagree with you? The cashier that gives out the wrong change? The waitress having a bad day? Where do you draw the line?"

"It won't be like that, Loren."

"Hate never dies, Harvey. Anger never fades unless you find something else to replace it." He held Soriya's hand against his chest, his heart pounding. "Friendship. Someone to believe in, someone to trust. A partner."

"That's enough." Light beamed along the stone, the Bypass shaking behind Harvey—screeching as the floating orb swirled light at the pillars surrounding it.

"These people you killed didn't hate, didn't fight, didn't do anything. They had hope. They brought light to Portents. All you've brought are shadows."

"Believe what you want, Loren." Harvey focused on the Bypass, his sidearm still by his side but lowered.

Loren pulled at Soriya's shirt. The wound along her right side continued to spurt, the blood thick and dark. There was no time to wait. He struggled to lift her.

"Loren…"

"Let's get you out of here," Loren said.

Soriya shook her head. She pointed to the Bypass and the sparks along the pillars. "The chamber. It won't hold. The Luminary was wrong to think otherwise. There's too much power in there."

"It doesn't matter, Soriya. If I don't get you out of here—"

"Even if you do…" She trailed off, her sad eyes washing over him. Her hand ran through his ruffled hair. "If the Bypass falls, none of us will survive."

She was right—she always was when it came to these situations. He trusted her in this regard. Their partnership, though cracked and torn over the recent months, cemented back into place as he laid her on the ground.

"What can I do?"

"Nothing," she said. She pulled him close, her hand slipping inside the breast pocket of his coat. He felt the weight of the object fall to the bottom, his eyes widening at its presence.

"Soriya," he urged, his voice shaky. "No. I…I can save you. I have to try to save you."

She smiled. "You already have." Small, painful exhales escaped her lips, fingers clenching tight to Loren's shoulder's as she worked her way to her feet. She kissed his cheek, a whisper in his ear. "You'll know what to do when the time comes."

"Don't do this," Loren called, scrambling after her. "You don't—"

"I do," she answered, unable to look at him. "It has to be me, Loren. You know it does."

Loren's hand fell, letting her go. Soriya faltered, swaying to her side. Pain caught in her throat, groans of agony at her failing body. Still, she continued, fighting for each step, every inch closing in on her target.

Harvey continued to stare at the orb, unable to work the stone properly, unable to contain the growing light from the Bypass. He was lost in its shine, in the hidden depths beneath the surface.

"Hey, Harvey!" Soriya yelled, her slow gait quickening with her resolve. "It isn't safe to stand that close to the light."

He turned, suddenly aware of her presence. "What are you doing?"

"Exactly what you wanted." She leapt at him with every ounce of strength left to her. "Ending this."

She slammed into him. He stumbled, unable to halt her momentum as the pair crashed into the box created by the four pillars. They fell forward, slipping across the threshold of the Bypass.

Then they were gone. Vanished in the blink of an eye. And Loren was alone, unable to do anything—unable to save any of them in the end.

CHAPTER SIXTY-SIX

The world melted away in a blur of blinding light. From only a few feet off the ground, the interlocked pair now hovered in endless space. The Courtyard was gone. Loren was gone. Only Harvey remained, struggling against Soriya. She fought for the stone locked in his grip, avoiding his wildly swinging gun, which fought an unseen current.

Around them, the veil pierced. Every door opened for them. The past. The present. The future. Soriya saw it all at once, the teachings of Mentor fading behind the wonder of the infinite. She witnessed the burning wreck that took her parents, the four-year-old girl emerging from the rubble unscathed. She saw Portents as it stood today, Ruiz and Myers standing triumphantly over the fallen hounds.

As the future opened, however, there was only darkness.

"It's… It's incredible," Harvey whispered, unable to tear away from Soriya or the world spreading out around him. She tracked his gaze to a younger man that held the same strong eyes. He stood beside a beautiful young woman, two children running up to them in mid-dance. Their laughter echoed in the void.

A vision of what could have been. A road not taken. He reached for the image and it slipped away, falling to shadow. More doors opened, the paths of a dozen Julian Harveys, choices never considered. Never pursued.

"So beautiful…"

"And you would steal it from the world," Soriya said. She clawed at his hand, fighting for the stone.

"It has to end. I have to end it."

"No," Soriya yelled. She heard the crunch of her elbow against his nose, feeling cartilage split from the impact. The stone flew free and she snatched it from the air. "I do."

Harvey snapped. "I have to be the one…"

Harvey's gun spun toward her. Bullets sailed wide, the booming thunder of the trigger deafening in her ear. With the stone clutched against her chest she lashed out, knocking aside the weapon.

Kicking off her elderly attacker, Harvey sailed deeper into the void. His body flailed, the visions fading to black around him. Fear took over. His screams faded as he fell into the infinite, lost to time and space forever.

Soriya cradled the stone, then turned toward the veil. Sparks of light and images covered the Bypass surface. Each and every one carried the same subject, matching her thoughts and causing her to smile.

"Loren."

He stood bright and beautiful against the stark colors of the glowing orb. So perfect. Her friend, her partner. She hoped he understood her final gift, the only thing she could possibly offer someone who had given her so much joy over the years.

In spite of the secrets. In spite of the doubts and the fears and the endless threats battering them from all sides. When it was the two of them; just the two of them against the world, it was perfection.

Nothing would ever change that.

Her smile grew, a glow emanating from the surface of Noah Jordan's Greystone. Every last ebb of strength and will channeled from her body into the stone, the light expanding and surrounding her.

She let the stone loose, watching it hover before her. The Greystone spun majestically, whirling faster. The light shifted but never faded, intensifying with each act, with each push of her will. Her strength came from within and without. Loren, his image dotting the veil, propped her up when she needed him the most.

Like he always did. Like he always would.

It was time to make the right choice. For everyone's sake.

The stone continued to glow, the surface cracking in bright white. At its height, with nowhere left to travel, no ounce of strength left in her, Soriya pulled the stone back.

Then threw it toward the veil.

Her eyes tracked the stone, watching the shrinking object soar through the infinite toward its destination. Loren would know; he would understand. Why she had to be the one, why it was always going to be her choice.

Soriya Greystone closed her eyes and fell deeper into the Bypass. Her strength failed but her smile never faded.

Even at the end.

CHAPTER SIXTY-SEVEN

The Bypass screamed. Waves of light split from the floating orb, slapping through the air. They cracked the sides of the makeshift barrier, the columns struggling to keep the infinite locked within.

Tears stung Loren's cheeks, his body unable to move from its position along the ground of the Courtyard street. Blood—*her* blood—covered his hands and shirt.

"Soriya!"

His call went unanswered, lost to the cries of the orb, which spun wildly before him. She had been gone for only a moment, a second, yet time stood still for him. As if in that second, lifetimes passed.

"Soriya!" he yelled again, taking to his feet. The Bypass responded in kind, light flaring along the surface. Escaping strands shot like bullets, cracking the closest pillar in two. The shattered inscriptions of a dozen dead languages rocked back and forth before collapsing, heading straight for the detective.

Loren dove, covering his head as he hit the street. All breath left him, the stonework continuing to spread toward him. He scurried along the center of the Courtyard, fighting for every inch, struggling to outrun the collapsing world.

The box was open; the cage set up an utter failure. There was no containment for the Bypass. There was no controlling it. There was only understanding it, and none of them truly did. Not after so long, not after the myriad questions asked, had any of them come close to figuring the damn thing out.

Now their lack of understanding might have been the end of them all. Not the Heads of Cerberus. Not the Charon. Not

Nathaniel Evans or the hundreds of threats over the years. None of them had the power to do it. None but the Bypass itself.

"Come on, Soriya," Loren muttered. On his feet once again he reeled back from the freewheeling orb continuing to lash at its barrier, wiping it from the world in its rage. "Fix this, Soriya. You're the only one who can."

In response, the Bypass expanded. Twice then three times the size, the orb swelled overhead. Energy sparked along the surface and the growing shadows flitting across the light snapped the air like electricity. The columns collapsed from the added pressure of containing the growing mass.

Loren continued to back away, squinting against the brightness of the infinite. *Like the sun. It's like the sun.*

A small flick of light broke through the surface. It popped clear, sailing in the air before crashing against the pavement. The object skidded to a halt inches from Loren.

A Greystone.

The light upon its surface faded, falling silent. The Bypass screamed once more. Not in expanse, not with willful destruction at its cage in mind.

The cry was one of finality. A death cry.

Buildings collapsed around him; the world shattered and debris showered the road. The great orb swelled once more then imploded, blinking out like a star. Those dotting the sky above reappeared, the bright beam from the infinite gone and silenced.

The Bypass was no more.

"No…" Loren bent low and retrieved the stone, its light gone. He held it out, trying to will its power back to the surface. Nothing happened. Nothing worked. "Please. I have to save her. I have to…"

He squeezed tighter, tears blanketing his cheeks. He screamed, falling to his knees. Still, the stone resisted.

"Greg!"

Ruiz stood at the entrance to the Courtyard. Blood covered his arm, sweat and mud caked to his skin. He rushed toward him, careful to avoid the large chunks of debris filling the street.

"Greg, are you—?"

"I'm…" Loren placed the stone delicately in his pocket, careful to keep it away from the final gift offered by Soriya before the end. "I don't know what I am."

Gravel crunched under the footsteps of another arrival. Samantha Myers peered around the Courtyard, eyes aglow at the sights of eras long since gone running the length of a dozen blocks yet hidden from the city.

"What the hell is this place?"

"Not now, Myers," Ruiz said, helping Loren to his feet. "Are you sure you're okay?"

Loren nodded.

"What happened, Greg?" Ruiz asked. "Is Soriya—?"

"She's gone, Ruiz." Loren turned toward the collapsed columns and the emptiness left by the passing of the Bypass and its protector. "I lost her."

EPILOGUE

CHAPTER SIXTY-EIGHT

Three Months Later

Myers took the stairs, hand to the railing. Her leg still ached in the morning hours but it was getting better. The scar was little more than a talking point and one she proudly shared if the correct amount of drinks were purchased in advance.

Normality returned in much the same fashion. Slow and steady. Crews worked during the daylight hours, restoring shattered storefronts and burned-down homes. Citizens traveled down from the coves to assist, working side by side with professionals in an effort to put the darkness behind them. For most, it was a simple matter to throw on a smile and get back to work.

It took longer for Myers.

Weeks of recovery meant time to question things, to doubt her place in Portents. Ruiz refused to take them into account. Not after everything the pair went through at Heaven's Gate Park. Not after surviving the crucible set before them by the Heads of Cerberus and Karen Winters.

Her badge gleamed under the hallway lights. It caught her eye and she stopped to admire the shine, grazing a finger over the shield to make sure it was straight on her jacket. It meant more now—more than just protecting her father and their past. This was her choice at last.

Not everything was settled. Ruiz welcomed her back with open arms, as did the shattered remnants of the department, but she still needed to make things right with others. She visited Mathers' grave, offering little more than an apology at her manipulation of him. When his wife arrived during her visit, the grieving widow

"

introduced herself with a slap to Myers' face followed by a hug. He always instilled that conflict in people and it showed on the teary-eyed face of the woman he left behind.

Pratchett's grave sat close by, tucked in the center of a large sun-kissed field dotted by dandelions. Myers placed a bouquet against the stone marker. No jokes slipped from her lips. No chiding of his driving or his lame sense of humor. She simply stood there, wishing for another second with him, another glimpse of his damn goofy grin.

She missed him more with each passing day.

He certainly would have made her visit to Six Mile Correctional more tolerable. Part of her never wanted to see Robert Standish's sneer again. The other part of her knew it was a necessary evil. Not a face to face, though. She wouldn't go that far. Instead, she monitored him from a distance, standing in the security hub. The former cop sat alone in the cafeteria, his solitude broken by the arrival of a less-than-friendly gang of cellmates that decided they didn't care for the man's look.

Myers couldn't help but smile at the brawl that left Standish cowering on the floor, his only defense the less-than-sympathetic guards who hesitated before arriving to end the fight.

Closing doors brought her relief and comfort. It drove her forward, accepting new beginnings rather than being dragged back by the baggage of the past. Her father remained one such door and would have to, for his safety and her own. But his time was coming, the conversation playing out in the back of her mind in preparation.

Loren came first. The way he should have when they were partners, when she wanted to tell him about Standish, about the blackmail and the evidence accumulated in secret. Loren saved her and she betrayed him in return. A situation that needed rectifying, especially in light of the new day ahead.

Stares from the neighbor across the hall welcomed her to the building and Myers waved, trying not to comment on the burning smell wafting from the old woman's apartment. Boxes lined the hall outside his door. Two men exited the place, heading for the stairs with their own set, each labeled in black marker.

"I think that is the last of it," Loren said within the apartment. Myers stopped in the doorway, unable to shed the look of surprise on her face. Loren's hair was trim, his cheeks cleanly shaved. His eyes beamed, aware and awake.

The couch was gone as was everything else in the living room. Four small crates sat in front of the mantel matching the two next to her in the hall. Loren grinned to the third and final mover present who threw a curious glare at the client.

Loren laughed, patting his back. "Yeah, I know. Light work. Don't complain or—"

He turned toward the door, his words trailing off at the sight of Myers. His smile faded.

"Hey."

"Hey," Loren replied. The mover cleared his throat and Loren tossed him a key before heading for the door. "I'll meet you at the new place."

"You sure?"

Loren nodded. "Don't break anything."

The man laughed, the boxes of books left offering little in the way of breakables. He picked up the closest one and started out of the apartment, passing the curious detective before heading down the stairs. Myers stopped Loren at the door as he put on his coat.

"New place?"

Loren shrugged. "Not far." He took a long glance at the empty living room, from the mantel to the kitchen off the left hand side. "Time to put Beth to rest."

"Soriya?" Myers asked before clamping down on her tongue. "Sorry."

"No. It wasn't Soriya."

"Then who—?" Myers shook her head, waving away the question. "You know what? Doesn't matter."

"Not anymore." Loren closed the door behind him. The pair started for the stairs, Loren offering a quiet wave to his neighbor.

"Loren, I…" Myers fell silent, unable to find the words.

"We're way past apologies, Myers."

She nodded.

"Ruiz told me what you did for him. What you did for everyone at the precinct—trying to rally them together."

"I channeled my inner *Braveheart*," Myers said. "It didn't work."

"It did enough. We're still here."

They stepped out to the sidewalk. Loren reached into his pocket and pulled a stick of gum from the sleeve. He went to put it in his mouth, then paused. He walked the stick and the pack to the garbage can by the side of the building and threw both inside.

Myers' shoulders slumped when he returned.

"What?"

She held out a pack of peach mango. "I had a peace offering."

"I quit."

"Just now."

Loren laughed. "Bad timing?"

"The worst."

She still held the pack out and he smiled. "Keep it. You might need it."

"Doubtful."

He pointed to the patrol car parked in front of the moving van and the woman sitting in the passenger seat. "Never know when you'll have to annoy the crap out of your new partner."

"True." Thel sat in the passenger seat, waiting impatiently with her head resting against the window. "She's not so bad, though. I've had worse."

"I believe it."

She started for the car then stopped, wheeling around. "There's a place for you at the precinct. The charges have been dropped. The evidence destroyed... I mean, 'missing.'"

"Thanks for that."

"We know now," Myers started, staring down the block and watching the sun rise over the skyline. "I mean, the two of us have for, well, *years* for you. But the department stands with us now. Better training, better preparation for what is really out there."

"Sirens for partners," Loren interjected.

"A new day, Loren. To keep Portents safe. You could be a big part of that. Ruiz would want—"

"He does. He's told me so many times. Annoyingly so." Loren tucked his hands in his pockets, his head low. "I'm sorry, Myers. There may be a job for me there but not a place. Not for me. I don't think I could ever fit there again. To trust..."

"Right." She understood, wishing his words didn't hurt so much.

Loren pointed to her badge. "Head Detective? Congrats."

"Ruiz's idea."

"Good for you." The moving van started down the road. "I should probably..."

"Yeah, of course," Myers said, stepping aside and letting him through to the sidewalk. She called after him as he passed the curious stare of Thel from inside the patrol car. "Loren?"

"Yeah?"

"I am sorry. About everything."

Loren nodded then walked up to her and offered her his hand. She took it, sharing a smile with the man she once called partner and friend. He leaned close.

"Stay safe, Myers," Loren whispered.

"I will," she said. "What are you going to do now?"

"What Beth always wanted me to do." He started down King's Lane for the Knoll, head held high against the sunlight. "Live."

CHAPTER SIXTY-NINE

The thin beam of the flashlight led him through the dark tunnel. The door was ajar slightly, a help considering the weight behind the metal junction just off the C-Line. Stairs clanged, his new shoes carrying him deeper into the depths under the city.

Until the Bypass Chamber stretched before him.

Loren stood at the base of the stairs, the flashlight scanning the vast space. Large webs filled the corners, running along the walls and down the four thick pillars in the center. Months of neglect did nothing to help the space.

He meant to come sooner but hesitated. This wasn't his place. It belonged to her—Soriya. She had a life here once, a family. Loren stood outside the domicile in the corner, swiping at the webs snaking along the frame of each door. They were windows into her world, a past he would never truly understand. Mentor and Soriya. Teacher and student yet more—more than one ever intended but remained because of her love for him.

Father and daughter.

Books ran the length of the right-hand wall. Mementos and notes from their journey together. Boxes of keepsakes were locked in the corner. For almost two decades they were a family and called this place home. Now it held no purpose, other than as a memorial to their sacrifice.

And a way for Greg Loren to say goodbye.

He missed her. Since her death, Loren missed everything about their time together. The adventure. The utter terror, usually due to some error on his part. The fun of their journey now at an end.

Loren vacated the life shared by two of the most interesting people he ever met for the white columns in the center of the chamber. He left the flashlight near the domicile, letting it guide him through the dark. No lights sparked along their surface. No rune cast among the thousands etched on their surface. The chamber and everything that came with it had fallen silent.

Bending low in the center of the four pillars, where the Bypass once floated majestically, Loren reached into his pocket. Soriya slipped the object there in her final moments, a gift for him. One he held close for months but now chose to relinquish. He placed her Greystone on the platform and stood.

"This doesn't belong to me," Loren said in the shadows of the chamber. "I thought about it. Hell, all I do is think about it. The stone. The city. You."

Loren took a shaky breath and jammed his hands into his pockets. "Dammit, Soriya. It wasn't supposed to be this way. Not after everything."

So many threats, so many dangers overcome. Until the last.

"I miss you." Loren closed his eyes, biting his lip. "The stone, though, belongs here. In this place. It was yours and always will be."

From his right pocket he sensed the warmth of the second stone. Another gift, this one cradled in his palm. *You'll know what to do when the time comes.*

"I thought about merging them. Had them humming like crazy at the prospect but I couldn't. It should stay here. Buried and forgotten." He squeezed tighter, putting the stone back in his pocket. "But I think I know someone who might need it."

A smile spread on his lips. Loren crouched over the stone, grazing a finger across its surface. "You gave me so much, Soriya. What did I ever do for you except turn you away? I didn't deserve you and now I can't tell you that. Can't tell you anything."

Standing, Loren looked over the vast space one last time. "You saved me, Soriya. Forget the city. Forget Portents and Beth and everyone else. You saved *me*."

He wiped a tear away, then bent down to retrieve his flashlight before heading for the stairs. There was a path ahead of him. Maybe that was why he felt compelled to pay his respects now compared to the weeks and months prior. It was time. Time to honor her memory. Time to make a difference again.

He stopped at the stairs, peering back at the resting stone, a final remembrance of its bearer.

"Goodbye, Soriya Greystone."

CHAPTER SEVENTY

Sweat dripped down his face, his arms aching from another late night of painting. Tearing down walls, revitalizing old woodwork. Ruiz loved every second of it.

Standing in front of Saint Sebastian's Church, Ruiz wiped his brow. Weekends vanished in the project of rebuilding and restoring the church to its full glory. Months of work, a massive undertaking, but one well worth the effort.

Saint Sebastian's was hit hard during the long night. Hell, the staple of the city's faith had been devastated over the last year. The death of Edgar Rusch was the starting point, one that continued to trail Ruiz's thoughts whenever he thought about a Sunday service in the grand church of his childhood.

When the Heads of Cerberus arrived, when they took their long night to the innocents of Portents, they also brought their violence and bloodshed to the city as a whole. Landmarks were totaled, the statue of William Rath before the Central Precinct still missing key pieces including the man's head. The church, a point of pride in a community that required its faith, was an obvious target. The hounds ripped and sheared masonry from the edifice, smashing pews and tearing down woodwork dating back over a century.

Ruiz refused to let that stand.

Months of nonstop work and Saint Sebastian's gleamed with the dawning light in the distance. Another night ended, his eyes tired yet anxious for the new day ahead. He stood at the corner, peering up at the tints of navy blue filtering out the black of night, smiling at the twin towers jutting from the main structure of the church, proud at the work completed by all involved.

Including the woman at his side.

"Water?" Hady Ronne asked, handing over a bottle. He took it, cracking the small lid open. He savored a long sip.

"Thanks."

Hady patted his shoulder. Her thin hair was tied back in a tail, recently trimmed. Once-pale skin now colored from long days in the sun and sunken eyes brightened in the company of others. Months of change and not all for the city itself. They were all the better for it.

"I can't believe it's done," Ruiz said.

Hady shook her head. "Still plenty of touch-up. The confessional needs a facelift but the carpenter can't get back here for another week. Painting will probably take—"

"Hady." Ruiz stopped her. She took the project in hand the day after the battle in Heaven's Gate Park. Where everyone else struggled to pick up the pieces, the other inmates of Pratchett's secret prison using the opportunity to return to the shadows, Hady rallied around the singular icon from their childhood: a project to bring people together.

"It's okay, Alejo," Hady said, catching his concern. She worked ceaselessly. Day in and day out, she coordinated with dozens of professionals and volunteers to bring the church back to life. To bring the people back to Portents.

"You've really done something amazing here," Ruiz said. "Working with the church, city officials…everyone."

"Edgar would have loved this."

"Yes. He would have." Her joy was another surprise. The quiet, muted introvert that felt more comfortable with the dead was gone. Ruiz noted it immediately, holding back the growing idea until the time was right. "You know, Hady, there's room at the coroner's office if you—"

"I appreciate the offer," Hady replied. "I think I should stick with the light for now."

"Is it ready?" a voice called from the street.

Both greeted the new arrival with surprise as Ruiz's wife, Michelle, wrapped her arms around him and kissed him.

"What are you doing here?"

She cocked an eyebrow. "You think I'd miss this?"

She wore a T-shirt and shorts. Paint stains marked both, her contribution to the long-term project worn like a badge of honor. "Hady."

"Michelle." Hady embraced her old friend. Then she stepped back, showcasing the towers to the church and the waiting dawn. "Have at it."

Ruiz paused. "You're not?"

Hady shook her head. "Portents needs you two, what you have, more than me. Don't you think, Commissioner?"

Commissioner. Never what he wanted with his career, at least not since his younger, more ambitious years on the force. When Zoe was born, after learning about the true city, Ruiz wasn't sure being a cop was where he needed to be. But he stuck it out, working to keep the people safe from threats human or otherwise.

Making captain before the birth of Teresa was the pinnacle for him and he took it graciously. The stress of the last few years, the strain on every relationship because of the work, because of the secrets, made him wonder if it had all been a mistake.

No longer. He stood beside his wife and his childhood friend, grateful at the day ahead and the opportunities therein. The chance to fulfill dreams of a better world.

This was their chance. Ruiz wasn't about to let it slip away. Not again.

"Race you," Michelle said, pushing him lightly as she ran for the stairs of the closest tower.

"Seriously?" he yelled.

She laughed, already starting her climb.

"Hey!" He followed suit, rounding the church for the second tower on the far side of the block. He heard his wife's mirth echo across the gap, catching sight of her through the windows along the tower.

Reaching the top, Ruiz stared out at the city. Pink and orange hues streamed from the rising sun in the east. Ruiz circled the large bell in the center of the tower, fully restored after being silenced for years from age and decay. Forgotten by the city and her people. Like everything hidden in the darkness. As if they could be ignored, as if that was an option anymore.

Fingers ran along the plaque, recommissioned and now adorning both towers. A remembrance of days long past and brighter ones ahead. The promise he made with each sunrise. One he intended to keep. He read the words slowly, the quote from Walker sending a chill up his spine.

These bells will signal the departure of any shadows that may fall over Portents and ring in the return of the light for all.

"Ready?" Michelle shouted across the gap. Slender fingers held tight to the ropes overhead, fighting the urge to pull. Ruiz held up a finger, staring out at the flourishing light. As the sun ascended from behind the skyline, gleaming against the front of the church he nodded to his wife and grabbed the ropes.

"Ready to face a new day."

The bells rang together for the first time in years, the dawn finally arriving for Portents.

CHAPTER SEVENTY-ONE

"Please!"

The cry rang out in Lowtown. A young man with tattoos the length of his arms ran from two others down the crowded streets. Cars whirred by, horns blaring as they avoided the pedestrians in the middle of traffic. The two pursuers, muscle-bound with blazing eyes, caught up to their prey. They battered him back and forth until he tripped along the sidewalk. His cheek led the rest of his exhausted frame, skidding against the concrete. The pair pulled him up and dragged him into a nearby cul de sac.

"Let me go," the tattooed soul shouted, kicking his legs to no avail.

The sound of the growing traffic in the city faded, the dead end's few establishments closed for the night. People were getting braver. The citizens of Portents took their streets back, refusing to follow curfews or unwritten laws.

The two men dropped their load along the gutter of the dead end. The young man rolled, the air forced from his lungs on impact. When he peered up he saw a third figure arrive, cracking his knuckles loudly.

"You stole from me, Pedro," the new arrival said. Bald and wearing gold chains around his neck, he approached the kneeling target, towering well over six feet. His hands were the size of the kid's head, his arms as thick as tree trunks.

"I screwed up, boss," Pedro pleaded. "Just give me another chance. You have to—"

"Teach you a lesson," he said. The boss slapped him across the face. Pedro slammed into the ground, his head connected with the curb. The enormous figure lifted Pedro back to his knees, a finger running the length of the large gash spouting crimson from the top of his head. He licked the blood from his finger and smiled. "And I am."

"Really?" a voice called from behind the display. All peered at the newcomer in a hooded sweatshirt carrying nothing more than a grin and a bad attitude. "I have to say, your teaching method sucks."

The boss dropped Pedro, leaving him behind like damaged goods. "Who the hell are you supposed to be?"

The two goons rushed at the newcomer, who pulled back his hood. Gabriel Jordan ducked under their clumsy swings, kicking out as they passed. The man-mountain to the right tripped on the leg, falling face first to the street. A second strike connected with Gabe's arm, but the kid took the hit, then jumped at the man.

The goon swung out but Gabe was too close. The kid jabbed his attacker in the throat and delivered a crippling punch to the jaw that sent the man reeling. He staggered, hands to his throat as he fought for breath. A pile of garbage snuck up on him as he crashed into it, sending black bags of refuse sailing through the air.

"Yes," Gabe cheered. He took a deep breath then returned to the fight, just in time to see the boss running toward him. "Crap."

The towering behemoth's punch knocked Gabe off balance, and when his second connected with his chest, Gabe soared across the street into a mailbox. The kneeling victim stared at the kid's struggle back to his feet.

Gabe pointed for the open road. "You can run now."

Pedro stared at him, then shuffled for the closest shelter. Gabe watched him depart, shaking the pain rising from his back.

"You're welcome," he muttered.

"You're not very good at this, are you?"

"I…" Gabe spit blood to the pavement. "I do all right most of the time."

The boss lifted him up by his hood. "Not tonight, kid. You spoiled my meal."

"Meal?" The man's eyes shifted to red, sharp teeth protruding from his lips. "Oh, crap."

"Down, Fido."

Gabe fell from the beast's hand, grunting as his body met the street once more. He recovered, wheeling away from his attacker, never taking his eyes off the massive figure.

The red eyes of the beast continued to stare at him for a long second. A thin line sliced along his neck, drips of blood running along his chest before his head toppled down his side and his body collapsed in a heap.

Loren stood behind the creature, sword resting against his shoulder. "Good boy."

"What did…? How the…?" Gabe stood, dusting off his pants and shaking away the piercing eyes of the dead thing in the street. He turned to Loren. "You? Where did you get a sword?"

"Borrowed it from the library," Loren said. "Don't worry about it."

"Thanks, but I would have been fine," Gabe said, fixing his hoodie and moving down the street.

"Not the way it looked to me, kid."

He had been tracking Gabe for weeks. Watching him from the sidelines some of the time, helping him out without being seen by others. Tonight, there was no choice but to take a more active role. The kid was capable. His attitude was a little too cocksure and his fighting style a little too "as seen on TV" than actual training, but Gabriel Jordan had something no one else had from Loren's perspective.

Potential.

"I'm not your kid," Gabe snapped.

"Right." It was part of the problem. The loss of his brother had sent the sixteen-year-old reeling. Loren tried to help but his offers were rebuked. He backed off, letting the system handle it. New home. New family.

Gabe asked to stay in Portents. With all other options on the table he decided to remain in the city that killed his family. Loren knew the roads left to him, the anger down each one, and the light at the end if he chose to accept it.

"Gabe." Loren ran to his side. "Come on. Hold up."

They continued to the intersection before Gabe stopped. "What the hell was that thing?"

Both glanced at the headless beast of a man in the street. "Wendigo. Some variety of it, anyway. They're usually hairier, I guess."

Gabe ran his hands over his face. "You sound absolutely insane saying that with a straight face."

"Don't I know it."

"And only swords can kill them?"

Loren lowered the blade, blood dripping from the tip. "One of the surefire ways, yes. I've been reading up."

"Must be some library."

Loren smiled. "Oh, it is."

Gabe shook his head, starting down the block. "Well, if you don't mind, I have things to do."

"Like get your ass kicked nightly?" Loren yelled. "Instead of homework and chores? All those normal things you wanted so badly?"

"Those people—"

Loren turned him around. "Are your foster parents. They took you in, gave you a home."

"I lost my only home," Gabe shouted. "My entire family. Because of freaks like that."

"Different situation," Loren said. "One you aren't even close to understanding."

"I can handle this just fine on my own."

"Maybe. Or you can't and you'll end up dead from it."

Gabe huffed, pushing away from Loren. Traffic whirred by, the sights and sounds of the city covering his anger as he rushed for the bus stop.

"How would you like to be more than a punching bag?" Loren asked. The bus skidded to a halt at the end of the block and Gabe waited for the door to open. "I've been where you are, Gabe. It's a dark and lonely road, but it doesn't have to be."

"Man, what do you want?"

"For you to have a life. A home. A decent school. Family. Friends. And a purpose."

"This is my purpose!" He stepped from the platform back to the sidewalk. "It's what my brother did and it's what I can do. This city—"

"Needs help," Loren interrupted. He reached into his pocket. "And so do I. If you're willing to listen. If you're willing to learn."

He opened his palm. Gabe's eyes widened at the sight of the stone resting within.

"Is that—?"

"Your brother's," Loren answered. "He would want you to have it."

Gabe inched closer, reaching for the object. He took it from Loren, running his finger over the surface. "It's warm."

"Sweaty palms," Loren grinned. "Kidding. It does that."

"I don't...I don't understand any of this."

"I know."

Gabe held the stone out. "What do I do?"

Loren's hand closed around Gabe's. "We'll figure that out together. Now put it away before you electrocute me accidentally."

"Who said it would be accidentally?"

Loren laughed, heading down the road deeper into Portents. Gabe paused at the corner, his hand cradling the stone. His eyes were heavy, tears held back in memory for those lost along the way.

"Well?" Loren called. "You coming or not?"

Gabe slipped the stone in his pocket and chased after him. "Where?"

"Moon's up. Time to get to work."

CHAPTER SEVENTY-TWO

Deep in the heart of the city, under the shine of skyscraper and monument, there once was a wellspring of light. Below the streets stood a place where humanity sang. A secret place, those held most treasured by the city of Portents, hidden from all.

Silenced now.

While life continued in the city, in the out-of-sight junction off the C-Line only darkness remained. The four pillars of stark white lost to shadow, the crackling embers of the pair that once lived within the vast chamber faded to ash.

No more laughter filled the space. The lectures had ended, the lessons passed on to new protectors. The chamber was empty, except for the lone object resting in the center of the four columns.

The Greystone.

Time meant little in the solitude of the chamber. Ever so slowly it inched along with no change, no deviation from what had come before.

And from what would come next.

In the blink of an eye everything changed. A flicker of light snapped against a pillar. Small, ineffectual and all but lost to the space's mounting shadows.

Then another light. Brighter, held over a longer span of time, still scant seconds. Another light joined the first, this one from the opposite pillar. Both grew from the spark with the addition of a third light and a fourth until the pillars' luminescence filled the chamber.

From the cold concrete of the floor, the stone shook. The earth rumbled underneath, an impossible breeze shifting through the vast space. A breath of air grew into a whirlwind between the four columns.

The lights danced, the symbols of dead and forgotten languages searching. With each marking, a new light, and with it a chance at the right sequence. The correct key. All four snapped audibly, the runes locked in place, the symbols keyed into the columns.

And the Greystone came to life.

For a moment, silence blanketed the chamber. And in the next, the orb of light returned to its center.

The Bypass floated in pristine glory. The fluctuations, the shadows were gone from its surface. Perfection remained, the infinite glory shining throughout the hidden space beneath Portents.

The wellspring of light returned and with it, what all looked for with the dawn—

Hope.

ABOUT THE AUTHOR

Lou Paduano is the author of the Greystone series of urban fantasy adventures, which follow Detective Greg Loren and Soriya Greystone as they hunt myths, monsters, and legends in the city of Portents.

He is also the author of the conspiracy thriller series, The DSA, a serialized tale about a clandestine government agency trying to discover the true power behind humanity's future.

He lives in Grand Island, New York with his wife and three daughters. Sign up for his e-mail list for free content as well as updates on future releases at loupaduano.com.

AVAILABLE NOW

BOOK ONE - SIGNS OF PORTENTS

Portents is a city like no other—and one that Detective Greg Loren can't wait to escape. Since his wife's death years earlier, Loren has looked forward to the moment he can leave the city of Portents for good—and never look back.

But fate has another plan for Loren. Called back to duty, Loren finds himself embroiled in a series of murders that has shaken the city. Together with Soriya Greystone, a young woman with unearthly powers, Loren must work quickly to find the otherworldly being that is killing citizens of Portents one at a time. Loren is tasked with deciphering the mysterious signs left at each of the crime scenes…even if it means traveling to worlds not his own to do so.

BOOK TWO - TALES FROM PORTENTS

Six tales of monsters, the dead rising, and the terrors of Portents.

The beasts Detective Loren and Soriya Greystone battled in Signs of Portents were just a hint of what lurks in the city. Tales from Portents explores the city's immersive history, including stories of Loren's descent after his wife's death—and his opportunity to have her rise from the grave. Among the pages, Soriya battles gremlins, navigates lessons with Mentor, and meets the werewolf Luchik. Follow new characters with expansive histories as they come face to face with the horrors of Portents—both human and otherwise.

AVAILABLE NOW

BOOK THREE - THE MEDUSA COIN

Death has come to the city of Portents.

Setting aside the aging case on his wife's murder, Detective Greg Loren has returned to the city with the task of stopping the bearer of the Medusa coin—an artifact with power over Death himself—from continuing to slaughter the people of Portents.

Soriya, no longer able to control the enigmatic Greystone, grapples with the decision to forge ahead in the case on her own, leaving Loren behind. But without the two counterbalancing each other, Death may be the force that levels them both.

BOOK FOUR - PATHWAYS IN THE DARK

The dark pathways of Portents tell of frightful demons and characters' surprising histories.

Discover new monsters in Portents, including a phoenix, an onna-bugeisha, and the cult of Anubis. Delve deeper into Detective Samantha Myers' secretive past, and follow Captain Ruiz as he continues to be plagued by the demons of Portents, even during his leave of absence.

As Loren and Soriya battle the city's monsters and their fractured relationship alike, they come to realize that everyone has two stories…and that nobody can be trusted, no matter how well you think you know them.

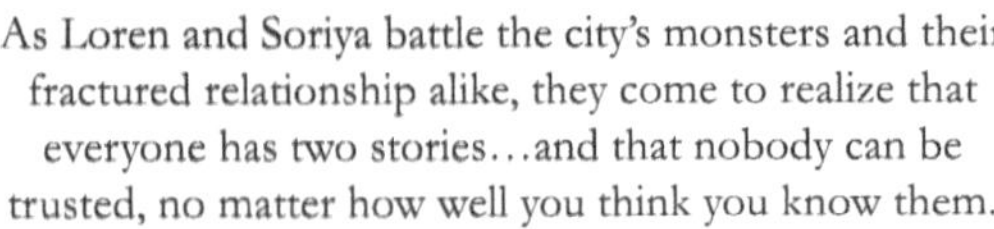

GREYSTONE CONTINUES IN…

It's her first case and it might be her last.

Soriya has worked her entire life to become the Greystone—protector of her city, Portents, against the growing shadows of myth and legend. All her efforts are in jeopardy when she is struck down by the destructive power of the Minotaur.

Soriya must now find a new path. Only one thing is certain—she's going to need help.

Beth, a researcher with insight into the city, has been locked in her own mystery—hunting for the recently stolen hammer of Hephaestus.

Working together to unravel the secrets hidden in Portents, Soriya and Beth must learn to trust the other's unique perspective. However, they aren't the only ones seeking answers as the Minotaur turns his rage on the city… starting with Soriya's beloved teacher.